SKYLA GRAY

An Acquired Taste

Contents

Chapter One

I *have been alive for two hundred years, and I have never met anyone like you.*

I sigh as I flip through the glossy pages of *Fangs* magazine, looking at images of vampire celebrities and their chosen valentines. Pampered and gorgeous, the human companions are almost as glamorous as the undead aristocrats.

I pause on the "Bite of the Week" photograph and pull it so close to my face that my nose brushes the page. The vampire and valentine couple is entwined on a couch at one of the many glitzy vampire balls. Her legs are on his lap, his mouth on her neck. A glimpse of his fangs sends a shiver down my spine. The blissful look on her face makes me clench my thighs.

…And the smell of smoke reminds me that I'm cooking dinner.

"Oh, shoot. Shoot, shoot, shoot." I toss the magazine on the counter, turn off the stove, and grab the handle of the pan, only to burn myself on the scalding metal. I wince as I set it aside.

Still… I may have burned my thumb and set off the smoke alarm, but dinner is done. And not just any dinner, but our celebration dinner for Declan finally accepting a job offer. I can't wait to surprise him.

I know he isn't the biggest fan of my cooking. Let's be real, I'm not crazy about it myself. But we can't afford a big night out. I make enough at the diner to cover rent and essentials, but only barely.

Now, though, Dec has finally made it to the finish line: a nice job that pays more than twice what I'm making. It took some time. He graduated last summer, and I was starting to panic after months of him declining job offers that "weren't a good fit" and spending all of his time "networking" to no avail. But the waiting paid off. Now we'll find a nice house, and my sister Maisy will move into our spare room while she starts at USC. She'll never have to struggle and delay her dreams like I did… and I'll finally have a chance to focus on my writing. Just like Declan and I planned four years ago, when we fled our small town in Nebraska to come to LA together.

My life has felt like a constant uphill battle for as long as I can remember. But now the hard part is over.

Smiling at the thought, I serve up two plates of spaghetti, set them on our tiny IKEA dining table—which has a piece of cardboard stuck under one leg to balance it—and grab my magazine again as I wait. I skim through articles about "Most Eligible Bachelors at the Valentine's Day Ball" and "LA's Most Exclusive Vampire Nightclubs."

God, I hope Dec will be in the mood tonight, because this stuff *really* gets me going, and we've been stuck in a dry spell for a while. I know it's just because he's been stressed, but my vibrator can only keep me sated for so long.

I pour another glass of wine and debate about changing into lingerie. Then I remember Declan saying it makes him feel *pressured*, so I sigh and flip to another article. I'm halfway through it by the time I realize that the food has gotten cold.

I frown, checking my phone. Declan said he'd be home by six, and it's nearly seven—even adjusting for the fact that I always set my phone clock ten minutes fast. With my chronic time-management issues, I was worried that I wouldn't be able to finish dinner on time, but now I'm more worried about *him*. He said he was just going to grab a drink or two with his classmates, but I know how things can get with those insufferable business bros.

Just when I'm about to call him, I hear the telltale click of the front door unlocking. I hide my magazine under a stack of unpaid bills and whirl to face the door with a wide smile.

"Welcome home!" I call as he steps inside, splaying my fingers in a spur-of-the-moment jazz hands sort of thing. I immediately regret my decision, but oh well, it's already happening.

Declan shoots me a weary smile. He looks tired and rumpled in his oversized blazer and lopsided tie, but still handsome. I fell in love with his floppy hair and big brown eyes the first time I saw him in high school, and I've adored him ever since. "Hey, Amelia. Thanks." He shuts the door behind him and then pauses, sniffing. "Is something burning?"

"Oh, uh—" I glance at the kitchen just to make sure. "No? I made dinner, though."

"Really? I was thinking we could order..." He pauses, catching the look on my face, and changes course. "I mean, I'm sure whatever you made will be great. That's really, uh, thoughtful. Thanks."

He follows me over to the table, sits down, and digs into his spaghetti. It's cold at this point and was never a five-star meal to begin with, but honestly? I think I did pretty good. "Maybe we could watch a movie or something tonight," I suggest between bites. "Have some… private time? You know?" I waggle my eyebrows but stop as I catch his expression. "I mean, no pressure, I know you've been tired lately, but…"

I trail off and shove spaghetti in my mouth. Declan sets his fork down. He clears his throat, looks at me across the table, and says, "Amelia, I think we should talk."

I choke, cough into a napkin, and set my utensils aside. My heart is pounding as I look at him, my eyes darting to a red splotch of what must be spaghetti sauce on his collar. I feel a hint of anxiety, but mostly the rising giddiness of expectation. This must be it. The big heartfelt speech I've been waiting for ever since I started supporting him. The moment he *finally* tells me how much he appreciates everything I've been doing for him over the years, and apologizes for all of the ways he's let me fade into the background while he focused on his education and career. He'll tell me he did it all for me, and now me and my sister will both get to live easy for a while. I'll forgive him, we'll kiss, have some passionate and long-needed sex. Maybe we'll even talk about marriage again. I didn't exactly anticipate this conversation happening over cold plates of spaghetti, but I'll take it!

"What is it?" I ask, trying to keep down a smile.

His expression goes unreadable, and a sick, panicky feeling lurches in my chest a moment before he says, "I think we should break up."

I plaster on an awkward sort of half-smile, and squeak, "What?"

Declan looks at me with those big brown puppy-dog eyes I fell in love with five years ago. "This is really hard for me."

"What?" I ask again, dumbly. My head feels like it's full of static.

He sighs. "I know you've been feeling the same way that I have. We've practically become roommates over the last couple of years."

I shake my head. It hurts to look at him. I look down at my own hands in my lap instead, rubbing one finger over the throbbing burn mark on my thumb. There's some truth to what he's saying, but it's only because I've been so busy single-handedly supporting us. I work long, weird hours as a waitress in a twenty-four-seven diner and handle most of the cleaning in the apartment, too. I haven't had the free time to write a word in years.

And I'm not the one who stopped trying. Dec always brushed me off, saying he was too tired or stressed. First he used school as an excuse, and then it was his job search.

So why is *he* the one breaking up with *me*?

"It seems like you have no time for me anymore," he says, and I look up. "For us, I mean," he corrects himself, as if that makes it better.

"Dec, *all* of my time is spent on us," I say, still too confused to be angry yet. "I work for us. I clean for us. I cook for us."

He grimaces at his plate of soggy spaghetti, and it finally sparks some anger through the haze of my shock.

"Because that was our deal," I say, my voice rising. "That I would take care of everything until you were finished with school, and then..." And then he was supposed to take care of *me*. I was supposed to have time to actually write, instead of scribbling ideas on napkins between pours of coffee.

And more importantly, he was supposed to help my sister. I paid our rent, did all the chores. I wrote his goddamn résumé.

All for… this?

"I know we made a lot of plans," he says. He's still using that mild, oh-so-reasonable tone that makes me want to fling my plate of terrible spaghetti at him. "But things change, you know? Feelings change. *We've* changed. We're not the same people that we were when we first got together five years ago. At least, I know I'm not."

I flinch because it's true: I'm still stuck in the same dead-end waitressing job, still wearing the same thrifted clothes. He's the one that's going to come out of this with a degree and a future. The future that was supposed to be *ours*.

If it were just me he was screwing over, then… fine. I'd deal with it. But it's not just me. I think of my sister, who already accepted her offer at USC and hasn't been able to stop talking about how excited she is to get out of our parents' stiflingly religious house and come live with me. How am I supposed to tell her that it's not happening anymore? How am I supposed to watch her struggle the same way that I have, all because I couldn't keep my promise to support her?

"Right," I say. My anger is still growing, sharpening, and I'm thankful for it. On the verge of drowning in despair, I cling to the lifeboat of rage. "Because when we met you were living on Mommy and Daddy's dime, and now you're living on mine. Such *progress*. Such *maturity*."

The look he gives me is so full of condescending pity that it makes me feel sick to my stomach. "Jealousy isn't a good look, Amelia."

"Jealous—" I bite off the word, grimace down at my plate of food, and then raise my eyes to glare at him again. I'm done trying to make myself small and push away my anger. I deserve to be angry.

I focus on that splotch of red on his collar, trying to feel some petty glee at his expense. But upon a closer look, I realize it isn't spaghetti sauce at all.

"Is that *lipstick* on your shirt?" I ask.

Declan flushes as he follows my eyes to the damning red against his white collar. "No, it's—" He pauses, fumbles, seems to think better of the lie. "Listen, Amelia. We haven't slept together in *weeks*."

"Three months and six days," I say. There's a faint but growing buzzing in my ears, and I feel like I'm watching this scene play out on a television screen rather than living it. It's just so... so *cliché*. Like something that would happen on one of those shows he makes fun of me for watching. "Because you reject me. Constantly."

He winces. "I was going to tell you, I swear..."

The rest is lost in the buzzing. My mind is somewhere far away, wondering how the hell I got here. The past is easier to think about than the vast, dark expanse of my unknown future alone. A future where I'm stuck in dead-end jobs and never have time to write again. A future in which my sister has to suffer and struggle the same way I have. Declan goes on, talking about some woman he met in his program, and how he cares about me but isn't in love with me anymore, and blah, blah, blah.

"I've wasted my life on you," I blurt, cutting him off halfway through a thought. He stops with his mouth open, blinking at me, and I slowly raise my eyes to meet his. "I... I can't believe I was so stupid." I know I'm not a perfect person. I can be messy and forgetful and easily distracted. I'm a god-awful cook. But I know that I deserve better than this. "Get out," I say. The words come quietly, but they're enough to earn a startled look from Declan.

"Huh?"

"Get out," I say again, louder. "Get out of my apartment." I'm the one who's been paying the rent all year, after all.

The look he shoots me is wounded, but there's something else underneath. Something smug. "Actually... I'm sorry, I wasn't going to bring this up, but... The apartment is in my name. Remember?"

I blink at him, ready to argue. I'm the one who pays all the bills and deals with the landlord, but... oh Jesus. This is *student* housing. We *had* to put it under his name because he was the only one enrolled at the university, and this was the only place we could afford that was close to campus.

"Oh, God," I say. I sink down in my chair and put my head in my hands

"I'm happy to let you sleep on the couch for a couple weeks," he says. "But..."

I let out a small, helpless, defeated laugh.

I am well and truly fucked.

Chapter Two

God, I'm such a cliché: sitting on the LA metro with no destination, a single, sorry suitcase clutched on my lap. I'm still too numb for the sadness to really hit, so instead, I mostly feel… lost.

My phone buzzes and I'm reminded that there is *one* thing that's certain: I have to tell Maisy that I don't have a place for her to stay anymore. Just seeing her name light up my screen makes me feel sick. I decline the call, lean my head back against the window, and try not to panic.

Around me, life goes on. Other passengers chat with each other or watch videos on their phones or hum to music. A couple argues about what movie to watch. A drunk slumps over and snores with his mouth open. It all seems distant, like I'm trapped in my own bubble where time has stopped.

I built my life around Declan, thinking that I was setting the foundation for a life *together*. It's been years since I tried to imagine a future that didn't involve him. And now, here I am, suddenly picturing myself as an old woman alone. The future stretches out in front of me in a horrifying stretch of bleak, joyless, lonely years.

How do I recover from this?

Returning to my hometown with my tail between my legs is not an option. I never thrived in the rural Midwest, and my parents' belief in crazy conspiracy theories has grown even stronger than their belief in the church over the last few years. I know how much they'd judge me for this. Especially since I'd have to go from no contact with them to calling and begging for a plane ticket across the country. Plus, if I get sucked back in to their lives, I fear that Maisy will lose the willpower to leave. I always felt guilty for leaving her behind; I'd feel even guiltier if I was the reason she stayed.

But staying in the city feels pointless, too. I could call up a friend and crash on their couch for a few days, but… then what? I've never liked LA. I was only here for Declan. I was willing to put up with the daily grind and the traffic and the ridiculous rent prices when I thought it was temporary.

So where does that leave me? Where am I supposed to go?

My eyes snag on a poster on the other side of the subway. It features a gorgeous young man lounging on a huge canopy bed with a glass of wine in one hand. His eyes are half-closed, his slender neck arched to reveal the puncture marks on his pale skin. The very image of decadence and sin. I know what he is even before I read the text on the ad. A *valentine*. A vampire's companion.

Valentines dedicate their bodies to their vampire patrons through frequent blood-giving… and lots of hot, kinky sex, if the gossip mags are to be believed. It's probably not true that *all* of them are banging, but the relationships certainly seem intimate. In return, valentines are pampered and cherished. Given the best food and drink and clothing, and brought to high society vampire parties that are otherwise inaccessible to humans.

Basically, they're sugar babies who give blood.

These ads are everywhere, of course. New valentines are always in demand, and LA is a hotspot for finding them. Some people travel here in the hopes of being hired as one. I never would've considered such a thing when I was with Declan, of course; he would guilt me about even enjoying books and TV shows about the lifestyle.

But right now, this ad feels like a sign.

A pipe dream is better than no dream at all. I find my hand wandering to my neck, touching the sensitive skin there. Wondering what it would be like to feel teeth sink into my flesh. Perhaps the thought should be frightening… but the thrill it gives me is more pleasure than fear. I have always wondered what it could be like. Like most girls, I grew up obsessed with vampire romance books and movies, poring over the gossip magazines filled with sordid details about the undead aristocrats and their luxurious, secretive lifestyles. I also grew up with a pastor shouting about vampires being soulless and valentines being "the devil's whores" every Sunday, but given the type of teenager I was, that only heightened the appeal.

Still, I never went any further than daydreams. Never truly considered the lifestyle. Instead, I chose what I thought was the safe option… and look how that turned out.

It's crazy to be considering it. I can picture Declan's sneer, my parents' shocked disapproval. Even Maisy would be surprised. And yet… What do I have to lose?

I'm sure the valentine life is not as glamorous as the magazines make it seem, but they make good money. It would grant me enough to fulfill my promise to Maisy and a step up with rebuilding my life. Plus, it's early February, which means we're quickly approaching Valentine's Day—the biggest vampire event of the season.

Before I'm even aware I've made the decision, my phone is in my hand and I'm typing out the contact number written at the bottom of the ad.

I hold my breath as the line connects—only to let it out in a disappointed sigh as I get a canned message that they are *currently closed to applications.* But before I can lose hope again, I notice a tiny sticker beneath the poster in the shape of a red rose. *The Valentine Society*, it declares itself in pretty cursive.

The ad looks so small beside the giant poster. One corner is peeling off, and the color is fading. Never thought I'd see the day I relate to a sticker, but here I am.

And I've got nothing to lose, so I type in the new number and try again.

"Valentine Society, Lissa speaking."

"Um, hi. I was wondering if you're…" What's even the proper word? "Hiring?"

A pause. "First of all, some common questions: No, we are not affiliated with any of the vampire courts. No, we do not guarantee patronage. No, we are not a matchmaking service. What we offer is training and chaperoning for new valentines." She says it with the air of someone who had repeated these words a thousand times, but it might as well be gibberish to me.

Training? I didn't know valentines needed training. But I'm unwilling to give up now. "So… that's a yes?"

"It's late in the season." Another pause. "But we're open to applications, yes."

Chapter Three

I'm sweating once I arrive at the address, both because of the walk from the metro station and the anxiety roiling in my gut. I peer down at my phone, then up at the gigantic, wrought-iron gate in front of me. Behind it waits a picturesque Victorian-style house, all pitched roofs and towers and stained-glass windows. There's no sign, but this is exactly what I'd picture a vampire's house looking like: sexy and gothic and a little spooky.

I bite my lip and consider turning back one more time. Then I picture the disappointed but unsurprised looks on my parents' faces when I walk in the door with nothing but a suitcase in hand, and Maisy's expression falling when I tell her she's on her own in LA. I gather my courage and jab at the intercom button near the gate to announce my presence.

A woman waits out on the wraparound porch. She's dressed smartly in a pencil skirt and silk blouse, and she's not a vampire, judging from the tan skin and warm pink of her cheeks. I guess she could be in spray tan and makeup, but from what I've seen, white vampires love to play up their natural pallor.

"Amelia?" she asks, and I nod. I'm tongue-tied with nerves.

She stands for a moment with her hand propped on her hip, eyeing me and my sad suitcase. "I'm Lissa. Welcome to the Valentine Society. Benjamin will meet you in the parlor."

Will you walk into my parlor, said a spider to a fly, my brain supplies, sending a trickle of unease down my spine.

I swallow. This is normally where I'd make some kind of dumb joke to alleviate tension, but I'm too anxious right now. Instead, I meekly follow Lissa through the door. She shuts it behind me, and I stare around at the foyer. It looks more modern than I would've imagined, sparsely decorated but still speaking of expense, with real hardwood floors and beautiful paintings adorning the walls. I stop for a moment to stare up at one—an image of a dark figure looming over a beautiful young woman's bed—before Lissa clears her throat and gestures for me to follow her.

The parlor holds a large, round table with a delicate floral tea set. The table is accompanied by a lovely velvet chaise and matching chairs. The window has heavy curtains drawn across it, so the room is lit only by an array of old-fashioned sconces and a chandelier.

"Oh my God," I blurt out as I drag my suitcase into the room. "This is… unreal. Like something straight out of a book."

"Yeah, I suspect that's what he's aiming for," Lissa says, looking unimpressed. Then her brusque attitude shifts as she shoots me the smallest smile. "But don't tell him I told you."

"Don't tell me what?"

My laugh shrivels in my throat at the sound of an unfamiliar, British-accented voice behind me. I whirl around, one hand pressed to my chest, to find a man standing in the doorway that leads further into the house. He wasn't here when I walked into the room, and I didn't hear him arrive.

Vampire. I know it instantly, intuitively. I've never been this close to one before, but it's like my body knows it's in the presence of a predator. My pulse rises and my hair stands on end. The man doesn't look like the cliché of a vampire, with his golden-brown skin, black beard, and round-rimmed glasses, but there is an unnatural stillness to him that makes me shiver.

"Lord Benjamin Acharya," he introduces himself, extending a hand without moving forward. Leaving my suitcase behind, I hesitantly cross the room. With someone else, it could be a power play to make me walk to him, but judging from his gentle grip and the way he looks at me, I suspect it's more that he's trying not to alarm me. Yet the shock of his cold fingers makes me have to stifle a gasp.

"Amelia Burton," I say, barely managing more than a whisper. Somewhere deep in my brain, I know I'm making a fool of myself, shaking like a leaf over a perfectly polite man who happens to be undead, but I can't seem to regain control of my body.

Benjamin gestures to the table in the center of the room. Every movement is polite and slow, and yet my muscles tense every time. "Please, take a seat." He glances at Lissa. "I'd appreciate it if you could stay for a few minutes."

Lissa sighs and smooths her skirt as she sits on the chaise. I take a seat beside her, my movements awkward and stiff, like I'm a marionette rather than a person. God, what is *wrong* with me?

"Your nerves are perfectly normal," Benjamin says, as if he can read my mind. I guess he *can* hear the nervous pitter-patter of my heart. He sinks into a seat opposite me with smooth grace, pours a cup of steaming tea into a porcelain mug, and slides it across the table to me. "Have some chamomile tea. Give yourself a few minutes to adjust. First time meeting a vampire, I presume?"

I nod, wrapping one hand around the cup but not able to bring myself to drink yet. Lissa's arm brushes mine. Despite her brusqueness, her presence steadies me, especially since she seems at ease around Benjamin.

"Right," Benjamin says. He pours himself a cup of tea, as well. Then he takes out a vial from his pocket, uncorks it, and pours the red liquid into the tea. *Blood*, I realize with a lurch.

He's all nonchalance, like he's adding sugar or cream instead of human blood. But I guess this *is* perfectly routine for him. He raises the cup, takes a sip, and looks at me over the rim.

"You're doing well," he says as he sets the cup down, even though I've broken into a cold sweat. "Vampires are a natural predator. Your bodies have evolved to fear us. Some have stronger reactions than others; they will panic and flee from our presence. Others are too squeamish and will be ill at the sight of blood, let alone one of us drinking it."

"So you're saying I have weak survival instincts?" I croak.

He smiles. "Maybe so, but it's a boon, given your interest in this line of work."

I relax. So I've passed the first test. Maybe this idea wasn't as crazy as it first seemed. Once I no longer feel like my heart is in my throat, I manage a small sip of tea. It's nice and hot, with a mellow sweetness. My pulse gradually slows.

"Very good," Benjamin says. He nods at Lissa, and she stands. Part of me wants to ask her to stay, but I know I am being tested, and so I bite my tongue. She pauses beside Benjamin, her fingers grazing his arm—and from the way his eyes linger on her as she leaves, I have a sudden inkling that there's something a little more than an employer-employee relationship there.

I am *so* tempted to pry, but once I'm alone with a vampire in the room, my nerves surge and render me tongue-tied again.

"Now, Ms. Burton," Benjamin says, returning his attention to me. "I'd like to thank you for contacting us. The Valentine Society is a new endeavor of mine; this year's Valentine's Day Ball will be our debut into vampire society. I set out with the intent to make this line of work safer for valentines, and that means I am particular about who I will sponsor. With only one week until the ball, I must inform you that I'm looking for something very special if I'm to bring you there with so little training."

"So, no pressure," I squeak.

He smiles. "I'd like to ask you a few questions. What attracted you to this line of work?"

"Well, I, uh—" I start, and then stammer, suddenly unsure about what the protocol is. "Am I supposed to call you 'my lord,' or something?" I know that vampires consider themselves nobility, since each of them has a trace of blood from the original vampire: Count Dracula, descended from King Attila of the Huns.

"Benjamin is fine," he says. "Some vampires are sticklers for that sort of thing, but I find it all a bit embarrassing, if I'm being honest."

"Okay. Benjamin." I brush my hair out of my face, stalling as I try to think of a good answer. Should I be formal, or honest? Can vampires really tell from your heartbeat if you're lying? Do half-truths count as lying?

"There's no one good answer," Benjamin says. "There are

many reasons that people come to this line of work, and regardless of what yours is, I will not judge you. I am simply trying to get to know you better."

"Right. Sorry." I laugh, a little breathless. "I've always been fascinated by vampires. As a little girl, I loved the gossip rags, the romance novels, all of it. I still watch *A Day in the Life of a Valentine* every Friday." Heat rises to my face. Maybe too honest? I try to redirect my nervous blathering. "But there was always a reason not to try it. Always some safer option to take."

"So why are you here now?"

"Because the safer option turned out to be not so safe after all," I say. "And I'm so tired of just scraping by. I want something better. So I just feel like… fuck it! I want to do something just because I want to, not because I *should*."

He nods, his expression thoughtful. "So the lifestyle appeals to you?"

"Yes," I say emphatically. "It just seems so romantic. The luxury, the social scene… even the danger. It makes me want it more." I look away, cheeks warming. "I probably sound unhinged."

"Not at all," Benjamin says. "Trust me when I say that all vampires are grateful that humans like you exist."

"People with little to no survival instinct?" I joke.

"People who enthusiastically consent to meet our needs," he shoots back with a sliver of a smile. I blush more deeply but don't argue.

"So…" I cock my head. "Is this the part where you bite me?"

He chokes on his tea, sputters, wipes his mouth with a napkin. "Well… yes, I suppose so. You certainly seem… calmer. Let's see what we're working with."

I grin despite my nerves. My heart is leaping again, with some anxiety, yes, but mostly with excitement. I slide over to make room on the chaise. No matter what he says, I still feel like a freak for being *excited* at the thought of being bitten... and more than a little turned on. I hope that his heightened senses don't work quite like they do in spicy novels.

It's not like I'm going to jump Benjamin's bones, especially not when I suspect there's something going on between him and Lissa. But still... I've imagined this moment for most of my life. Now it's time to figure out if reality can live up to the fantasy.

Benjamin settles beside me, leaving a few inches of space between us. He takes a small metal kit out of his pocket and sets it on the table: I spy a sanitizing wipe, bandages, and a vial of smelling salts, along with a second vial containing a thick dark liquid.

I brush my hair off my neck, tilting my head to the side, but Benjamin stops me with a raised hand.

"*Never* offer your neck to a stranger," he chastises. "It's dangerous. Far too easy for someone to overindulge. And it is also intimate, best saved for someone you trust."

"Right," I say, face heating. "Then, where...?"

"The wrist is standard." He reaches out, gently takes my hand in his, and flips it over to expose my pale blue veins. "May I put my other arm around you?"

I nod. He holds my wrist with one hand and slides his other arm around my waist.

"Sometimes, people faint," he says. I stare up at him, meeting his dark eyes. He's so businesslike about this, but my mouth has gone dry, my heart thumping rapidly. I knew what I was getting into, but now that the moment is here, I'm more nervous than I thought I would be. And more excited, too.

"May I bite you now?" he asks, lifting my wrist to his mouth.

My heart skips a beat.

I'm so enamored by the sight of two canines sliding out from behind his slightly parted lips that I almost forget to answer. His fangs gleam in the light, white and sharp and all too enticing. "Yes," I breathe.

"Try not to tense," he murmurs. His voice is thicker and has the slightest hint of a lisp with his fangs out. "It will make it hurt more. Take deep breaths. In through the nose, out through the mouth."

I suck in air and let it out, trying to heed his advice. "Easier said than done," I mutter. "Like when they tell you to relax when they're about to stick you with a big-ass needle and—*ah*."

An involuntary noise escapes me as he sinks his teeth into my skin. There's a bright burst of pain in my wrist and then—

And then—

Pleasure. It floods my veins like a drug. Heat rises to my face, and my head goes fuzzy. Tension oozes out of me until my entire body feels loose and relaxed, like being tipsy but better.

"Oh, damn," I mutter. Everything's going hazy around the edges. Holy shit, am I actually swooning? I didn't think that happened in real life. Benjamin's hand tightens on my waist, his arm holding me steady even as my body goes liquid and boneless in his arms. I can feel his tongue pressing against my skin, the *pull* as he drinks from me, my pulse. An ache between my thighs throbs in rhythm with it, and I bite back a moan.

Then the pressure of his fangs disappears. The heady rush fades a couple of seconds later. I stiffen, cheeks burning. I was always turned on by the thought of being bitten, but my god, I still didn't expect it would feel *that* good. I'm breathing hard, and it takes a few moments for me to sit up again.

But my pleasant haziness fades as I glance over and notice the look on Benjamin's face—brow furrowed, lips slightly puckered, like he just sucked on a lemon. Except he just sucked on *me*.

"That bad?" I ask, chuckling nervously.

He smooths his face into indifference. Still, the silence ticks on for an uncomfortable couple of seconds. He takes the dark vial from the kit, puts a drop on a small cloth, and dabs at the puncture marks on my wrist.

"This is vampire blood," he murmurs. "It has healing properties. Ingesting it can have its dangers, but applying like this is safe."

But I barely notice the sting or the fascinating sight of my puncture wounds closing within a couple of seconds. I'm too busy trying—and failing—to read Benjamin's expression. "*What?*" I burst out. "Is something wrong?"

"No, no." He swipes his tongue over his teeth, which are smooth again, his fangs retracted into his gums. "It's just that your taste is very... distinct."

I let out an uncomfortable giggle. "Gee, you really know how to butter a lady up."

"It's... hm," he says. "Certainly unique." He pulls a black handkerchief from his pocket and dabs at his lips. "I've never tasted anything quite like it."

"In a good way?" I ask, my voice creeping higher along with my nerves.

"There is no good or bad when it comes to taste. It is all a matter of preference."

"That's a bullshit line if I've ever heard one," I say. Doubly so when I notice he leans over to take another sip of his tea and swirls it around his mouth, as if to wash the taste of me from his tongue. Panic flares in my chest and erupts in more nervous words. "Is there something wrong with me? Am I… diseased?"

"No." When he says it this time, it feels far more honest. "I didn't taste anything medically wrong with you."

"So I've just got bad blood? Am I all rotten inside?"

He sets his tea aside, folds his hands in his lap, and scrutinizes me. I squirm and bite back another retort as he considers for a few long seconds.

"Your taste is… different," he says. "I cannot deny that it may be a challenge to find a match for you. I can think of one or two patrons to whose palates you may appeal, as a novelty, but…" He shrugs. "I will not lie. I am not sure if the life of a professional valentine is in your future."

My heart sinks. Despite my nerves, I wasn't ready for him to say *no*. I thought there would be more steps to the interview, at the very least. I thought I was doing well, passing his tests. I *liked* being bitten. How is it possible that I could taste so bad that it wouldn't even matter?

This was my last, desperate attempt at salvaging my life. That thin thread of hope has just been snipped. So what am I supposed to do now?

Yet, just as I feel a surge of heat behind my eyes that promises an embarrassing rush of tears on its way, Benjamin continues. "However, I think your blood is distinct enough that many would like to sample it. So, if it is acceptable for you… I would be interested in sponsoring you for attendance at this year's Valentine's Day Ball."

I suck in a breath, heart soaring, but he holds up a finger. "As I said, I can't promise a long-term position. This would be a contract for one night only."

My teeth worry at my lower lip. One night? It's far from the luxurious life as a pampered valentine; this feels more like being a cheap hooker. Speaking of cheap… "How much would that pay?"

He purses his lips, face creased with thought. "One week of crash-course training, and working a Valentine's Day Ball… hm." He taps a finger to his chin and then looks me in the eyes and says, "I'm prepared to offer five thousand dollars."

I blink at him. Blink again. "Say what?"

"I'm not interested in negotiating. You're a unique case, and that's what I'm willing to pay, so—"

"Yes," I say, before my common sense can make me second-guess myself. "I'll do it."

Five thousand dollars for one night… I'd be willing to do just about anything for that price, let alone something I've just learned that I very much *enjoy*. But even as I break into a grin, there's a voice in the back of my head whispering that I should've anticipated this. *Of course they only want you for one night*, it says. *Declan didn't want you, and the vampires don't either. You're a short-term thing. A fling, and nothing more.*

But… five thousand dollars is better than nothing. It's more than enough for a rent payment for me and my sister while I figure something else out. I'll tell work I'm sick for the week or something.

When Benjamin offers his hand, I take it.

Chapter Four

"There will be thousands of people applying to be potential valentines this year. Perhaps fifty will be chosen to attend the Valentine's Day Ball."

I nod and sip my tea like my life depends on it. Benjamin decided to launch into my training as soon as I signed the contract. There's no time like the present, he said, especially because I only have a week to train and adjust my sleep schedule to stay up all night. I sometimes work night shifts, so I have a bit of an advantage… except that I worked this morning at the diner.

"How many people are you sponsoring?" I ask, trying to stay focused.

He pauses. "Just you."

Now *that* jolts me awake. "What? Why?"

He shrugs. "I told you I was particular," he says. "Most potential valentines went with the larger agencies, I suspect. And out of the few who applied, I found none suitable except you."

I should probably find that flattering, but instead, my pulse rises. What in the world is he thinking? Surely, choosing me will lead to disappointment. I'm about to ask *why* when Lissa enters with a tray of tiny sandwiches, and my stomach lets out a very loud grumble. The only thing I've eaten today was a muffin at the diner this morning and a few mouthfuls of rubbery spaghetti.

Benjamin huffs out a laugh. "Please, help yourself."

I don't need more encouragement than that. I sample a couple sandwiches—one cucumber with cream cheese, which is delightfully refreshing, and another with roast beef and spicy horseradish. It's hard to get used to eating while Benjamin just sips his blood-infused tea, though.

"Do vampires eat?" I ask once I've polished off my second tea sandwich.

"We can if there is blood mixed into the food, but most vampires choose not to, save for special occasions. Blood sustains us." He shrugs. "It usually tastes better, too."

"Except for mine, apparently."

He levels me with a disapproving look. "That is the sort of thing you are *not* going to say at the ball," he says. "I'll be touting you as a unique delicacy, which you are. Do not devalue yourself."

I take another sandwich and say nothing. Apparently, that's our segue into the etiquette lesson, because Benjamin reaches into his pocket and pulls out a paper folding fan with a wooden handle. "Do you know what this is?"

I almost choke on my mouthful of egg sandwich in my haste to answer. "A blood card!"

He smiles, holding it out. I wipe my hands on my napkin before taking it in a reverent, two-handed grip. "That's right. You'll have one at the ball."

I flip the fan open. The paper is thick and creamy, the wood polished and solid, and there's a black silk ribbon tied around the end of the handle that attaches to an elegant quill pen. I feel luxurious just holding it and can't resist the opportunity to fan myself and grin. I've seen blood cards on TV, read articles about those belonging to famous valentines, but never seen one in real life.

"On one side, we will write the name of your patron—or your chaperone, in this case—and some tasting notes for your blood," Benjamin tells me. "The other will hold the time slots where vampires can sign to claim a drink from you. But always remember it is *your* choice, first and foremost, of who you allow to taste you."

I snap the fan shut and hand it back to him. "How many time slots are there?"

"Six," Benjamin says. "The party will last from dusk till dawn, approximately twelve hours. So you may be bitten once every two hours. Each one will take only a brief taste, so you will give a pint of blood total. Well within a safe range, and I will be with you, ensuring you stay fed and hydrated."

"You'll be with me all night? I didn't realize the chaperone thing was literal." It's a relief to know I won't be all alone in a party full of fanged predators, but still... "Don't you have better ways to spend your time?"

"Than keeping you safe? No, Amelia. Nothing is more important than that." He gives me a stern look. "That is the main purpose of these lessons. But the two most important rules you should know are these: you must never leave my side at the ball. And you must never let anyone bite you outside of the designated time slots on your blood card."

"Right," I say. "But... is it going to be an issue to keep me *safe*? I thought there were all kinds of laws protecting valentines."

"There are. Valentines are cherished and safeguarded in our

society, but it is their patrons who guarantee that. Till you are claimed, you exist in more of a legal gray area."

I swallow. My nerves flicker, but instead of scaring me off as they probably should, they only make me more curious. "So how are you going to keep me safe?"

He smiles. "With impeccable manners, of course."

* * *

"I thought you were kidding," I groan an hour later as Benjamin corrects my posture once again. I'm sweating from holding this stiff pose. Actually sweating. I didn't think being polite would take so much effort. "There's no way anyone actually cares about this stuff."

We've moved from the parlor to the "sitting room," because apparently that's a thing that rich people have. Lissa has taken up a spot at the grand piano, and we've pushed the furniture to the sides to open up the center of the room as a makeshift ballroom. By *we*, I mean that Benjamin moved all of the furniture with an effortless strength belying his slim build, showing off the heightened abilities of a vampire.

I can't lie, it was pretty hot to see him lift a couch with one arm, but I still don't intend to get in the way of whatever is going on between him and Lissa. They keep stealing glances at each other when the other person isn't looking.

From there, it's straight into dance lessons. Even after witnessing the strength in Benjamin's hands, I still feel safe with his palm resting on my lower back. I've gotten used to being in a vampire's presence quickly, which I suppose bodes well for the ball, when I'll be surrounded by them.

"That's where you're wrong," Benjamin says, coaxing my spine into the proper position. He is always polite, but he is also goddamn relentless.

"Huh?" Shit. I already forgot what we were talking about.

He shoots me an exasperated look. "Tradition is important to vampires. It is, in many ways, what binds us. A way to preserve our long, shared history. Some see it as what separates us from humans."

"Sounds like some snooty, elitist shit," I grumble.

Benjamin favors me with a smile. "Indeed," he says, which draws a laugh out of me. "But it's not without its merits. Adhering to social standards helps us to subdue our baser instincts. At our core, we are creatures of endless hunger and necessary bloodshed. It is important to prove to ourselves and to each other that we can overcome that. That our willpower is greater than our animal impulses. And, yes, there is a sense of proving we are superior to the humans we feed off."

I roll my eyes to show him what I think of *that*. But I can't complain. I've heard of the terror and chaos of the early days after vampires revealed themselves to the world in the '50s, and before that—the stories of drained bodies found in dumpsters, and vicious court wars tearing cities apart. The fuss and frippery of today's vampires is certainly better than that violence.

Still, etiquette is not my strong suit. Neither is dancing. Even Benjamin's valiant patience seems on the verge of breaking after the fourth time I stomp on his foot while learning to waltz.

"You keep trying to lead," he grumbles, rubbing his temples. "Which would be fine if you had any sense of rhythm…"

I sigh and flop onto the nearest chaise. "Maybe I'm just not cut out for this," I complain, staring up at the ceiling. "Nobody's going to like my blood, anyway."

Lissa stops playing the piano. After a moment, Benjamin settles onto the chaise beside me. "It's possible," he says.

I groan, flinging an arm across my eyes. "You're supposed to make me feel better."

"I'm not here to lie to you," he says. "But… I will say that you already possess the most important quality of a valentine. The rest is just stage dressing. If you can find someone who *matches* your particular flavor, I believe you will do quite well."

I let the arm slip off my face and steal a glance at him. "Isn't taste the most important part of being a valentine, though?"

"No," he says. "It's the enjoyment of being bitten. One is either born with it or not, and you have been." He favors me with a small but genuine smile. "The rest can be learned, I assure you."

I smile back at him. It's not the strongest pep talk—there's still that big *if* about finding a proper match—but I appreciate that he's not bullshitting me.

"Alright, alright," I say, sitting up. "Get back to teaching, then. We've only got a week."

Lissa strikes up a lively tune on the piano, and I enthusiastically waltz all over Benjamin's feet again.

* * *

When I fall asleep on the chaise during a break, Benjamin gently shakes me awake and offers the guest room for the night. I stumble over myself trying to express my gratitude; I almost forgot I don't have anywhere to stay tonight.

As I crawl into bed at six in the morning and rest my aching feet, I realize I have a string of missed messages waiting on my phone. For one traitorous moment, I find myself hoping one of them is from Declan saying he misses me. But of course, I still haven't heard from him.

Instead, it's my sister blowing up my phone. My heart sinks when I see the first of her string of messages today: *Just bought my plane ticket!!*

Maisy must be so excited. She's been scrounging and saving money behind my parents' backs for months, since she's supposed to be moving out to live with me before school starts in August. After the initial excited declaration, Maisy's messages have become increasingly worried—the latest reads *HELLO, STILL ALIVE??*

If she reaches out to Declan because I'm not answering, then… crap. I can't bear the thought of her hearing the news from him instead of me.

But if I tell her about the breakup, she'll start panicking about where she's going to live. And I don't know if I'm ready to tell her about this whole valentine situation. Especially not before the ball, when having *her* worry is just going to make me *more* worried.

Maybe I can delay the inevitable conversation. Pretend that everything is fine until I get through the ball and have money to get an apartment for us. Some good news to temper the bad can't hurt, right?

I swallow my nerves and dial her number.

"Amelia?" She picks up on the second ring. "What's wrong?"

"I—" I stammer for a second, caught off guard. So much for

my plan to pretend that nothing is amiss. Immediately, my voice starts going high-pitched and strained. "Wrong? What? Ha, no, nothing's wrong."

Great. Super convincing.

"Amelia, I sent so many texts! So! Many! And now you're calling me at six a.m., what the hell is going on?" Her voice rises to match my own panicked squeaking.

Shit. Not a good start. I didn't even realize the time. "I, um, well…" I consider telling her the truth, but I'm so tired, my eyes ache, and I'm so thoroughly unprepared for that conversation. After a second's indecision, my mouth starts moving before my brain can catch up. "Oh, right, I forgot to tell you. I'm… out of town this week. On a… writing retreat."

"Oh." My sister sounds puzzled but not suspicious "Well, geez, okay, you could have at least answered a text."

"Yeah, my bad… You know how forgetful I am."

She blows out a breath. "Whatever. A retreat, huh? That's cool. But you're gone for Valentine's Day? What about Dec?"

This lie tastes especially bitter in my mouth. "The retreat was a present from him, actually. For supporting him over the years."

"That's sweet." I hear her shift, yawn. "So what kind of crazy retreat has you up at six in the morning?"

"I was… up all night, actually. With my new, um, writing friends. Super inspiring." I wince and pinch the bridge of my nose. "So I can't talk long. Really tired. Sorry. I just, I didn't even think about what time it was, I just saw I had missed a bunch of texts and…"

"Oh, that's okay," she says. "I just wanted to check in about me moving in and everything." There's a pause as I scramble for something to say, and I hear her start to get anxious again.

"I'm excited about getting out of here. Mom and Dad have been really… you know. Them. And when you didn't answer, I started getting all in my head, worrying that something had gone wrong, so…"

"There's nothing to worry about." I shut my eyes, pushing the truth down. There's no going back now. I'm burying myself in lies. But I tell myself I'm doing what's best for my sister. "I promise everything's gonna be fine."

As she sleepily says goodbye, I hang up and tell myself that no matter what, I'll find a way to make sure that, at least, was the truth.

Chapter Five

When Benjamin said he was going to train me to be a valentine, I thought it would be exciting. Maybe even sexy. But instead, it's all a blur of practicing curtsies and dress fittings with Lissa and reading about vampire society until my eyes cross. Part of me is grateful for the intense training regimen. It keeps my mind off Declan and provides a good excuse to accept Benjamin's offer for me to stay at his place until the ball. I have to admit it's nice to have a break from constant work and chores, too. Though I can't shake the sense that I'm out of place here, intruding on Benjamin's and Lissa's privacy.

But it's hard to worry too much because then, just like that, Valentine's Day is here. It's time for the ball.

I pull myself out of bed a couple hours before sundown. Thank *God* I had a week to adjust my sleep schedule so I won't be stumbling around half asleep all night. I'm just getting out of the shower when there's a knock at the bedroom door.

"Come on in," I call, wrapping my hair in a towel. When I walk out into the bedroom, Lissa is waiting, with a rare smile instead of her usual resting bitch face. She gestures, and I turn.

I gasp when I see the dress draped across my bed. Actually gasp out loud, like a soap opera character. But I can't help myself. This is the most beautiful thing I've ever seen, and it's hard to believe it's for me. It looks like yards of rich burgundy silk, and when I reach out to touch it, it's impossibly soft.

"I want to wrap it around myself like a blanket and wear it forever," I say, finally tearing my eyes away from the dress to beam at Lissa. It fades after a moment, though. "But I'm going to trip over my own feet."

"Maybe you'll surprise yourself. You've done well in training."

I shrug, unconvinced. Still, in a dress like this, it seems like even tripping over my own feet would somehow manage to be luxurious. Like I'll swoon right into some handsome vampire's arms.

"Put it on," Lissa urges, already stepping out the door to give me some privacy.

I end up calling her back in for assistance tying up the corset back, but after some struggling, I manage to get the dress on. I pull on my matching red-bottom heels, turn to face myself in the mirror, and watch my own eyes widen in shock. I hardly look like myself. The corset bodice cinches my waist in beautifully, while the sweetheart neckline *really* shows off my assets. The silk hugs my hips before slipping down over my legs, making them look longer than they've ever looked before, and the knee-high slit provides a flirty flash of thigh.

"Damn," I whisper, running my fingers over the material.

"Agreed," Lissa says. "Ah, and here. I got you some jewelry as well." She tucks my hair behind my shoulders and helps me put on a pair of dazzling earrings, real pearls dangling from delicate golden chains. There's a choker to match, featuring delicate layers of gold filigree around my neck, and a thread of pearls that hangs down into my cleavage.

"Shit, I feel expensive," I say, looking at my reflection again. I didn't know I could look this good, or *feel* this good. I can't remember the last time I thought of myself as *sexy*.

"You look amazing," Lissa says, and I preen under the rare praise from her. She's warmed up to me since I've been staying here, but she's still not exactly sunshine and butterflies. "Now, you *better* let me do your makeup and hair so you don't ruin the effect."

I sit at the vanity table without protest.

"Bold, or natural?" Lissa asks. She sets a bag on the table and unzips it to reveal a dazzlingly wide array of makeup products.

I hesitate. I've never worn much makeup—my mom always called it *trashy*, and Declan always said things like *who are you trying to impress?*—but tonight is about making an impression. "Bold," I say, meeting her eyes in the mirror.

"That's what I was hoping you'd say," she murmurs, and gets to work.

I watch myself transform in the mirror, and my confidence grows by the minute. Lissa has a magician's touch, drawing attention to all of my best features. Under her expert hand, the smoldering, dark eyeshadow and plum-colored lips don't look overdone, but captivating. I look like a new version of myself: mysterious and alluring and confident.

She does an incredible job with my hair, as well. She coaxes a never-seen-before glossiness and bounce out of my curls, and then pins everything into place so it looks elegant rather than out of control. I look like an old-school movie star, or maybe like one of those '50s pinup girls, in the best of ways.

"Everyone's going to want a taste of you," she says when she's done, standing back and admiring her handiwork.

My stomach flips, and my expression crumples.

"But what if nobody likes me?" I ask. "Or what if they like me too much?" Oh, God. I've been so focused on learning etiquette and worrying about the way I taste that I never processed the fact I'm going to be surrounded by people who want to *eat* me. Not even people, really, but undead immortals who are faster and stronger than I am. What if they take it too far and hurt me? What if I don't know when to ask them to stop? What if…

Lissa squeezes my shoulder, and it stops me from spiraling. "You're going to be fine," she says. "Benjamin will look after you, and nobody is going to hurt you on his watch. He knows what he's doing."

We both attempt to compose ourselves as Benjamin walks in. He takes one of my hands, lifts me out of my seat, and spins me in place. "You look absolutely striking," he says.

His presence is steadying, a reminder that I'm not going into this alone. I dip into an exaggerated curtsy. I'm surprised how graceful I feel doing it, even as a joke; before Benjamin's training, I'm pretty sure I would have managed to fall over while doing this. In heels, nonetheless!

"Ah, one more thing," he murmurs. He pulls something out of his pocket and holds it up to the light: a metallic pin in the shape of an anatomical heart, colored white and gold. He carefully attaches it to my dress, right over where my own heart beats. "A white heart indicates an unclaimed valentine," he says as he steps back to admire me. "If someone chooses to offer their patronage, you will wear a black one at your next ball."

We both know that isn't going to happen. But still, as I gaze at my appearance in the mirror, I can't help but dream… and that dream is *almost* enough to let me forget that I'm about to be surrounded by vampires from dusk till dawn.

Chapter Six

The size of the grand ballroom is dizzying. Every time I look up at the high, domed ceiling, vertigo washes over me, making me feel like I'm going to tumble right down the staircase. Now *that* would be quite an entrance to the Valentine's Day Ball.

The floor is black marble shot through with gold. More gold adorns the furniture arranged around the edges of the room, the tables, the old-fashioned candlesticks, the delicate railing winding around the staircase below us. Classical music from a live string quartet floats over the background murmur of the crowd. Moonlight streams in through a wall of floor-to-ceiling windows, caught and amplified by crystal chandeliers to lend a dreamy shine to everything in the room. All of this is so gorgeous and luxurious that it hardly seems real.

The moment our ride pulled up to the driveway of this sprawling Victorian mansion, I knew I was out of my league. Now, there is so much going on, I hardly know where to look. I cling to Benjamin's arm as we descend the staircase and enter the buzzing crowd.

Even surrounded by glamor, most stunning of all are the party attendees—and there are hundreds of them. Vampires and humans alike sweep through the party with perfect poise, on-point makeup, and exquisite finery. Each person I see is more beautiful than the last, and I gawk unabashedly. If not for Benjamin navigating us through the ballroom, I'd surely be bumping into furniture and people left and right, because it's so hard to look away.

I cling to my chaperone, heartbeat rising until it's louder than the music in my ears. My anxiety is going haywire in the presence of so many vampires, but also over a thought that keeps repeating in my mind: *why am I here?* I'm going to stick out like a sore thumb amid all of this beauty and poise. Even wearing Lissa's well-crafted disguise of elegance, I'm just… me. Just an achingly normal woman who *really* shouldn't have received an invitation to a place like this, and I'm surely going to screw it up somehow.

Desperate for something to ground me, I latch on to Benjamin's training tip about using vampires' outfits to determine which of the courts they belong to. As he explained in one of our lessons, there are four prominent vampire courts in the United States, and they're bound by values rather than blood.

Camelia Court, whose motto is "strength in beauty, beauty in strength," represented by a dagger piercing a rose. They're made up of models, actors, and fashionistas.

Vulpe Court, "the endless thirst for excellence," with a snake wrapped around a goblet's handle. The artists of the vampire world.

Solomon Court, "keepers of the unwritten," represented by a skull with a moth over its mouth. They enforce vampire law, and "protect our secrets," which Benjamin refused to elaborate on.

And Celeste Court, "they who remember," with the symbol of a quill and crescent moon. The recorders and preservers of history.

Though some are more subtle about it, many of the vampires' outfits make their courts apparent. I spy dramatic capes designed like moth wings, golden quill earrings, and silver snake bracelets. Camelia—roses and daggers—and Vulpe—snakes and goblets—are the two most prominent courts in the crowd, which makes sense for a party like this.

Eventually, Benjamin pauses beside an unoccupied chaise on the edge of the ballroom. A few pairs are already twirling around the dance floor, but the majority of partygoers, like us, are watching from the sidelines. Many of them are humans, blood cards gripped in hand and white hearts pinned to their chests, waiting to be approached by someone.

None of them seem to have chaperones, which makes me feel self-conscious. Yet when I feel him starting to pull away, I clutch Benjamin's arm in sudden fear. "Do. Not. Leave me here," I hiss at him, panic fluttering in my chest. Despite the glamor, I'm well aware that I'm prey surrounded by predators, and Benjamin is the only one I trust to keep me safe.

He gives me a sympathetic look and eases my grip off his bicep. "I promise you're not in any danger here. Just stay put for a minute. If anyone asks for a dance or a bloodletting, please politely inform them you're waiting for your chaperone."

I take a breath and try to steady myself. Right. I can do this. He's not going to throw me into the deep end. This is just a dip into the kiddy pool. And he's paying me for this, so I better play my part. "Okay," I say, and force myself to let go of him and sit on the leather chaise, smoothing my dress under me.

"Just a minute," he repeats. "I'm going to make the rounds and see who's present. You'll be fine." He steps back, pauses, adds, "Don't eat or drink anything," and then disappears into the mix of people, leaving me alone.

Watching from the chaise is slightly less overwhelming than being in the thick of the crowd. Once I get over my nerves, I begin to enjoy people watching. I watch two very handsome men spin around the dance floor together as if they've done it a thousand times before, and then try my best not to gawk at a man drinking from a woman's wrist on a love seat across the room. I can't tell from this distance if she's his valentine or a free agent, but the sight is more than a little titillating.

It reminds me why I'm here. Why I *want* to be here. I take my blood card out of my pocket and fan myself with it to ease my anxious sweat.

"First time?"

I start as I realize someone is speaking to me, and flush. "That obvious?" I ask, glancing up at the woman who spoke. She's a lovely blonde draped in pink tulle, with a white heart indicating that she's an unclaimed valentine.

"You're staring," she says. Her smile has a mean edge. Then she glances at my blood card, clutched tightly in one hand, and gestures. "Do you mind?"

"Oh… no?" I hold it out to her.

"Lord Benjamin *Acharya*?" she reads, frowning. "Your chaperone doesn't even belong to a court?"

"No…" I resist the urge to snatch back the fan before she continues on to the tasting notes I've already memorized. Her eyebrows lift as she reads them to herself: "Lively and intense; a unique flavor for a refined palate." She glances at me, lips

41

curling in a smirk. "That's… interesting."

Before I can take the card back, she turns and gestures to another hopeful-valentine. He walks over and peers over her shoulder, huffing a laugh as he reads my blood card.

My face must be nearly as red as my dress. "What do your notes say?"

"'Sweet and fruit-forward, with a velvety mouthfeel,'" the woman quotes without glancing at hers.

"I'm 'savory, earthy, and decadent,'" the man says with a smirk to match his friend's.

"Well, best of luck tonight," the woman says as she hands back my blood card. "You're going to need it." And then she drifts away with her companion, both of them concealing laughter behind their hands.

I stare down at my blood card, heart sinking again with the reminder that I'm not cut out for this world for more reasons than one. Their tasting notes sounded appealing, but mine… would *not* be a description that would entice me to buy a bottle of wine. The more I read it, the more I think about Benjamin's puckered expression after the first time he tasted my blood. Honestly, the description is just a fancy way to write *"tastes like a steaming pile of shit."* So why did Benjamin bring me here? Am I being paid thousands of dollars to be publicly humiliated?

The shreds of my self-worth are screaming at me to leave. But I'm already here. The worst that could happen is that no one wants to try me, and I get paid for nothing. Right? Benjamin and Lissa assured me there was no actual danger here, and I can handle a bit of humiliation.

"Amelia." I look up to find Benjamin standing over me. "Thank you for waiting." He scrutinizes me, and then follows my glance at the still-giggling valentines who are now gossiping with a small crowd. He frowns. "Some of the valentines get unnecessarily competitive about these events. Don't let them get to you." He offers an arm. "Please, come with me, I'd like to make some introductions."

I bite my cheek but nod, and force myself to rise and take his arm.

Being paraded around the room feels worse than sitting in the corner. Benjamin introduces me to a few different vampires. Each time I curtsy and greet them, I feel more like a show animal putting on a performance. All of them are shockingly beautiful and dressed to the nines, and each makes the same confused face while reading my blood card. None of them offer to taste me, and Benjamin always politely excuses us after a few minutes of uncomfortable conversation.

Uncomfortable for me, at least. Benjamin slides smoothly from circle to circle, always seeming to know the right thing to say or ask, but soon I'm embarrassed and sweating like a pig under this expensive fabric. I fan myself with my blood card.

"Too early to call it a night?" I half-joke, but Benjamin ignores the comment and continues on with the same unshakable confidence.

Next, he approaches a stunning woman who is lounging on a black leather couch in the corner. She's surrounded by a circle of both human and vampire admirers. Some of them are kneeling on the marble floor just for a chance to be near her. And I can see why.

She's strikingly beautiful, with blue eyes so pale, they're nearly colorless, fair hair cropped into an elegant pixie cut, and legs for days. She must be at *least* six feet tall, and her elegant black dress fits her perfectly. But almost as striking is the human draped over her lap like an accessory. He's wearing a deep red velvet suit with a black heart pin displayed proudly on his chest, and has almost the same ethereal beauty as the woman he's with.

When he turns to face me as I approach on Benjamin's arm, I realize with a jolt that I recognize this man's striking green eyes and perfect bone structure. He's the model from the ad that gave me this idea in the first place. Jonah Montgomery, the valentine poster boy. He's even more beautiful in person, his hair elegantly mussed and a hint of stubble on his sharp jawline.

"Lady Viktoria de Camelia," Benjamin says, bowing to the vampire who I assume is Jonah's patron. "May I present Amelia Burton?"

The vampire's pale eyes shift from him to me. So do Jonah's, but though Lady Viktoria's gaze feels curious, Jonah practically burns a hole in my cheek with his glowering. I shift from foot to foot and glance down, working on committing the name to memory. Camelia. Right, the roses. Roses and daggers, beauty and strength. It makes sense for these two heartthrobs and the fawning mob around them.

"Who are you?" the vampire asks—directed not at me, but at Benjamin.

"Lord Benjamin Acharya," he introduces himself.

She gives him a once-over. "My, my. I thought courtless vampires were extinct. How on Earth did you secure an invitation?"

Her tone makes me squirm, but Benjamin is as unflappable as ever.

"Courtless does not mean friendless," he says. "And I could

not miss an opportunity to offer this lovely delicacy." He places a hand on my lower back, and I try not to wither as the vampire's piercing attention falls upon me.

"I have no desire or need for a new valentine," Viktoria says.

"Oh, please be certain, I have no intent to replace your dear Jonah, if such a thing were possible," says Benjamin. "All I am offering is a taste. I think you will find it… refreshingly novel."

Viktoria's lips twitch in amusement. "I'm three hundred years old. I've given up on novelty." Still, she holds out one delicate, long-fingered hand.

Benjamin clears his throat and nudges me. I finally realize what she wants, and flush as I hand over my blood card.

Her eyebrows lift as she snaps the fan open and reads the notes about me. She lowers it, looks up at me, and taps the tasting card against the arm of her chaise. "Very well," she says, after a moment. "May I, dove?" She speaks directly to me for the first time, stunning me with the intensity of her pale gaze. I nod, unable to muster up words. She grabs the pen attached to the card and writes her name in the first slot with a flourish. "Move aside, please, my love."

Jonah sighs and sits up, glaring daggers at me as he perches on the edge of the couch, as though he can't bear moving any further from his patron. I think of him as a cranky shih tzu removed from his owner's lap and have to suppress a giggle.

His isn't the only gaze on me. Viktoria's entire fan club is watching: some vampires with thinly veiled interest in their eyes, other humans almost as sulky and jealous as Jonah. I swallow a nervous joke and sit on the couch near Viktoria. She grabs me and pulls me onto her lap instead; after a darting glance at Benjamin, I let myself be situated there. The vampire moves me all too easily, an iron strength in her deceptively slender arms.

My pulse leaps, my body reacting to being so close to a vampire. Still, it doesn't feel so bad to be held by her like this. It feels pretty good, actually, and I can't fight the stir of interest deep in my belly. Her mouth is close enough to my neck to make me shiver, but as I recall Benjamin's warning, I hold up a wrist in offering instead. She grips it with cold, pale fingers and brings it to her mouth.

She bites like a snake, a quick, darting moment, two needle-thin pinpricks of pain flaring to life on my wrist only to die just as quickly as that heady pleasure sinks in. But it barely lasts a second before she pushes my wrist away.

I stiffen and half turn to see Viktoria grabbing the wineglass she set aside. She brings it to her mouth and spits out a mouthful of my blood.

Judging from the shocked silence, this is unusual. I slide uncertainly off her lap as she sets the wineglass aside. Viktoria doesn't even look at me, but up at Benjamin instead, disgust plain on her face.

Then she tosses her head back and laughs. Her mouth is still stained red with my blood. "A *unique flavor*, indeed! God, what a prank." She presses the back of her hand to her mouth, shoulders shaking with amusement, as she glances around at the onlookers. "Apologies for the manners, but trust me, you'd do the same. I've never tasted anything quite so abhorrent."

Abhorrent. The insult hits me like a fist to the stomach, and it's all I can do to hold back tears as I get to my feet. Vampires and humans alike are glancing at me, chuckling, whispering behind their hands. Jonah is smirking at me from the couch like he's won something.

"My precious, come here, help me get that taste out of my

mouth," Viktoria calls, and he moves over to her. She pulls him against her in a sensual embrace; the sound he makes when she bites his neck borders on obscene.

The display would fascinate me if it weren't only heightening my humiliation. I turn away from them, seeking out Benjamin, who looks at me with sympathy and not a hint of surprise.

I take his proffered arm with a bit more force than necessary, squeezing myself tight against his side as he leads me away from Viktoria.

"You knew that was going to happen," I hiss at him. "Why put me through that?"

He places a hand on my arm and gives me an apologetic look. "Look around and see."

Huffing out an annoyed breath, I glance around. But that anger soon shifts to surprise as I notice all eyes on me. Heads turn to follow our slow progression through the party.

"Viktoria made you a spectacle," Benjamin murmurs, low in my ear. "And vampires *love* a spectacle. Trust me, Amelia: the night has only just begun."

* * *

Benjamin turns out to be entirely goddamn right.

It takes all of two minutes for another vampire to approach us, this one a gorgeous Black man in an all-white suit. He politely requests to take the next spot on my blood card, two hours from now, and leaves only to be replaced by another: a pretty blonde valentine with a black heart pin, asking for the third spot on behalf of her patron.

"I don't understand," I mutter, beelining to the buffet table as soon as I get a chance. Benjamin grasps me by the elbow and steers me away from the one I was aiming for—which I realize, on second glance, must be the blood-infused desserts for vampires—and toward another. "Viktoria made it very clear that I taste disgusting."

The food is as dazzling as everything else. Platters of candied fruit arranged like a work of art, golden serving trays piled high with tea cakes and bite-sized tarts. Right now, I desperately need some sugar to get the bitter taste of humiliation out of my mouth.

"Imagine being hundreds of years old and hearing that you could experience something entirely *new* for the first time. Wouldn't you be tempted, even if it wasn't a pleasant experience?" Benjamin pauses to side-eye me as I shove an entire pink cupcake into my mouth. He sighs, grabs a porcelain dish, and fills it with a few choice options from the table before shoving it at me. "Beef carpaccio, spinach, potatoes," he tells me. "You need iron and b-vitamins, not sugar."

"Everyone else is eating sugar," I retort. All around me are hopeful valentines snacking on delicate pastries, and chocolate-covered strawberries, and pretty little fruit tarts.

"Everyone else is aiming for *sweet*," he says with a roll of his eyes. "Because they do not have the benefit of your distinctive flavor." I'm about to tell him exactly how much I value this *distinctive* flavor and what it's gotten me when his tone softens and he adds, "And they don't have someone looking after them."

I hate that it gets to me. It's like a knee-jerk response for my heart to go all warm and melty whenever someone shows me the slightest bit of care. I don't think I realized how long I had spent clinging to scraps of affection with Declan.

But that softness has never gotten me anything but trouble. "Aw, thanks, Daddy," I tell him with as much sarcasm as I can muster. I take the plate and pop a thin slice of meat into my mouth with my fingers.

After rolling his eyes at me, Benjamin leads me on a spin around the dance floor, and I surprise myself by only stepping on his feet a couple times A few others ask to dance as well: a very serious man in a slim-cut suit, a shy woman with big blue eyes and a puffy dress to match, a gorgeous vampire of indiscernible gender wearing some kind of tuxedo-and-cape outfit I can't make heads or tails of. Just when I'm starting to have fun, the time comes for my next blood appointment.

As I sit on the chaise and offer my wrist to the Black gentleman who took the slot on my card, I can't help but notice that a small crowd of onlookers has gathered. The vampire is all gentility and softness as he takes my hand, and I barely feel the bite. But I *do* feel the sting when he pulls back, his expression puckering in a way that stands at stark odds with his usual politeness. He manages to compose himself and thanks me for the taste, but I'm beet red as he pulls away, especially when I notice the tittering of the onlookers behind their hands.

Feeling lightheaded either from the blood loss or the embarrassment, I spend the next couple of hours lounging while Benjamin fusses over me and brings me food.

All too soon, my next appointment arrives, and the crowd is even bigger this time.

I dislike the look of this smirking vampire with his dark

hair slicked back, but I've already agreed, so I politely offer my wrist and a thin smile. He bites into me hard enough that I wince, and then pulls back just as quickly, letting out a theatrical sound of disgust and leaving blood spurting from my wrist. Benjamin is at my side quickly, dabbing at me with vampire blood to heal the wound, but that can't take away the embarrassment.

The crowd laughs as I bleed. Louder this time, emboldened by the vampire's mockery of me as he pretends to gag and retch. He slinks into the crowd without another glance, loudly describing the *foul* taste of my blood to anyone who will listen.

I suck in a breath and will myself not to let despair show on my expression. I will not let these people see that they're hurting me. And there's no need to be hurt, not really. It's not like I can control it. And I'm getting paid either way. So why do I feel this way? Why does it feel like the sharp sting of rejection, over and over again, bringing me back to that door slamming in my face as I left Declan's apartment?

I shut my eyes, fighting back tears. Benjamin touches my shoulder. At first, I think he's offering polite comfort, but when I open my eyes again, I see that he's also getting my attention because two more vampires are coming my way to politely inquire about my blood card.

I force my head up and plaster on a smile. If nothing else, at least I am a novelty.

Chapter Seven

I wobble on my heels as I make my way away from the latest vampire who made a mockery of me. It seems like a game to them: who can have the most over-the-top reaction and entertain the ever-growing crowd the most. The dress that once felt beautiful and luxurious is now stifling and restrictive; the ballroom full of glitz and glamor is inducing a headache.

Benjamin is close behind me, one cool hand resting on my upper back to steady me. I groan, sinking down into a plush armchair by a window, as far away from the dance floor and the crowd as I can manage. Yet even here, I can feel the eyes on me. I can sense the hunger.

Benjamin was right; these people do value me as a novelty, if nothing else. I can't say he didn't warn me. But I didn't expect it would leave me feeling so… used. Valentines always seem cherished, pampered by their patrons in a way that makes it seem like a more than fair exchange. But this doesn't feel like that. This makes me feel like I'm just a *thing* to them.

Still. I just have to fill one more slot on my blood card. Go through this one more time. Then I can dry my tears with the pile of cash I'm making.

"Can I get some air before the last one?" I ask, looking up at Benjamin.

"Of course." He offers his arm, and I follow him outside onto the back patio.

The cool air sweeps over my too-warm skin with a delicious prickle. The music and chatter of the party are muted now, not so overwhelming. The garden is beautiful and well-manicured, with rows of decadent rose bushes bursting with lush petals in various colors. And there's an *actual* hedge maze. I didn't think they existed in real life, and I can't help but wander in, Benjamin trailing behind me. The whole area is strung with fairy lights, so that it is pleasantly dim but not dark enough to be menacing.

"*Help!*"

A cry shatters the peaceful night. I exchange a wide-eyed look with Benjamin.

He hesitates. "You should go inside."

"What? No." I tug at his arm. "We have to help!"

He reluctantly obliges. We head deeper into the hedge maze, toward the noise.

Around the next corner, a woman crouches beside a huddled form. When she looks up, I recognize the tear-streaked face of the human woman who was mocking my blood card earlier. Crumpled on the grass is the man who ridiculed me alongside her.

Benjamin strides forward. "What happened?" he asks, crouching to scrutinize the bite mark on the man's neck. "Was he attacked?"

"N-no. He was… we were…" The woman is too distraught to make sense. I rub her back as she sobs. She may be a bitch, but I can't help the urge to comfort her when she's so upset.

"He must've given too much blood," Benjamin says. "But he's fine. His heartbeat is steady." He looks from the unconscious man to me. "I should get him inside, but…"

"I'll be right behind you," I promise. I tug the woman's arm, helping her to stand. "Both of us will."

Benjamin nods. He lifts the man into his arms with ease and is gone in the blink of an eye.

I pat the woman's hand and lead her back toward the party. "Come on. It'll be okay."

But just as we're about to turn the corner toward the hedge maze's exit, two figures in matching gray suits step in front of us.

They move smoothly out of the shadows, a liquid grace in their steps that would scream *vampire* even if I weren't at a party like this. For a moment, I swear I glimpse a third in the darkness, a pair of pale eyes watching me—but I blink and they're gone, and I focus on the two approaching us. The woman at my side stiffens.

Most vampires look as though they were turned in their mid or late twenties, but these two appear younger than me, like college kids. Both are, of course, gorgeous, but something about their smiles makes my alarm bells ring.

"Well, well, if it isn't the lady of the night," one says. He has dark hair, a ring pierced through his lower lip, and a skull earring dangling from one earlobe. He reaches forward and plucks my blood card out of my hand without asking. He scrutinizes, and then mutters, "Only one spot left." His gaze flicks up to meet mine. "But surely you won't deny us?"

"Oh, um…" I look from face to face—the smirking one with the piercing, and a fair-haired man with an expression as cold as ice and a moth tattoo wrapped around his throat. "My chaperone—"

"Chaperone? How old-fashioned." The dark-haired vampire gives an exaggerated look around the garden. "But I don't see a chaperone. Do you, Dante?"

"No chaperone," the blond agrees.

"He'll be right back." I glance toward the maze exit—and see that the woman I was with is inching toward it, making her escape since the vampires are focused on me. Our eyes meet, and I shoot her a pleading look. She turns her back and leaves.

Well, fuck.

My chest feels tight. I thought my body had become accustomed to being around vampires, but that was with Benjamin at my side to protect me. Now I'm alone, and these two are setting off those age-old instincts that scream I'm in danger.

"My name's Dominic," the dark-haired vampire says. "I saw Viktoria feeding on you. You like it, don't you? You had that look." He moves closer, as close as he can without touching me. "I bet you haven't been fed on by multiple people at once," he says with a dangerous smile. "I bet you'd like it even more. And we're good at sharing." His gaze flicks to the quiet blond man—Dante, he called him—who is watching me intently.

Part of me thrills at the sense of being so obviously *desired*, even if it's just for my blood. But I can't stop thinking about Benjamin's warnings… and the sight of that man crumpled on the ground. Are these the vampires who did that?

"I think I should wait for my chaperone," I say in a small voice.

Dominic chuckles, the sound low and dangerous. "You're no fun," he says. He doesn't reach for me, but he and his friend are still blocking my exit.

All I can do is wait for Benjamin—but can he protect me? He's a single vampire without a court, and judging from the skull earring and moth tattoo, these two belong to Solomon. *The secret keepers. The most dangerous of the courts.*

I try to remember what Benjamin told me about vampire weaknesses. Sunlight, silver, and decapitation. Nothing that will help me right now. I'm only armed with my manners. Benjamin insisted they would help keep me safe, which was a lot easier to believe in the glitz and shimmer of the ballroom.

"Please let me pass," I say.

A beat. Nothing happens. And then—

"You heard her."

Both vampires' spines stiffen. Their heads whip away in the direction of the mansion. I can't see anything in the darkness of the hedge maze that way, but their eyes widen.

A moment later, another vampire steps into the light, and my mortal eyes find him, too.

He's tall with broad shoulders and a lean build, thick dark hair styled neatly. The tuxedo he wears is all black. His eyes are so dark, they look black as well, like two pools of darkness in his pale face. And what a face… even among the vampires he would stand out, with cheekbones like a marble statue and a shadow of facial hair perfectly accentuating his sharp jawline. He is *shockingly*, timelessly handsome, and the intensity of his gaze only heightens the effect he has on me.

"Lord Sebastian," Dominic says, his voice formal now, all the playfulness gone. "I didn't know you were attending tonight's ball."

"What do you want?" asks Dante. His voice is sharp, bordering on threatening. His shoulders are tense and his eyes narrowed, like he sees the man as a threat. But what could possibly threaten a vampire? A *pair* of vampires, nonetheless?

This "Lord Sebastian" comes to a stop about a yard away from me. He does not look at the man at my side, or the one who seems on the verge of ripping his throat out. Instead, he looks at me, standing frozen, a deer surrounded by wolves.

"I would like to claim the last spot on your blood card," Sebastian says.

Chapter Eight

Dominic and Dante are tense, muscles coiled, as though they're expecting a fight. But Sebastian walks over with his hands in his pockets and his posture relaxed, as if he hasn't a care in the world. To my shock, the two others peel away as he approaches, retreating with a haste that almost feels like fear. They exchange glances, but Sebastian is not even looking at them. His arresting gaze is locked on mine. He stops a couple of feet ahead of me and holds out his hand palm up.

"May I?" he asks.

I reach for where my blood card should be before realizing Dominic still has it.

"I, um, he…" I mutter, glancing over at where the duo is looking on unhappily.

Sebastian follows my gaze, and his expression sharpens. When he speaks again, I catch a glimpse of fangs catching the moonlight. "The lady's blood card," he demands.

There's a swollen moment of silence. Then Dominic steps forward, jaw clenched, and holds out the fan to Sebastian, getting only close enough that the other vampire could reach out and take it.

But Sebastian doesn't move. "It doesn't belong to me. It belongs to her," he says.

My breath hitches. Dominic's lip curls. For a moment, I swear there's going to be violence. But then Dominic turns to me, steps forward, and holds the blood card out to me instead. "Here," he mutters.

I swallow hard and take it. "Thank you."

Glaring daggers at Sebastian, the two vampires step back into the night they appeared from. Sebastian watches them go before turning to me. His posture is ramrod straight, his bearing solemn. Most vampires seem to be masquerading as the nobility they claim to be, but with Sebastian, I can see it. He seems, every inch of him, a king among peasants.

He looks at me expectantly. I stare back for a moment before I remember that he asked me a question. He wants permission to sign my blood card and claim my final spot for the night. I should wait for Benjamin… but I can't deny that I'm intrigued by this man, and I feel safer around him than I did with the other two vampires. I peel my clenched hand off my blood card and offer it to him.

His cold fingers brush against mine, and I suppress a gasp as electricity zips through my veins.

But instead of signing the card, he only scrutinizes it. "Where is your chaperone?"

"He should be back any minute," I say.

He taps a finger against the paper. *"Benjamin Acharya."*

I fold my arms across my chest. I'm not thrilled by Benjamin myself after how tonight has gone, but I still don't like this vampire's judgmental tone. "Let me guess, you disapprove because he's courtless?"

Sebastian glances up at me. "I disapprove because he's not

here."

"There was a situation. It's not his fault."

"You could've been hurt."

"But I wasn't."

His jaw clenches. "That's not the—"

"Amelia!"

We both turn at the sound of Benjamin's voice. My chaperone rushes into the hedge maze and looks me frantically up and down before he seems to note the other vampire's presence. Then his eyes widen and he hastily drops into a bow. "Lord Sebastian," he says. A sideways glance encourages me to show similar respect—but I'm too annoyed with both of them.

"Took you long enough," I say to Benjamin. And then, to Sebastian, "Are you going to sign my blood card or not?"

"*Amelia,*" Benjamin chastises under his breath.

Sebastian gives me a long look, my blood card still in his hand. Then he flips the fan open, grabs the pen, and writes his name in the final spot. I hold out my hand, and he walks over and surrenders the blood card to me. Our eyes meet one last time—his gaze dark and intense—before he turns to Benjamin.

"You ought to keep a closer eye on her," he says.

Benjamin bows his head, not even making eye contact. He looks small beside Sebastian. "I will. My apologies."

Sebastian nods, and just like that, turns to leave.

What the hell?

Blood boiling, I ignore Benjamin's warning look and call out before I can think better of it. "You're not even going to try my blood?"

Sebastian pauses but doesn't turn back. "Consider it a

reprieve. An easy night."

Righteous indignation flares in my chest. "I'm not looking for an easy night," I say, tapping my blood card against my arm. "I'm looking for a patron. And I get that you swooped in here thinking you were saving me, but in actuality, you might have ruined one of my last chances to find one."

He pauses, posture stiffening, and slowly turns to face me again.

"Please excuse—" Benjamin starts, but he goes silent as Sebastian raises a hand.

"No," Sebastian says. "She's correct. I signed her card. It's only right for me to drink from her."

He gestures to a nearby, wrought-iron bench. Chin held high, I lift my skirts and walk over to settle myself on it, trying to pretend my heart isn't pounding at the realization of what I've gotten myself into. Benjamin stands back as Sebastian comes to join me.

All of the boldness goes out of me once he's near. I remember that I'm challenging a vampire who just scared off two of his kind with barely a few words.

This close, I can see that Sebastian's eyes aren't truly black, but a very deep brown. Closer scrutiny reveals that he is not quite as perfect as he seemed from afar. He has a distinctive, aquiline nose. Shadows under his eyes and a perpetual furrow to his brow make him look older than most vampires. And, goddamn it, somehow it only makes me more attracted to him.

I tear my gaze away to glance down at my blood card again and process the name he wrote: *Lord Sebastian de Celeste.* I try to rack my memory for which court that is, but I'm too distracted by his nearness, the sensation of his eyes on me.

My eyes flick to his all-black outfit, and I find a hint in the shape of a small metallic moon pinned to the pocket of his suit. *Moon and quill. "They who remember."* That's right—Celeste is the court I deemed "old and boring" in Benjamin's lesson.

Sebastian does not give the impression of being either. I flush at the thought, swallow hard, and hold out my wrist to him.

But instead of taking it, he reaches into his pocket and pulls out a syringe. "I'll be using this."

I don't know much about vampire culture, but this definitely feels like an insult. Maybe he's so repulsed by me that he can't stand the thought of putting his lips against my bare skin. Part of me wants to turn him away for the snub, but judging from his cold expression, that's exactly what he wants. So I stubbornly set my jaw, keep my wrist extended, and nod, my gaze holding his.

At least I'll get a laugh out of watching his surprise at the taste of me. He didn't even read my notes.

Sebastian drops his eyes from mine as he sets the needle to my skin. His other hand holds me steady, and goose bumps ripple under his cold touch. He works with surprising care and gentleness. I barely feel the needle enter my skin, and watch as he fills the syringe with my blood. It doesn't feel anywhere near as intimate as when the vampires drank from me directly, and nowhere near as pleasant, either, but it's oddly fascinating to watch my blood fill the small tube.

Once the syringe is full, he makes eye contact with me again as he raises it to his mouth. He tilts his head back, full lips parting, and empties the syringe into his mouth in one long push. Only when he has a full mouthful does he swallow, hard and fast like he's forcing down a pill.

Surprise flickers across his face, so fast, I wouldn't have caught it if I weren't studying him. He's close enough for me to see the way his eyes dilate, pupils growing so large, his eyes look black once more. His tongue glides over the sharp tips of his fangs before he closes his mouth. But a moment later, his expression smooths over into cold disinterest.

"There," he says. "Are you satisfied?"

I blink at him. Blink again, waiting for a shudder of disgust or loud exclamation of shock. "That's it?"

His brow creases. "What did you expect?"

"I…" I bite my tongue. Of course, he's just being a gentleman. Probably trying his hardest to maintain a poker face. I clear my throat, stand, and offer him an exaggerated curtsy. "It's been a pleasure, Lord Sebastian." I rejoin Benjamin where he stands waiting, hoping Sebastian didn't notice the heat crawling up my neck.

Before I can make my hasty escape, he calls out once more. "And your name?"

I stop, glance back over my shoulder. "What?"

"You didn't tell me your name," he says, his gaze steady as he looks at me.

I resist the urge to roll my eyes. It was right on my blood card, but of course, he barely glanced at the thing before scrawling his name there. And I'm not sure why he cares, given that this is the last time we have to experience one another's company. "Amelia," I tell him, anyway. "Amelia Burton."

As I walk inside on Benjamin's arm, I feel Sebastian's eyes following me.

Chapter Nine

The frantic pace of the party slows as dawn approaches. Couples and groups drift out the door, some to more exclusive after-parties, like Lady Viktoria de Camelia and her beautiful coterie. I don't see Sebastian again, so I assume he left after our encounter in the garden.

I'm not sure why I can't stop thinking about it. Nor why I'm disappointed. He's the one vampire who tasted my blood and didn't humiliate me over it, but somehow his cold disinterest was even more of a letdown. Like the one person who could stomach my blood without making a face still wasn't interested in me. My terrible blood seems to be the only thing that anyone found noteworthy.

The vampire duo I met in the garden certainly aren't interested in me anymore, now that the opportunity to taste me has passed. I see them a few more times inside—flirting with the human bartender, feeding each other blood-infused pastries—but only Dominic glances at me, once, before frowning and turning his back to me.

The only person continuing to tolerate my presence is Benjamin. He's hovered over me since the moment we stepped back inside, practically incoherent with concern, especially after I told him what happened with the two Solomon vampires.

As the night winds down and the ballroom empties, I resist the urge to ask if we can leave yet. I *am* getting paid for this, after all. I drape myself in what I hope is an alluring way across a chaise but only succeed in nodding off multiple times. Then a cold hand squeezes my shoulder, and I jolt awake. I glance up at Benjamin and then follow his gaze to another vampire standing over me. For a moment, the stranger's pale eyes look familiar, but I brush it off; I must have seen him around the party earlier. It'd be hard to overlook such a beautiful man. There's something elfin and enchanting about him, with hair so fair it's nearly white, and a sharp intelligence in his blue gaze.

"She's done for the night, I'm afraid," Benjamin says. I'm surprised at the clipped, cold nature of his voice.

"I see." I realize, with a start, that the stranger is holding my blood card. It must have fallen from my hand while I dozed off. Those pale eyes study my tasting notes and the names written to claim my bloodlettings. "Amelia Burton," he reads, and his eyes shift to meet mine. I freeze, caught by the piercing quality of his stare. "I've heard a lot about you. It's a shame I didn't have the chance to get a taste." His eyes linger on my neck, and then on my lips.

I flush, but the attention is not entirely unpleasant, especially after that encounter with Sebastian left me feeling raw and vulnerable. I smile up at the stranger and then look at Benjamin.

"Would it really be so bad to have one last bloodletting?" I ask.

There's a hard set to Benjamin's jaw. "I'm sorry. It's not

possible."

I open my mouth to protest but cut off as the fair vampire laughs. "Far be it from me to challenge your chaperone," he says, returning my blood card to my hand. "But perhaps he would allow you one last dance with me?"

"Of course he would," I say, before Benjamin can get a word out.

After a moment, Benjamin releases my shoulder. "One dance," he says. "Then we had best be off."

I hand my blood card to Benjamin and accept the fair vampire's hand. He lifts me to my feet without an ounce of effort. I giggle with delight as he sweeps me onto the dance floor, all gallantry and grace. He's like a real-life prince.

"I'm sorry, I forgot to ask your name," I say as he leads me in a waltz around the nearly empty dance floor.

"I am Lord Alexander de Solomon," he says.

I miss a step and nearly stomp on his foot, but he lowers me into a dip that renders me dizzy. When he lifts me back up, I study his face. He's not wearing anything that indicates his court, and I would never have guessed from that charming smile that he belongs to the court of secrets. The same as those two men who frightened me in the garden earlier. Of course I can't judge him for that when he wasn't involved, but still…

"I'm guessing your chaperone didn't have the kindest things to say about my court," he says. "The days of the war are behind us now, but vampires are slow to forget and slower to forgive."

I nod. I don't really understand, but Benjamin did say that the courts had a tangled history, and I'm sure that includes old grudges. Maybe Benjamin doesn't like Alexander just because he's from Solomon?

Alexander seems perfectly charming to me. He treats me kindlier than just about any other vampire has tonight. As the song comes to an end, I'm reluctant to step away from him. But instead of releasing my hand, he nods in the direction of the bar, mischief in his eyes.

"Maybe we can steal one drink together before your chaperone catches us?"

I bite my lip. It *would* be a shame to end the night just as it's getting good, wouldn't it? "Just one," I say, and follow him to the bar. As he gets us drinks, I scan the crowd for Benjamin. He's caught up in a conversation with a few other vampires but tries to catch my eye across the room. I turn away, pretending I didn't see him, and accept a glass of champagne from Alexander with a smile.

"Cheers to your first ball," he says, and clinks his glass against mine. To my surprise, he throws his drink back quickly, so I laugh and do the same. When I lower the empty glass, Alexander is staring at me. I flush; it's a heady feeling, to be so blatantly wanted. He leans close, one hand grazing my hip. For one mad moment I think his mouth is moving toward my neck, but instead he whispers into my ear.

"It is a shame I didn't get a taste of you," he says, his voice sending a delicious shiver down my spine. "But we could—"

"Pardon," a voice interrupts. "I believe your one dance is up."

Alexander and I both turn to see a very annoyed Benjamin standing beside us. I'm torn between mortification at being caught in an intimate moment, irritation at being interrupted, and relief that he probably stopped me from doing something rash, because Alexander's seduction is *definitely* working.

I step away from our embrace. Alexander grabs my hand

and presses a quick kiss to my knuckles before releasing me.

"It seems you had best go before you turn into a pumpkin, or whatever it is your chaperone fears," he says with a wicked smile that makes me blush all over again. "I hope to see you again, Amelia Burton."

Tension hisses between Benjamin and I as he leads me toward the door. I fully intend to give him a piece of my mind, and I suspect he means to do the same. But when I stumble over the step and nearly fall, he grabs me around the waist to hold me up, and his stern expression softens.

"You must be exhausted," he says. "It's almost dawn. Come, you can spend one more night at my house."

I want to insist I can find my own bed for the night, if only for politeness's sake, but my attempt is stifled by a yawn. My head is suddenly spinning; my exhaustion must finally be catching up with me. When Benjamin gives me an encouraging smile, I rub my eyes and nod.

"One more night," I agree.

* * *

I don't remember much of the ride home. Then comes a vague memory of strong, cold arms holding me, and Lissa grumbling about missed sleep as she helps me out of my dress and into an oversized sleep shirt.

When I wake again, I'm tucked into the guest room at Benjamin's house. I'm lost as to what time it is, and a glance at the window doesn't help, because it's covered by blackout curtains. I groan, fumble along the nightstand until I find my phone, glance at the time, and then do a double take. It's six p.m. Jesus Christ. I can't believe Benjamin didn't come kick me out of his house already.

The sweet, sweet smell of coffee draws me down to the parlor where we had our whirlwind of lessons over the last week.

Benjamin and Lissa are sitting at the table with the coffeepot, along with small containers of cream and sugar. Lissa is in a pink nightgown, and Benjamin in flannel, which I would probably make several jokes about if I wasn't dead tired.

"Please tell me there's coffee without blood in it," I burst out in lieu of a greeting.

"There is," Benjamin says, inclining his head toward the pot. "But I have to warn you that I made it today, so it may not be up to your usual standard." He glances over at Lissa and gives one of those soft smiles that has resulted in me shipping the two of them together ever since I arrived. "It's her day off."

"That's right," Lissa says. "Everyone can make their own damn coffee today."

I grin and serve myself, add some cream, a sugar cube, and then another sugar cube because I deserve it. I take a big sip, sigh, and then rest my face on the edge of the table.

"God," I groan. "I feel like I got hit by a truck."

"It was quite the party, no?" Benjamin asks, sipping his coffee.

I grumble incoherently, still face down.

"You'll need your recovery vitamins as well," he says. "They'll help more than the caffeine, I promise."

I lift my head to eye the container of colorful pills he's pushing over.

"And plenty of water," he says, nudging a glass toward me.

I stick my tongue out at him but do as he says, swallowing the pills one after another. Once I start drinking water, I can't stop until the glass is empty, and only then do I return to my caffeine.

A couple of minutes pass in the quiet as we sip our coffee and wake up. Then Benjamin clears his throat and sets down his mug. "I suppose I should pass along the good news."

"If 'good news' means 'the five thousand dollars I owe you,' I'd be delighted to receive it." And now that this is over, I can start apartment shopping and figuring out how to admit my lies to my sister. Time to go back to my sad but *safe* reality.

Benjamin cracks a smile. "Your payment has already been deposited in your account. But there's more."

I finish off my coffee and eye him, unsure what to expect. He reaches into his pocket, pulls out an envelope, and slides it across the table to me.

"Is it a bonus for being so overwhelmingly charming?" I ask as I pick it up. The envelope is thick and expensive-looking. My full name is written in beautiful red calligraphy on the front, and there's an actual wax seal on it. I feel bad ripping it open, but I do it anyway, and pull out the luxurious, cream-colored stationery from within. I squint, struggling to read the old-fashioned cursive. Then my eyes widen. "Wait... is this..." I glance up, my gaze darting between Benjamin and Lissa, who are both beaming.

"Yes," Benjamin says. "I'm delighted to report that you've received an offer of patronage."

Mouth hanging open, I give up on translating the cursive and skip to the bottom of the letter to find a name. I fully expect to see *Alexander de Solomon*, the name that's been lingering in my mind since we danced. I'm pretty sure I had naughty dreams about those last words he whispered to me.

But that's not what the signature says.

"Lord Sebastian de Celeste," I breathe, stiffening. I remember the darkly gorgeous man from the garden, his bland reaction to my blood. "But… he… He didn't even *like* me."

"It appears he very much did."

I squint down at the letter. "Or he's trying to lure me to his mansion so he can murder me."

"This is not like a party, where there is the threat of something happening to an unclaimed valentine. With a contract signed, you will be legally protected by the Celeste Court." Benjamin smiles. "And also, I assure you that I would never try to arrange you with a patron whom I did not trust."

I can't stop running my fingers over the silky paper, as if reassuring myself that it's real. Still, my expression feels stuck somewhere halfway between a smile and a grimace. My mind keeps flashing back to Alexander's smooth smile, comparing it with Sebastian's dour scowl. "I don't suppose I got any other offers?"

Benjamin frowns. "Lord Sebastian is a highly respected vampire of the Celeste Court," he says. "He may not live the sort of decadent social life you were expecting, but he is an honorable man. I trust that he will treat you well."

"No, sorry, you're right. I just…" I set the letter on the table and tap my fingers on the wood beside it. "I'm surprised, I guess. I got the impression he couldn't stand me. You saw it. He didn't even want to bite me."

Benjamin's brow furrows. "Drinking from you with a syringe was a quirk, I'll admit. The contract is for six months rather than a full year, which is… also rather less common. Plus there's a clause for you to sign indicating that you have no desire to be turned into a vampire. That's a legally tricky, physically dangerous process as it is, so I would suggest agreeing."

"That's not a problem," I say, shuddering at the thought. As much as I'm enamored with vampires, I've always pictured myself as the bitten rather than the one who bites. A lifetime without the sun? Without being able to eat chocolate unless it has blood in it? No thanks. "But the rest is weird, right? I don't understand why he'd choose me."

Benjamin shrugs. "I'm sure you can ask him his reasoning yourself if you accept his offer."

What choice do I have? I want to ask. But I hold back because I know that's not true. I *do* have choices. I could run back to my parents' house, or use the five thousand dollars I made last night to start a new life with my sister here. But even though I have my reservations, I can't deny that this choice is the one that holds the most appeal for me. I came here wanting to be a valentine, and after getting a taste of it last night, I'm only more intrigued.

I'm intrigued by Sebastian de Celeste, too, as loath as I am to admit it. If it were a *choice,* I probably would've gone for Alexander, but still… I can't get the image of those almost-black eyes out of my head. I want to know more about what lurks in those dark depths. I want to know why he chose to make this offer after our less-than-stellar first meeting. I want to know if he isn't as disgusted by my blood as everyone else, or if he's just better at hiding it.

Worrying my lower lip, I look at Benjamin. "What do you know about him?"

"He's said to be reclusive," he says. "He lives in a mountain estate that has been in his family since before he was turned, which was over two hundred years ago."

"*I've* heard he's very handsome," Lissa chimes in with a wink. I grin at her, nodding.

"He also played a significant role in the last court war as a young vampire," Benjamin continues, choosing to ignore that commentary. "Solomon attempted to absorb the Celeste Court, and likely would have succeeded if not for some prominent members such as Sebastian who fought fiercely to retain their independence. But he was also, as I recall, one of the first to call for an end to the war. Since then, he's retreated from the public eye."

Trying to wrap my head around that makes me dizzy. Over two hundred years of history, and such a significant history as all that… What could someone like him see in someone like me?

I can't possibly imagine. But I would like to find out. I run my finger over his signature on the offer letter and then glance between Benjamin and Lissa. "Will you go over the contract with me?"

Chapter Ten

Everything moves quickly after I agree. It only takes a couple of days for Benjamin to file paperwork with the vampire courts to make sure I'm protected. He's kind enough to encourage me to stay with him during the waiting period—and I'm starting to think he knows I don't have anywhere else to go, even though I haven't admitted it. I ask him if I should text or call my new patron before I head to see him again, but to my stupefaction, Benjamin says that Sebastian doesn't have a cell phone.

I pass one day working a final shift at the diner because I feel guilty leaving them stranded, and then hand in my resignation. On another, Lissa insists on taking me shopping for a few new outfits.

"You're officially a valentine now," she says when I wince at the price tags. "You should look the part."

But even when I'm draped in silk and diamonds, I feel like an impostor. I swear that any second now, Sebastian is going to retract the offer and declare it was a cruel prank.

Yet all of a sudden, I'm on a plane, and then in a limo with tinted windows, being transported to Lord Sebastian's mountain home as his official valentine.

When Benjamin warned me about how remote Sebastian's estate is, I thought it sounded luxurious and romantic. Yet a couple hours into the ride, with nothing but classical music playing over the speakers for company and the city lights far behind us, I find myself wondering if it's more of a gothic horror story that I'm waltzing into.

But oh well. I'm here now, and the extensive paperwork is signed. There's little to do except lean back in my absurdly plush seat and sip from the bottle of champagne that was waiting for me in a little ice bucket.

"Fancy as heck," I mutter, wiping my mouth with the back of my hand and putting my bright yellow sneakers up on the seat next to me.

But then I remember: there is still *one* more thing to do. I take another sip of champagne to fortify myself and call my sister.

"Amelia! How was your writing retreat?"

"Good. Great, actually." And as impromptu as that lie was, it set the stage for my next one. "Matter of fact, it led to an even better opportunity for me. I'm not allowed to talk about the details quite yet, very hush-hush, but… I'm traveling up to the Bay Area for six months for a contract job I'm excited about."

There's a brief pause on the other end. "Oh," she says. "That's really great! I'm happy for you, but…"

"You're worried about where you're going to stay for school," I say, before she has to say it. "Don't worry, I've got you. Matter of fact… the money from this new job means that I'm able to rent you an apartment of your own."

"What? Seriously?" Maisy's tone teeters between concerned and excited. "That sounds expensive. I really don't need— I mean, I'm grateful, but—"

"Seriously, don't worry about it. I want to help you." I pull the phone away from my ear and text her the information about the apartment I'm arranging. It's a cute two-bedroom spot near the university. It *is* expensive, but the rent is doable with my generous valentine salary. And it works out perfectly, really—my six-month contract with Sebastian will be done in August, the same month that Maisy starts school.

In addition to securing a safe place for my sister to live, I'll have somewhere I can travel to if things don't work out with my mysterious patron. After what Declan did to me, I never want to end up stranded again.

"The one condition is that if things don't work out between me and Declan, you'll let me move in," I say, disguised in a joking tone, but testing the waters.

"Oh my God, don't even joke!" Maisy says. "We all know you two are destined to be together forever."

I swallow a lump in my throat. "Right." I guess that's what I get for keeping the worst parts of my relationship from her. I never wanted Maisy to worry about me. Which is maybe why I want to keep the breakup and this valentine gig a secret for just a little while longer. She has her upcoming move and the start of the school year to worry about.

"But seriously," she says, catching a hint from my tone, "you're welcome whenever you want. Though I can't promise I won't try to pry details about this mysterious new job out of you."

I smile to myself. If only she knew… and one day she will. But not today. I excuse myself soon after that and finish off the rest of the bottle of champagne as a reward for the conversation going well.

After that, I'm feeling pleasantly hazy. With nothing else to do, I doze off.

* * *

When I wake again, there is a castle outside the window.

At least, that's what it looks like. I expected someplace fancy the moment I heard *vampire*, and even fancier when I heard *estate*, but I didn't expect it to be so close to my gothic daydreams. With the redwoods towering around us and mist draping the grounds, there is a dreamlike quality to the whole thing. We traveled only a handful of hours away from busy, sunny Los Angeles, but Northern California might as well be another world. I sit up in my seat and press my nose to the window, impatiently wiping at the glass when my breath fogs it.

The three-story house is painted dark gray, with deep crimson windows and doors. A porch wraps around the outside, supported by stark white pillars. Towers form sharp silhouettes against the sky, and the windows are huge and ornate and plentiful.

It's beautiful and old-fashioned and… rather spooky. My heart beats faster and faster as it looms closer through the gloom.

Then the car stops, and the driver—a stooped, achingly polite old man who introduces himself as Vincent—opens the door and takes my hand. I step out of the limo and start shivering, unprepared for the cool, damp mountain air. Vincent leads me onto the winding stone path up to the front porch, and I feel as though I've been whisked away from my normal life and into a fairy tale.

Vincent opens the front door before heading back to grab the single suitcase I brought. I step into the foyer. A candelabra-style chandelier hangs overhead, and the floor is made of real, polished wood. The ceiling is at least a dozen feet tall and arched like a cathedral. A curving staircase on the left leads up to the second floor.

And straight ahead, a blur of white and black fur is barreling toward me. I have barely a second to react before impact. I pinwheel my arms, stumbling back, and barely manage to keep my footing.

"Barnabas!" A woman rushes down the staircase only to come to an abrupt stop and go red in the face as she notices me on the threshold. I blink at her and then down at the large dalmatian staring up at me with his teeth bared, his whiplike tail wagging a mile a minute behind him. I'm not quite sure what to make of the mixed messages, so I stand frozen with my hands out.

"He's friendly, I promise," the woman calls. "He's just smiling. It's, er, a dalmatian thing."

I blink and then smile back at him. "Barnabas, hm? What a gentlemanly name." I crouch, offer him a hand to sniff, and then scratch him behind the ears. He pants happily, pink tongue lolling out.

The woman flashes me an apologetic smile as she approaches. The blush when she first saw me already made it obvious she's human, and I glean new details as she approaches. She has fair hair in a bob and a round face, but once she's closer I see faint lines around her eyes that indicate she's older than I would've guessed from a distance. She's likely somewhere in her thirties or forties. "I'm so sorry. He's excitable, and we rarely get company, so…"

"I imagine I'll be much the same after living here for a few months," I joke. Barnabas flops onto the floorboards and offers his belly, and I obligingly scratch it. One of his feet starts thumping as I find a good spot. "What a good boy!"

"Ah." The woman stops a few feet away from me. She looks me up and down—not in a mean way, but she does look puzzled. "You must be the new valentine, then?"

Right. She probably expected me to show up looking beautiful and fancy, but instead I'm dressed in jeans and a T-shirt with my wild curls tied in a messy bun. It seemed ridiculous to dress up in one of my nice new outfits for a car ride.

"That's me." As much as I'd like to continue rubbing Barnabas's belly for the rest of my life, I realize I'm being impolite and straighten, shaking off dog hair before offering my hand. "Amelia Burton. Nice to meet you."

"Ellen Anders," she says, shaking my hand and dipping her chin.

"Do you live here, Ellen?" I can't deny that it brings me some hope. The place seems so huge and cold and strange, it would be nice to have some friendly, *human* company, especially after the icy impression I got of Sebastian.

"I live in town nearby. But I'm here every weekday, keeping the place tidy."

"There's a town?" I perk up; the place seems so remote.

"Yes. Anville. Though my use of *nearby* may have been misleading. It's about an hour away by car."

"At least we're not *fully* removed from civilization," I say.

"Speaking of which," Vincent says, clearing his throat as he steps in behind me with my bag. "I should be making my way there to pick up groceries. Bridget will have my head if she doesn't have fresh veggies in time for dinner." He turns to me, sets the suitcase down, and takes his hat off to give me a small, formal bow. "It's a pleasure to meet you, and to welcome you to the estate."

"Thanks so much," I say, though I feel awkward, unsure if I'm supposed to bow or curtsy or whatever back. Should I give a tip, or is that insulting? Before I can break through my indecision paralysis, he's already shutting the door behind him. It's just me, Ellen, and Barnabas standing in the huge and unfamiliar house.

"Well, Barnabas and Vince both beat me to it, but allow me to welcome you as well," Ellen says, dipping in a small, elegant curtsy. I guess that's how things are done in a vampire's employ, so I curtsy back. "Let me show you to your room, and then I'd be happy to give you a tour of the rest of the house."

"Oh." I hesitate, surprised that Sebastian isn't here to greet me or show me around. But—*duh,* the sun is still up. He must be asleep. "That'd be nice, thank you."

I insist on carrying my own bag and follow Ellen up a winding staircase to the second floor of the house. The wooden steps creak beneath my feet but shine with polish; the portraits on the walls look ancient but don't have a speck of dust. Altogether, this place feels old but well maintained. Loved, even. As I watch one of Ellen's slender hands trail along the staircase and as she leads me through the maze of halls with a familiar ease, I suspect she is at least partially responsible for that.

I linger behind her, my eyes wandering from portrait to portrait. The stern faces and dark, dark eyes are all too reminiscent of Sebastian, and I suspect these must be his forebears, previous owners of the estate. But there's no time to ask, because Ellen is already carrying on ahead. I barely manage to catch up before she stops in front of one huge wooden door.

"This will be your room," she says.

I step inside, so shocked that I gape without self-consciousness. The room is huge and lavishly decorated. There's a gigantic canopy bed with lush silk sheets the color of fresh snow. Mahogany rungs shaped like twisting tree branches lead up to billowing crimson curtains stretched overhead. On the nightstand beside it, a single red rose sits in a porcelain vase. I walk over to smell it, smiling to myself at the gesture. Sebastian may seem cold, but perhaps there is a romantic side to him

Across from the bed sits a delicate, old-fashioned vanity table. Atop it sits an ornate mirror, its metal frame carved in the shape of roses. The armoire is so huge, I'm not sure how I could possibly fill it, *and* there's a walk-in closet and a personal bathroom. But I don't peek into either of those yet because my attention is caught by the huge windows that line one wall. The view outside is far more beautiful than anything even this decadent room could hold.

The grounds are nothing like the manicured garden of the estate that hosted the Valentine's Ball. These are more wild, more natural, and far more captivating. All rolling green hills lined with redwood forests. Even under the sunlight, the trees are dark and impenetrable from here, but rather than feeling intimidated by them, I feel a tug somewhere deep in my stomach, a pull to explore them.

"I hope everything is to your liking?" Ellen asks, and I tear my attention from the windows and turn back to her.

I'm smiling so widely, my face hurts. "It's amazing," I say. "This is amazing."

"Lord Sebastian is very generous," she says. "Would you like a tour now, or a rest first?"

As soon as she asks, I realize how tired I am. I'm not used to being awake during the day anymore. All of the excitement of my arrival gave me a burst of adrenaline, but now that it's fading, I'm realizing that my nap in the car somehow only left me sore and tired. That big canopy bed looks *very* inviting.

"I wouldn't mind some rest, actually," I say. "And maybe a bath." I feel sticky with stale travel sweat, and I don't want to encounter Sebastian before washing it off. Plus, as eager as I am to see more of this beautiful house and those incredible grounds, I have time. This is my *home* for the next six months, as amazing as that is.

"Of course." Ellen curtsies again. "Sleep well, Amelia."

I barely manage to yank off my shoes before tumbling into bed, clothes and all. *Just for a little rest*, I tell myself as my eyes drift shut. *And then I'll...*

Darkness takes me before I can finish the thought.

Chapter Eleven

A knock on the door wakes me. I pull myself out of bed, glance in the mirror, and come to an abrupt stop. I'm an absolute *mess*: my hair a rat's nest, my eyes puffy from sleep. I'm still dressed in my wrinkled outfit from the ride to the estate. I hastily finger-comb my wild curls, shimmy out of my clothes, grab a robe from the closet to wrap around myself, and grimace at my reflection. It will have to be good enough. If Sebastian wanted me to look pretty, he should've warned me.

But when I open the door, it's not Sebastian on the threshold. It's Ellen, smiling politely, holding up a tray with coffee and a breakfast spread. "Hello again," she says. "You slept through breakfast, so I thought I'd bring it to you."

I bite the inside of my cheek. As nervous as I am about seeing Sebastian, delaying it is only making it worse. I need to get some answers about why he chose me as his valentine. But I force on a smile and step aside to let Ellen into the room. "That's very kind of you," I say. "Thanks. Sorry for missing breakfast."

"That's quite alright. I assume it will take time to adjust to our schedule here." She sets the tray on my nightstand.

I glance at the window, realizing I don't know what time it is… and then, confused to find it dark outside, at the clock on my phone. "What… is the schedule, exactly?" I've already been nocturnal for my training with Benjamin, but I didn't consider that it might be a permanent arrangement for this lifestyle.

"Ah, right! I should've explained. The staff keeps a nighttime schedule here, as per the master of the house's natural sleep cycle. We take breakfast at sundown—six p.m., that is—tea at midnight, and dinner at two in the morning."

"Oh, jeez." I push hair out of my face, trying to wrap my head around that. "He requires that of the household?"

"We don't mind," she says, which isn't an answer.

"Right." I rub my eyes. Just the thought of permanently staying up all night and sleeping all day makes me tired, but I guess it makes sense, if I ever want to spend time with Sebastian. If he ever wants to spend time with me, I should say, because he's still not here to greet me. But I guess I should be grateful for that, given the state I'm in.

I pull myself out of my thoughts when I realize Ellen is still hovering near the bed with her hands clasped.

"Do you need something?" I ask, brow furrowing.

"Yes. Well, that is… Lord Sebastian requested some blood," she says, flushing.

"Oh," I say. I'm surprised—and flattered, to be honest. I was half certain he took me on out of pity at this point. "Where should I meet him?"

The flush in her face deepens, and she pulls out a syringe from a pocket of her uniform.

"Ah. Gotcha." It's a bit insulting that he can't even come get his blood himself, but I can't complain when this is my job.

It's his choice, ultimately. So I clear my throat, sit on the edge of the bed, and roll up one sleeve of my robe. Ellen steps to my side and ties a tourniquet around my upper arm.

"I'm a certified phlebotomist, don't worry," she says with a reassuring smile.

"Really? Was that a part of your job description?"

"Lord Sebastian paid for the certification program after he hired me."

"Huh," I mutter. I guess the use of a syringe wasn't specifically an insult to me, then. Still, it doesn't bode well for our relationship that he seems determined to go to extreme lengths to avoid taking blood himself. "Why doesn't he just… bite people?"

"Don't know," she murmurs. "Didn't ask."

Her fingers prod at the crook of my elbow until she finds a promising vein, and she slides the needle in. I avert my eyes—not out of queasiness, but in an attempt to think about something other than the fact that this feels like a massive snub from Sebastian—and eye my coffee until she's done.

"There we are," she says, pulling away from me with the now-filled vial of blood and removing the tourniquet. "All done. Are you feeling alright?"

"I'm fine." Just a bit jilted.

"Well, make sure to eat up and have plenty of fluids." She smiles at me. "Tea is usually casual. You'll find a spread in the parlor. Dinner will be served at two in the dining room, if you'd like to join us. Though you're welcome to take your meal in your room if you prefer."

I clear my throat, feeling ashamed of myself for being miffed. Sebastian may be behaving like a bastard, but that's not Ellen's fault. She's doing her best to make me feel welcome, and here

I am, acting like a child. "I'd love to join you for dinner."

* * *

While I'm eager to explore the grounds, I'm still tired, and my body is confused by the fact it's dark outside, so I find it harder to leave my bedroom than I would've liked. After taking my time eating breakfast—blueberry scones with clotted cream, fresh strawberries dusted with sugar, and a hard-boiled egg in a tiny glass cup—I spend a while lounging in bed, scrolling through social media on my phone. As I see pictures of friends and family, my former life feels distant already.

After I'm done wallowing over that, another thought occurs to me. I type in the search bar: *Sebastian de Celeste.*

Nothing. Of course there's nothing; Sebastian doesn't even own a cell phone. After a guilty, hesitant moment, I type again: *Alexander de Solomon.*

A profile pops up, one with a checkmark to verify his identity and a shocking amount of followers. My eyes widen as I scroll through his pictures and videos. The suave blonde vampire is just as handsome as I remember, and his feed evidences a life of extravagance. A yacht ride under the moonlight, a charming smirk over the rim of a bloody cocktail, the recognizable neon sign of a famous vampire club…

It looks decadent. Exciting. Fun. All of the things my life could've been if he had decided to become my patron. This estate is lovely, but it's also isolated and spooky and not at all what I imagined after reading all of those gossip magazines.

I feel terrible thinking that way, but I can't help it. I sigh and bring the phone to my face, bonking it against my forehead a few times to clear my terrible, selfish thoughts. Only when I glance at the screen again do I realize I accidentally liked one of Alexander's photos. A shirtless one revealing chiseled abs and a delicious V of muscle where his pants dip low.

Shit. I unlike it, realize it'll still be visible to him, and like it again. Then I like a different one so I won't *just* be liking the thirst trap. And I follow him so it doesn't look like I'm creeping. By the time I'm done, I feel like an idiot, and my face is hot. I don't know what I'm thinking. It's not like he'll notice, he has about a million drooling fans on here.

Eager to scrub my embarrassment off, I drag myself out of bed and into the bathroom to get ready for the day, or night. Whatever.

The bathroom is as awe-inspiring as I imagined it would be, albeit a bit old-fashioned. There's only a claw-foot tub instead of a shower. But it's hard to complain, especially since it's set next to a gigantic window that overlooks the grounds I'm so enamored with. They look even more magical under the moonlight.

I find luxury bubble bath product under the sink, and soon the bath is filled with foamy, steaming-hot, honey-and-coconut-scented water. I toss my clothes aside and sink in with a happy sigh, back arching as the heat floods my body and caresses muscles sore from sleeping in the car earlier. With my head leaning back against the edge of the tub and my eyes drifting out to my view of the grounds, I easily pass a full hour in the bath.

For the first time in years, I feel the desire to write stirring. My fingers itch to describe the fog-shrouded trees and the moonlit hills, the perfect crescent of the moon hanging in the sky. I drag myself out of the tub, dry off, and wrap myself in a gloriously fluffy robe waiting for me. Since I didn't bring any materials to write by hand, I flop onto my stomach in bed and open my old, clunky, much-abused laptop. My fingers hover over the keys and…

…And nothing. The words are gone as soon as I have a moment to write them down. I stare at the blank document, anxiety crawling up the back of my throat the longer my paralysis stretches out. I love writing… or at least, I used to. It's been so long since I had the time for anything more than a few stolen sentences scribbled on whatever paper I could find. Is it possible I've forgotten how to write? Has my creativity been eroded by the years of waitressing and cleaning and having barely a single second to think about anything else?

I'm not sure how long I sit there, but I'm not able to produce a single word. When I finally give up and shut my laptop, I realize that dinnertime is approaching. As I stand and look around the room, still dressed in only a robe, it occurs to me that I should've asked Ellen if dinner has a dress code.

And *then* I realize I have nothing more than a few grungy old T-shirts and ill-fitting jeans to wear. Just when I'm starting to panic, I remember the new outfits I bought with Lissa and breathe a sigh of relief.

When I open my suitcase, my jaw drops open. This is *way* more than the small handful of outfits I agreed to purchase. Lissa must have gone back without me to buy more. She also included the Valentine's Ball dress and the heels I wore.

One by one, I unzip each bag and hang the outfits in my enormous new closet. Velvet and silk, corset tops and voluminous skirts… the kinds of things I only ever dreamed of owning. The kinds of things a valentine would wear.

I *have* to dress up for dinner now. It would be a shame to let all of this go to waste. Ultimately, I'd rather be overdressed than underdressed, *especially* since I'm finally going to see Sebastian. I mean, surely he'll come to greet me now, right? Despite my lingering hesitance over this arrangement, I feel a surge of excitement at the thought.

I let my robe drop to the floor and reach for the first thing that catches my eye.

Chapter Twelve

All eyes are on me from the moment I enter the dining room. I expect it's partially because I'm late—I had to wander around the hallways, trying to find my way here—but I'd like to think it's also because of how I'm dressed.

The attention is intoxicating and embarrassing all at once. I hold my head high, keeping in my mind the image I saw of myself in the mirror. Cat's eye liner, red lips, an elegant burgundy gown that dips low between my breasts and shows off every curve. I'm not as magical with makeup and hair as Lissa, but I'm doing my best to coax out a shade of that bold and beautiful woman she transformed me into the night of the Valentine's Day Ball. I did all of this because I *wanted* them to look. Wanted *him* to look, specifically.

But when I raise my eyes to scan the room, I see Ellen, a couple of familiar faces, a couple of unfamiliar ones, Barnabas smiling and wagging his tail from the rug, and… that's it. No Sebastian.

Disappointment is a knife to my chest. I'm surprised by how much it hurts. Just when my feelings toward Sebastian had started to soften, resentment curdles in my stomach once again. Maybe he *is* just an asshole who invited me here to ignore me. But why the hell offer patronage, then? It couldn't have just been for my gross blood. I doubt he's even drinking the vial Ellen extracted from me this morning. Then is all of this out of pity? The thought is awful. Humiliating.

But for now, I plaster on a smile and find a seat. There are plenty of open ones; the long mahogany table is built to seat around a dozen, and there are only five staff members present besides me. But before I can sit, a young man lurches to his feet. He's curly-haired and covered in freckles and can't be any older than twenty.

"Oh, please, ma'am, allow me," he says, flustered, and pulls out a chair at the end of the table.

I smile at him—he blushes furiously in response—and take the offered chair. I'm a few seats away from the nearest dinner companion, but I have to assume that this is meant to be a seat of honor, rather than some kind of exile. Though it's hard to ignore that everyone else is dressed casually. I am indeed overdressed. It's also impossible not to notice how quiet the room has become since I entered, as though all of the conversation stopped. The grandfather clock in one corner ticks audibly in the silence. Were they talking about me?

I swallow back self-consciousness and seek out Ellen among the strangers. "Will Lord Sebastian be joining us for dinner?" I ask, unable to give up my hope completely.

Ellen shakes her head, looking apologetic. "I'm afraid Lord Sebastian prefers to take his meals alone, in his study," she says. "I'm sorry, I should've mentioned it. But we're so happy to have you here! And you look *stunning*."

Of course he wouldn't make an exception for me on my first day here, even knowing I'd be surrounded by strangers and he has yet to even greet me since my arrival. I suppress a sigh and try to smile instead. "Well, I'm glad for an opportunity to get to know everyone."

Ellen takes my cue and begins a round of introductions around the table. The boy who pulled out my chair for me is Trent, the groundskeeper's grandson and assistant. The groundskeeper himself is a gnarled old man named Tobias who greets me with a scowl, but since that seems to be his default expression, I try not to take it personally. I recognize Vincent, the driver who brought me here, and give him a small smile; he sweeps off his hat and nods back. The last is the chef, a stout, friendly woman named Bridget who gives off an energy younger than her streaks of gray hair suggest.

"And I already know this lovely lad," I coo, reaching under the table to scratch Barnabas under the chin. He whines, tail smacking against a chair.

Conversation starts in fits and spurts, peppered with glances in my direction, but soon returns full force. While I eat quietly and with no small amount of enjoyment—dinner is a crispy duck with plum sauce, butter-rich mashed potatoes, and roasted carrots—I observe the others at the table. I knew that a decent-sized staff would be required to maintain a big, old house like this, but I didn't realize that everyone would stick around for dinner, too. There's a cozy, familial vibe in the room. Yet it also makes me painfully aware that I'm a newcomer and the odd one out.

They try to include me. Ellen brings me into the conversation whenever she can, asking polite questions about my background. I answer honestly, even though I know it's far from exciting material, and part of me wishes I could make up a more alluring history for my glamorous new persona as a valentine. They all seem a bit shocked when I tell them I was working as a waitress at a greasy LA diner just a week ago.

"But you seem so glamorous," Trent says, and then flushes like he didn't mean to say it out loud. I beam at him, and he continues, "We were surprised to hear that Lord Sebastian had hired a valentine, but… it's easy to see why you caught his eye."

My smile goes a little strained around the edges. If Sebastian were enamored with me, he would be here. But I don't want Trent to know he struck a nerve.

"Is it really so surprising? Most vampires have at least one valentine, don't they?" I ask.

"Not Lord Sebastian," Trent says, shaking his head.

"What?" I ask. "Like… never?" I look around the table, but nobody answers. It seems so *strange*, especially given my room. The red canopy on the bed, the vanity table, the rose-framed mirror… it all seems outfitted for a valentine.

"The master's personal life is none of our concern," Tobias says with a grumble. "And especially not to be gossiped about with a *stranger*."

"She's not a stranger," Ellen scolds. "Show some respect."

Tobias grunts and spears a piece of duck on his plate with more force than necessary.

I am curious to know more, but I can tell that trying to pry right now would only put me on the cranky groundskeeper's bad side.

Instead, I say, "You seem loyal to Sebastian. How long have you worked here?"

Despite Tobias's suspicious glance, he can't resist the urge to answer. "All my life," he says, lifting his chin. "My father worked the grounds before me, and I've been helping look after them since I was a boy."

"And now you've brought on your grandson," I say, with another smile at Trent. "That's amazing. You must love it here."

"Can't complain," Tobias grumbles.

"I inherited this position from my father, as well," Ellen says. "And Victor's family has worked here for generations. Bridget is the only new one."

"New?" Bridget scoffs. "I've been working here for fifty years!"

"I think I speak for all of us when I say we're happy working here," Ellen says. "And we hope you'll come to love it as well."

The conversation drifts from there, and I am content to stay quiet and observe the curious mixture of people who are willing to give up daylight to work for Sebastian. And as I see how comfortable they are with each other, how like a family they seem to be, it comforts me to know that Sebastian can't be such a terrible person if he's created a home like this.

I only hope that I will find a place here, among them.

* * *

Back in my room, I remove my makeup and dress and crawl into bed. When I grab my phone, I'm surprised to see a notification. And I nearly drop the device onto my face when I realize that notification is from *Alexander de Solomon* following me back. Not only that, but he's in my DMs.

There you are. I was afraid I'd never get a chance to see you again.

I bite my lip. Type something, untype it. Type again.

You remember me?

His response comes startlingly quick.

As if I could forget such a lovely face.

If there was any doubt he still intends to flirt with me, it's gone. I squirm in my bed, not sure how to feel about it. If he wanted me, he should've made an offer to be my patron. And now that I'm Sebastian's valentine, it means I owe him my loyalty. Even if he didn't show up to greet me or get my blood for himself or join me at dinner. Right?

"Right," I whisper to myself, and shove my phone back under my pillow before I can change my mind. This life may not be what I imagined when I became a valentine, but it's what I've got. I signed a contract, and I owe it to Sebastian to try to make this work.

Still thoughts of vampire nightclubs and lavish parties plague my mind, and the silence of the estate weighs on me as I drift off to sleep.

Chapter Thirteen

I t's a strange experience, to feel pampered and ignored at the same time. I have leave of the beautiful estate, a closet full of dresses so luxurious, I never could have afforded them before this, and delicious food hand-delivered to my door. Plus my enormous room, the canopy bed, the claw-foot tub I use nearly every morning... it is all more than I ever could've wished for.

Sebastian ensures that I want for nothing. Nothing, that is, except for his company.

Sometimes, Barnabas joins me as I wander the hallways, his tail always wagging. The staff are always around, and polite. Yet there's a gap between us that feels impossible to breach, even when I do my best to be friendly. Ellen is kind, and when we sit and have tea, it feels almost normal, but when we say our goodbyes, it's impossible to forget that she's heading off to scrub floors and I have nothing to do but lounge in bed all day.

For my first week at the estate, I'm more than happy to do so. I can't remember the last time I had so much freedom to relax. I've been used to working long hours, keeping the apartment clean, doing everything for Declan and having no time to myself. It feels great to take long soaks in the bath and lie in bed whenever I want, and let my calloused hands and aching calves have a break.

Plus, it's been so long since I was able to look in the mirror and focus on *me* and what I want. Even knowing that Sebastian won't be at dinner, I enjoy getting ready every night. After several days of enjoying the luxury products in my bathroom, my hair falls into shiny ringlets rather than its usual mousy brown tangles, and my skin is radiant and soft. I revel in painting my face and trying on dresses just to watch myself spin in the mirror. It makes me feel beautiful, even if that beauty is only for my own eyes.

But after a while, it isn't enough. I have all the time in the world to write, but words still evade me. The long hours start to feel empty. I have to resist the urge to talk with my sister on the phone for hours, because whenever I do, I only end up making up more lies about my fake job, which makes me feel guilty and more alone than ever.

Benjamin texts me once to check in, but it feels more formal than friendly, and it's not like I have any *official* complaints about this arrangement. I try talking to Lissa, but she is the driest texter in the world and only responds a couple of times per day.

So my loneliness grows, and the feeling of freedom starts to spoil. I begin to wonder if I'm more of a doll than anything, prettied up only to be left in a closet, collecting dust. Ellen takes a tiny vial of my blood every morning, and other than that, it's like I don't exist to Sebastian. When Ellen replaces the rose on my nightstand on the seventh day, I realize even that romantic-seeming gesture was her all along.

It leaves me craving connection. Or is it attention? Is there a difference? I'm surprised by how little I miss Declan, but I do miss having *someone*. I think I missed that even when we were together, I just hadn't realized it yet.

With nowhere else to turn, I look to social media. My contract included the fact I won't disclose personal information about Sebastian, including the location of his estate. I can't, anyway, since I'm still lying to my sister about my job. But I post some subtle shots: one of the mist hanging over the forest, another of my freshly pedicured toes peeking out of the bubble bath, and a *slightly* risqué selfie of me in my silky night-robe.

I hate the rush I get whenever Alexander likes one of my photos. My mind wanders to the chemistry I felt with him during our one dance. What would have happened if Benjamin hadn't been there to interrupt, I wonder? And why didn't he offer to become my patron when he seemed to like me far more than Sebastian does?

Guilt is always close on elation's heels. It's not Alexander's attention I want. It's Sebastian, who seems intent on ignoring me. I want to know the man who brought me here. I want to understand him, and why he chose me, and why he brought me all the way out here to his estate only to leave me alone in my room.

Still. I should be grateful for the luxury and the money this position affords me, even if it's not what I imagined a valentine's life would be like.

To stop myself from going stir-crazy—and also hoping for a chance encounter with my mysterious host—I take to exploring the estate. The house is enough of a wonder to keep me occupied for days. I spend evenings wandering the long halls and admiring the paintings on the walls.

The estate has a certain age and gravitas that fascinates me. It's so different from the cramped apartments and modern stylings of LA. There's so much space, and so much personality. Sometimes I stand still and shut my eyes and just listen to the house creak and groan around me as though it's breathing. It's eerie and enticing at the same time. Especially when the staff goes home after dinner, and it feels like the entire world is silent. Every day, I aim to discover a new room. It makes me feel like an intrepid explorer, running my fingers over the spines of old leather books and peering into ornate mirrors at my reflection.

Sometimes I catch myself fantasizing about spending the rest of my life here, occupying these halls, learning every spot where the floorboards creak and all of the best windows to gaze out at the misty grounds. I discover the "music room"—what a thing to have!—with its grand piano, the drawing room with a stone fireplace and carved mantle. Most of the house is a relic of the past, perfectly preserved; the kitchen is the only room that seems to have been modernized, and Bridget semi-jokingly banished me from it after a disastrous attempt to help with dinner.

My first few weeks at the estate blur past like this. Yet, for all my wandering, I never run into Sebastian. His absence becomes like a sore tooth, a throbbing ache that is impossible to ignore. I don't even know which of the many bedrooms is his, or which rooms he frequents; he is just *gone*, with no more presence here than a ghost. Occasionally, I have the creeping sensation that I've entered a room that's recently been occupied. I've found an abandoned teacup with a hint of red on the porcelain, a book left open on a chair. Whenever I encounter a locked door, I stand there wondering if he's on the other side, listening to me breathe.

Sometimes, especially when I'm standing near a window, a shiver runs down my spine, and I swear I feel someone watching me. But every time I try to look out upon the dark grounds, there's nothing to see but trees.

My frustration grows, until I reach the only logical conclusion: it's no accident that I never manage to stumble upon Sebastian. He's avoiding me on purpose. In his own goddamn house. But *why*? He brought me here!

I know I'm not the easiest person to get along with. Yet no matter how I rack my thoughts, I can't come up with any way that I could've annoyed him. Surely it wasn't our first conversation at the Valentine's Day Ball, or else he never would have offered patronage… and since then, I haven't had a chance to offend him.

Instead, I am left to wander, alone in the quiet halls, wondering if I'm the one who's been reduced to a ghost.

* * *

Finally, I decide I've had enough. It's been *weeks* since I arrived. It'd be one thing if Sebastian were away on business, but according to the staff, he hardly ever leaves this place. Sebastian brought me here, to this isolated home; even if it was out of pity, the least he can do is look me in the face and tell me that himself. So after getting out of bed, I throw on one of my low-cut and most dramatic dresses, do my makeup and hair, and wait on the edge of my bed for Ellen to arrive.

As she walks in with breakfast and a syringe, I let her set

down the tray and take my blood before asking, "Where is he?"

She pauses, eyes flickering to my neckline before jolting back up to my face. I'm certain she knows exactly what I'm asking, but as if giving me a second chance to consider it, she asks, "Who?"

I hold my head high. "Lord Sebastian, of course. I wish to speak with him."

"I, um…" She stammers, still holding the fresh vial of my blood. I snatch it from her hand.

"I'll bring this to him," I say. When she still hesitates, I give her a pleading look. "I need to talk to him. I *deserve* a conversation with him. This is ridiculous."

She sighs and tilts her chin down the hallway. "I believe he's in the library. The big double doors on the right. But really, Amelia, he's—"

"Thank you," I say, cutting her off before she can make me doubt myself. She stiffens, and I pause, give her a small smile, and say more gently, "Thank you. Really. But this is something I need to do."

Then I take a deep breath, shove a pastry into my mouth to bolster my courage, and march down the hallway before I can lose my nerve. I pause in front of the wooden double doors, smooth my hair and my dress, and then push them open.

At least, I try to do so. They're heavy as hell, and I struggle to push them open inch by inch, with a little huff of effort. This is why I've always given up on it during my explorations, but now that I know this room is both a library and Sebastian's secret hiding place, I'm determined. By the time I get the doors open, I am breathing hard and feeling entirely off-balance. When I look up, Sebastian is sitting in an armchair, one hand frozen halfway through the motion of turning a page, his dark eyes locked on me.

I had almost forgotten just how good-looking he is. Dressed in a white linen shirt with the sleeves rolled up, with a book in his hands, he is *devastating*.

I swallow hard, attempting to moisten my suddenly dry mouth. I regret the pastry that now sits like a lump in my stomach. But before I can think of something to say, my gaze drifts from the man I came to confront to the wondrous expanse of the library around him.

There was part of me, of course, that expected this fancy-ass house to have a fancy-ass library. Still, this place is breathtaking. The walls are lined with beautiful, mahogany bookshelves that stretch from floor to ceiling. In one corner is a small spiral staircase leading to a loft with more shelves. The wall across from the entrance is made up entirely of stained-glass windows, with the curtains pulled open to allow moonlight to spill inside. Tiffany-style floor lamps add their own warm glow. The ceilings reach high above us and culminate in a dome; we must be in one of the towers I saw from outside of the house.

In the middle of this glorious room waits a round table holding a strange bronze sphere. It is surrounded by a love seat and two plush leather armchairs—one of which is occupied by Sebastian, who has now closed his book in his lap and is still staring at me.

I flush, realizing how long I've been gawking at the room after barging in on him. I clear my throat, press back my shoulders, and say, "Hello."

Sebastian blinks. His fingers curl around the spine of his book. "Hello."

I purse my lips and wait to see if he will apologize or make some explanation for the way he's been avoiding me, but he says nothing.

"So this is where you spend your days?" I ask, gesturing to the room.

"Nights," he corrects, and then, "but, yes."

This pedantic bastard. Ire rises in the back of my throat, but I push it down again. I did not come here to pick a fight. That would make me look like some immature girl acting out for attention. And that is *not* what I'm doing. I am politely *asking* for attention, which is… different. Right?

Doubt stirs in my chest, but I try to ignore it. It's too late to turn back now.

"Well," I say, and then pause. I had a speech half-prepared in my head, but now that I'm here, it feels like too much. He's still staring at me like I've committed some major faux pas. His hands have begun clutching his book so tightly, the leather cover is bending, and I am remembering that this man so clearly *hates* me.

How could I have forgotten? How could I have let myself think that I was wrong about that first impression? Just because he invited me here? He could have brought me here for any reason at all. Maybe he struck some secret deal with Benjamin. I don't know.

I should've just asked Ellen to deliver a note instead of coming myself. At least it would make it easier to bear the inevitable rejection. I'm already bracing myself for it, and the words are sticking in my throat. But, God, walking away now would only make me look weirder for barging in like this.

"Well?" he repeats.

I clear my throat… again. Drag my eyes from his polished

shoes to his just-as-dark eyes. I wish I could think of some excuse for coming here, but my mind has gone blank but for the question I came here to ask, and so I have no choice but to blurt out, "Will you have dinner with me tonight?"

He looks at me. Really looks, taking in my dress, my makeup, my hair, everything I did just to come here and ask this question. I feel ridiculous. He takes his time answering, and I wonder if he's trying to think of the politest way to reject me or a scathing insult. My throat constricts in preparation for humiliation.

"Fine," he says.

Fine?

I open my mouth, about to nonsensically repeat the word just to make sure I heard it right, but I snap it shut again. His attention has already returned to the book in his lap. He opens it and begins to read while I stand here awkwardly.

But he said *fine*. And, as much as I rack my brain for a way to interpret that negatively, I cannot find one.

"Well, okay then," I say. He does not look up or make any indication that he realizes I'm here. So, after a moment, I gather my dress and the shreds of my dignity and leave the library with my head spinning.

…Then I walk back and hand him the forgotten vial of blood. My fingers brush his in the briefest touch before I scurry out again.

* * *

My heart sinks as I step into the dining room and find that, once again, Sebastian is missing. At least the staff is as warm as ever, everyone except for grumpy old Tobias meeting my eyes and smiling in greeting. Yet I still feel separate from them as I take my usual seat at the end of the table. Especially given that I dressed up again. I should have learned at this point, but… I wanted to look good for Sebastian.

Perhaps it's time to admit that this is a foolish hope to nurture. He doesn't respect me enough to make good on his agreement to be here. I can no longer pretend he has anything akin to fondness for me. I doubt he cares enough to pity me. There must be something else at play here, something I don't understand.

As I sigh and lift my fork, the door opens. The conversation goes silent, much in the same way it did the first time I entered, but this time, the stares are not in my direction. They're at the door opening behind me. I'm seated closest to it, so I have to swivel in my seat to face it.

Sebastian stands there, looking heart-attack-inducing in a pinstriped vest and pants. He pauses in the doorway, oddly out of place, even though this is his home. I wonder if he's regretting his decision to come already. Then his eyes brush over the faces at the table before stopping on mine.

I smile. "Hello, Lord Sebastian."

He steps inside, stops briefly beside my seat. "Hello, Amelia."

To my disappointment, he then walks all the way to the opposite end of the table to take his seat. The entire length of the table and all six staff members sit between us. But still… he's *here.* I feel a fragile flicker of hope bloom in my chest.

"I'm so glad you joined us," I call across the table.

The rest of the staff echo the sentiment—except for Bridget, who looks as though on the verge of a fit.

"Lord Sebastian, I had no idea you'd be coming tonight," she sputters, starting to rise from her seat. "I can go and prepare you a plate—"

"No, no, there's no need." Sebastian raises a hand, and she slowly, grudgingly lowers back down. "You know I rarely eat."

Still, when someone passes over an unused wine glass, Sebastian doesn't say no. He pours himself before someone else can beat him to it, and then takes out a vial from his pocket. As he adds it to his drink, he looks across the table at me and dips his chin in the slightest nod. I smile back over the rim of my glass.

With the table and staff between us, there isn't an opportunity to converse more. Yet as Sebastian rises to leave when dessert is served, I turn to him.

"Will you join us again tomorrow?" I ask.

He pauses, glancing at me, and then at the staff who are all awaiting his answer.

"Fine," he says, and leaves.

It's a small step... but it's a step.

Chapter Fourteen

Sebastian continuing to show up at dinner feels like a triumph, at first. He still avoids me the rest of the time, but at least I get to see him now… except that it's always from the other end of the table, which makes it impossible to have a conversation. He always leaves early, too, preventing any opportunity for me to talk to him. The staff seems eager to speak with him as well, so I don't want to hog his attention. But after three days of barely more than a *"Hello, Amelia,"* I decide to move my plate to the seat beside his end of the table.

Then he shows up—late, as usual—and takes *my* usual place. Again, at the opposite end of the room. I fume through dinner, glaring daggers at him while spearing bites of steak, but he ignores me while carrying on a quiet conversation with Tobias.

After a week of similar treatment, I'm on the verge of texting Benjamin, begging him to get me out of this contract. Or Alexander, who seems far more eager to give me attention than the vampire who actually chose me. But a stubborn part of me is so determined to figure out *why* Sebastian insists on treating me like this.

"Lord Sebastian has always been aloof," Ellen says when I complain to her one evening, seated at my vanity table with her standing behind me. "He treats us well, but he keeps his distance. It's his way. Tobias occasionally draws him out, but Sebastian has known him since Tobias was just a boy."

She insisted on braiding my hair for me after I fell asleep with it wet and woke up with a bird's nest atop my head. I couldn't work up the willpower to say no; even though it's strange to be doted on like this, it feels so damn relaxing.

"But I'm his valentine." I sigh, leaning my head back and shutting my eyes. Her fingers running through my hair remind me how long it's been since anyone last touched me, even non-sexually, and it makes my chest ache with longing. "It's supposed to be different for me. I don't understand why he brought me here if he doesn't want to spend time with me."

Ellen doesn't answer for a few seconds. When I open my eyes and peek at her in the mirror, she's chewing her lip, looking as though she's debating saying something or not, but after a moment she shakes it off. "Maybe he's working himself up to it," she says, and I have the sense it's not what she first intended to say at all. "It's been a long while since he was close to anyone. It must be a bit daunting."

"Daunting for *him*?" I ask, brows drawing together in disbelief.

Ellen laughs. She sets the brush aside and bends down beside me, pointing at my image in the mirror. "Who wouldn't be intimidated by this?"

"Oh, shove it," I say, blushing.

Ellen's a hopeless flatterer. But still, it makes me think. If he truly has been alone for such a long time, maybe it's not coldness that keeps him at a distance. Maybe he doesn't remember how to act around people.

So I decide to take the initiative. That night at dinner, I'm halfway through my meal when Sebastian finally decides to make an appearance. He nods at me, and then, as always, takes his seat at the opposite end of the table.

But this time, I stand up, grab my plate, and walk over to the empty seat beside him. The conversations go quiet as everyone sees what I'm doing, but I shove down any hint of self-consciousness and slide into the chair to Sebastian's left. It is a blatantly obvious move, and probably an impolite one, but oh well.

Sebastian sits very still, watching me, and I have a distinct sense that he's tempted by the thought of leaving the room, all good manners be damned.

"Lord Sebastian," I say before he has a chance to flee. "I've been meaning to ask you something."

If he dislikes me rather than simply being reserved, now is a good moment for him to show it. He could leave me scorned and publicly humiliated if he wished, and even though I plaster on a smile, my stomach is in knots at the thought of it. I see the way he glances at the curious eyes on us and reaches the same conclusion. There's a moment where everyone seems to pause, waiting. He reaches for his glass of blood-tinged wine and swirls it idly.

"Yes?" he asks. At the rest of the table, conversations resume, albeit more subdued than before. Everyone seems to have an ear turned to our exchange.

"Are there a lot of depressed vampires?"

He pauses, glass of blood-infused wine halfway to his lips, to stare at me. "...What?"

"Well, if you never see the sun, it must be like having seasonal depression all the time," I say. "Though I guess it's not seasonal at that point. It's just plain ol' vanilla depression."

He continues to stare at me, the furrow in his brow deepening.

"Or maybe you get enough Vitamin D from my blood?" I ask, tapping a finger against my chin.

He slowly sips his wine. "I haven't the faintest idea," he says finally.

That's all I get, but I consider five words in a row to be a middling success.

After that night, Sebastian gives up on avoiding me at the dinner table, which I take as a victory. But the man is still damningly difficult to hold a conversation with. He won't speak a single word to me unprompted. Even prompted, it's difficult to get more than a couple.

It soon becomes a game.

I arrive at dinner prepared with new and increasingly ridiculous prompts. *Can vampires get drunk?* (Yes.) *Can you taste what I eat in my blood?* (Not really.) *Do you sleep in a coffin?* (That's absurd, Amelia.)

One night, I'm so thoroughly overjoyed by my chocolate cake that I almost forget to try speaking with him. The moist, rich cake, the silky frosting… I practically moan as I take my first bite. Then I notice Sebastian staring at me and realize I haven't asked my question of the night yet.

"Why do you hardly ever eat?"

"I don't need to."

"I don't *need* chocolate cake." I scoop up another delicious bite of it. "But what would be the point of life without it?" I place it in my mouth to demonstrate, humming in pleasure as I lick the last of the frosting off my fork.

Sebastian clears his throat and looks away, probably appalled by my table manners. "I've never been much of a fan."

I widen my eyes, dramatically pressing a hand to my chest. "Of *cake*?" No wonder he's so miserable.

Sebastian shrugs, glances at me, pauses. "You have, er…" He gestures to his lip.

I lick the frosting off, and he looks away again.

It isn't until he's gone that I realized he stayed all the way through dessert, which is practically unheard of. And I got *seven words* in a row!

Surely, it must be progress.

* * *

Life is certainly different than I'm used to, but it's surprisingly easy to fall into routine. Ellen collects my blood; I bother Sebastian at dinner; the rose on my nightstand withers and is replaced. Benjamin's check-ins become less frequent. Alexander's texts don't, but I don't reply quite as eagerly. I'm starting to get used to it here. It may not be everything I wished for, but it could be worse.

One day I realize, with a shock, that I've been here for two months already. Just like that, my sense of contentment begins to crumble. *Two months.* I wonder if I'm the first valentine in history who has made it two months without ever being bitten. Or kissed. Or *touched*…

I've been so pleased with myself for the tiny scraps of progress I've made at our dinners over the past couple of weeks. But now, sitting in my bed, I have to fight off the sudden threat of tears. God, I'm lonely. I need more than this.

I hold that thought in mind while I get myself ready for

dinner, slashing on eyeliner like war paint. *I need more.* And it's time to get it.

I set my plate beside Sebastian's seat, as usual, and wait for him to arrive. But instead of hitting him with one of my usual ridiculous questions, I flash him a bright smile. He pauses, looking almost alarmed by my expression, as if he senses something has changed.

"Lord Sebastian," I say, all too sweetly.

"Amelia," he replies, his tone cautious.

"I've realized, it's been months, and I still have yet to explore the grounds," I say. "But I'm afraid I'm intimidated at the thought of going out alone." I sip my wine and set it back down, trying to conceal the fact that my hand is shaking. There's no reason for Sebastian to know how nervous this makes me. I want to come across as cool, composed, confident. Sexy.

"I'm sure Tobias would be happy to give you a tour," Sebastian says, his eyes slipping away from mine.

But I will not be deterred so easily. "Oh, I wouldn't dream of adding more work to his duties," I say, widening my eyes as if the thought has just occurred to me. "He must be so busy already, tending to this place—" I drop my voice. "And at his age, nonetheless!"

Tobias side-eyes me but says nothing. Perhaps he's fonder of me than he lets on, or perhaps he just pities me.

"Trent, then," Sebastian says, but it's half-hearted; he's clearly realized the trap I've sprung.

"But then who will help poor Tobias with his duties?" I ask, frowning. Trent refuses to look our way, pretending to be deeply involved in a conversation with Ellen.

Sebastian regards me silently. It's so hard to read his icy features. His icy, *handsome* features. It's hard to be this close to him and not react to it; sometimes I almost forget how shockingly good-looking he is, with those high cheekbones and long, dark lashes. Those eyes that are nearly black when they meet mine.

"I suppose I could give you a brief tour, then," he says, finally giving in before it becomes *glaringly* obvious he's making excuses.

I smile at him. "Well, how nice of you to offer. That would be lovely."

* * *

The next evening, I wait in the front entrance, as we planned before parting ways last night. I'm surprised at my nervousness. I was the one who made this happen—insisted on it, in fact—but now I'm doubting myself. I told myself that I was only pushing Sebastian because he was too stiff and withdrawn to do it himself… but what if that isn't the case? What if this is going to be awkward and I'll regret ever pushing for more time with him?

But I can't keep chasing these thoughts around and around my head during all of these long, lonely hours. I'll use this rare private time with Sebastian to assess the situation, and then do whatever is necessary afterward.

Still, I hope that this encounter will prove the opposite of what my self-consciousness is telling me. I hope he is merely private by nature, and this will get him to open up to me. I want to believe that his kindness is real, not manufactured. And that someone like him could feel something other than pity for someone like me. It will prove that I'm worth more than being used and thrown away like Declan did. And, *God*, what an upgrade it would be to go from Declan to a handsome, powerful vampire lord... even if it's a temporary, contracted arrangement.

I peer at my reflection in a nearby wall mirror, biting my lip and patting my hair. It's a misty day, and my curls are already starting to frizz from the humidity, but there's little I could do about that other than tucking them under a slouchy knit hat that only makes the ends puff out more.

My whole outfit, which I agonized over endlessly, now feels haphazardly thrown together. I've gotten so used to wearing slinky dresses around the house that I feel like an over-stuffed dumpling with this long trench coat, the layers beneath hiding every curve from view. And my only shoes are heels or my old yellow sneakers, so sneakers it is.

Of *course* the one time I get a private moment with Sebastian, I have to cover practically every inch of skin. But Ellen did tell me to dress warmly.

It's too late to change now, anyway. Especially since I hear footsteps approaching from the hall. As the door opens, I whirl away from the mirror, unwilling to be caught staring at myself, and try to stand casually with my hands in my pockets.

My heart stutters as Sebastian enters the room. God, I thought I would be more impervious to him after he began gracing dinner with his presence—but this feels like a different ball game.

Especially right now, when he looks dashing in an all-black winter ensemble. A black, wool peacoat emphasizes his broad shoulders, and with a black sweater and black slacks beneath, he looks broody and imposing and ridiculously attractive. He even has a goddamn scarf, which should be hard to pull off but somehow suits him. With his dark hair pushed back and his dark eyes on me, he looks every inch the vampire lord of my fantasies.

Shit. I'm blushing. And my heart is galloping a mile a minute, surely broadcasting my feelings loud and clear. For a moment we just stare at each other, and I notice his eyes wandering over me in the same way mine did. But his face is unreadable, showing neither approval nor disapproval. His eyes stop on my sneakers and hover there.

I resist the urge to squirm.

"I know they don't exactly match my new wardrobe, but… they're comfy. And my favorite color. So."

He blinks, looks up at me. "I see."

I swallow. Try to think of something else to say. But before I can manage it, Barnabas comes barreling into the parlor, his entire spotted body wiggling with excitement.

It's a welcome break from the tension. I grin, crouching to take his soft, furry face in my hands, and plant a kiss on his nose. "Oh, hello, Barny! Will you be coming on our tour today?"

"Yes, he will be joining us, if that's alright," Sebastian says, watching us. There's something soft in his eyes that makes my ovaries do an excited flip. *Please, calm down, hormones,* I chastise myself.

"How could I possibly resist the company of such a handsome gentleman?" I coo, scratching behind the dalmatian's ears as he pants, tail thumping against a side table.

Sebastian turns and walks toward the front door without another word, Barnabas trotting happily after him. At the door, we pause for Sebastian to clip the dog's leash onto his collar, and then we head out into the darkness of the grounds.

It feels strange taking a walk at night. I never would've felt safe doing this in the city—or anywhere, really, on my own. Such is the peril of being a woman, and that's why I've yet to wander the grounds. But with Sebastian and Barnabas as my bodyguards, I have nothing to fear, and it feels like a whole new world has opened up to me. A misty, moonlit wonderland.

With the moon nearly full, no other lighting proves necessary. We stroll along in the quiet darkness, occupied only by the sounds of our footsteps and my breath, and Barny's happy snuffles as he moves along with his nose to the ground. Sebastian sets a quick pace that leaves little room for conversation, but I don't mind. All of my plans for this walk, my carefully constructed conversation topics and memorized flirtations, fall away as I get my first real sense of the estate's grounds.

It's beautiful here. I knew as much from staring out my window, but that was nothing compared to wandering through it. It's like stepping into a painting that I've long admired. All towering redwoods and moss and mist, so wild and green and *alive* compared to the gray concrete of LA.

It is also, however, quite cold. April in LA would be warm, but here, in the mountains at night, the air has more of a bite than I expected. Any thoughts that I may have overdressed for the chill are long gone after about ten minutes of walking. The tip of my nose stings, and I wish I could burrow down into the warmth of my jacket. Instead, I try to tug my collar up around my cheeks, but after a few tries, Sebastian turns and frowns at me, noticing that I've lagged behind and gone silent. He seems unbothered himself—but of course he must be used to the chilly mountain air, and vampires don't feel the cold, anyway.

"I'm fine," I blurt before he can even ask the question. Then I blush, realizing how obvious the lie must be. Surely, he will take this as an excuse to turn around and cut our tour short.

"I *told* Ellen to make sure you were dressed warmly," Sebastian grumbles. That catches me by surprise—I thought that was her being maternal, not instructions from him—but even more startling is when he steps closer to me. He undoes his scarf and leans down to wrap it around my own neck. The action shocks me into stillness—especially since he does it so casually, as though it barely occurs to him that this is unusual. As if he hasn't avoided any physical contact with me until this moment. He is very close, and very, very tall.

I can't bring myself to speak until he pulls away and studies his handiwork. "Better?" he asks.

I nuzzle my face into the scarf and breathe in the scent of him, woodsy and masculine. "Yes," I murmur, chest warming at the unexpected kindness. "Thanks."

Maybe he *is* just reserved. As beautiful as he is, there's an awkwardness about him, which I've observed not just in my presence but that of the staff. It must be hard to always stand apart. I've had the tiniest taste of what that isolation can feel like in my time here, and for Sebastian it has been a very, very long while.

So as we start to walk again, I start to feel daring. Rather than letting myself lag behind, I step up to his side and loop an arm through one of his. He stiffens, peering down at me, and I smile up at him.

He doesn't smile back. But neither does he pull away, and as we begin to walk again, he slows his pace so that it is easy for us to stay side by side. We don't talk much, but with his scarf warming my neck and his arm twined with mine, I don't mind.

* * *

By the time we return to the estate, I'm tired and mud-spattered from Barnabas's enthusiastic romping, but satisfied. Perhaps even happy. Barny is happier still, his paws covered in mud so thick, it's like he's wearing socks. Sebastian is as unreadable as ever, and somehow the only one of us that didn't get a speck of dirt on him, but I like to imagine he's secretly as pleased as Barny and I are.

Ellen, however, is less than thrilled to see us. She's standing at the top of the stairs when we enter the foyer, and lets out a shriek so startling that all three of us take a step back. Even Sebastian, who does *not* seem prone to startling.

"*Not* on my freshly cleaned floors!" she shouts, pointing an accusing finger at Barnabas. He barks, thrilled by the attention. "Straight into the bath with him!" A couple moments later she seems to realize she's shouting at the lord of the manor, but though color blooms on her face, she does not apologize or drop the finger.

"Yes, ma'am," Sebastian says. He bends to remove his shoes, then crouches beside the dog. In one smooth motion, he grabs Barnabas around the legs and scoops him up, as easily as though he were a toy rather than sixty pounds of wriggling dog.

I let out a startled laugh. Sebastian gives me a dour look, as if appalled at me finding amusement in the situation, but it only makes me stifle more laughter.

"Oh, but Lord Sebastian, your clothes," Ellen squeaks out from the top of the stairs, looking mortified. "I didn't mean— I can fetch Trent—"

"No need," Sebastian says. He strides down the hall with a delighted Barnabas in his arms, surely getting mud and dog hair all over his lovely, black outfit.

"No way in hell I'm missing *this*," I say, shrugging off my jacket and kicking off my shoes. I inhale the smell of Sebastian's scarf one more time before putting it aside and following him into the closest bathroom.

When I arrive, he is struggling to wrangle Barnabas into the porcelain tub. Cheerful as he was a few moments ago, Barny has clearly decided to be uncooperative now that he's aware of his fate. Unable to keep down a laugh, I step forward to help hold him in the tub. Once both of us are keeping him in place, he gives up the fight, and stands sullenly with his head down as Sebastian lathers him with suds and water.

I hold on to his collar to ensure he doesn't try to escape the second there's an opportunity. Then I glance sideways at Sebastian and snort out a laugh. His once-striking black outfit is now covered in mud and white dog hair. Sebastian follows my gaze down to his sweater and lets out a weary sigh.

"I don't know how I thought I could get away with wearing this," he murmurs.

"Your hubris is your downfall," I tell him, and he cracks a smile.

It's the first time I've seen him smile, and with his fangs withdrawn, I'm shocked at how *human* the expression makes him look. This whole interaction is so... *normal*, it's easy to forget that he's a stern and mysterious vampire lord who has been ignoring me for the past couple of months.

Afterward, the three of us—all damp and exhausted—retire to the drawing room and sit in front of the fire. Sebastian and I each occupy separate armchairs near the comforting warmth of the flames. Barnabas curls up at Sebastian's feet, his snout resting on one of the vampire's shoes, his tail thumping lazily against the floor. Sebastian reaches down and strokes the top of the dog's head.

"I never would've expected you to be a dog person," I say, unable to help the smile creeping across my face.

Sebastian glances at me. He doesn't quite give me another one of those life-changing smiles, but his expression is softer than usual. "He's not my dog. He's Trent's."

"Oh?" The way he and Barnabas look at one another says otherwise, but I hold my tongue.

"He's staying here while Trent is living in an apartment too small to handle him." Even as he says it, one of his hands drifts down to scratch behind Barny's ear. "His previous owner couldn't handle his energy. Trent wanted to help but couldn't keep him. He brought him here. I had never wanted a dog, but..." He pauses. "I had a dalmatian as a boy. Mags. A sweet girl who would run alongside our carriage." The word *carriage* jolts me. It's easy, sometimes, to forget that he is two hundred years old, and that his boyhood was during an entirely different era. His eyes go distant, and I bite my tongue to keep quiet, entranced by the sense he's finally showing me a hint of something deeper within himself. Something personal and true.

"Everything around me has changed so much over the decades, but dalmatians have stayed largely the same. Barnabas looks so much like Mags... he feels like a glimpse of the world I was born into. I had to let him stay." He blinks and seems to slide back into the present. As he looks down at his dog again, something troubled passes over his expression. Still gentle, but sad. "Though it is… difficult. Setting yourself up for heartbreak in such a way."

I nod. The mood change takes me by surprise… but I understand what he's saying. Dogs feel tragically short-lived even in comparison to my human lifespan. I can't imagine what it would be like for a vampire who can live forever.

"Like a flicker in the darkness," Sebastian continues, his eyes lowering to the floor. I can tell he's sinking inward, like he's retreating from something, or someone. Is it me? "A single match in an endless cave…"

"But a light, nonetheless," I say.

He blinks and looks up at me like he'd forgotten I was here. His expression goes thoughtful, and he nods. "Yes," he says. "And that is always something to cherish." His eyes linger on mine, and for a moment, I think I see something like gratitude in them.

Chapter Fifteen

"Come in," I call, expecting it to be Ellen here to deliver breakfast and take my blood, as usual. But instead, it's Trent who steps in with the tray containing my usual breakfast spread.

I sit up in bed, frowning. "Trent? Is everything alright?"

"Yes, ma'am," he says, his eyes on his shoes and his freckled cheeks aflame. "Just that Ellen's unable to make it until later tonight, so I'm helping out."

"I see." It's strange how quickly I've gotten used to our morning routine, but of course Ellen is her own person with needs. As soon as Trent shuffles over with the tray, I reach over to take my coffee. I sip it and lean back against my pillows with a sigh, eyes fluttering shut in pleasure. When I open them again, Trent is still standing there, wringing his hands.

"Um," he says. "I'm also… supposed…"

"Oh, yeah. My blood." I swap my coffee to my other hand and hold out my wrist for him.

Trent pulls out the tourniquet and syringe but hesitates. After a few moments of waiting, I glance up from my coffee to his face, and am alarmed to find him looking rather green-tinged and even more anxious than normal. "Is everything okay?"

"I… yes, of course," he says, looking very much not okay. "It's just that, um… I've never done this before. I'm certified, but, uh…" He grimaces. "I'm a little squeamish around blood, to be honest."

I huff a laugh at the ridiculousness. I would tease him about working in the wrong household, but he already looks like he's vibrating with nerves. And his anxiety is becoming infectious. I'm not so eager to have someone inexperienced prodding at my veins, especially when I need this done every morning. "Is there no one else who can do it?" I ask, pulling my wrist back.

Trent rubs the back of his neck with his free hand. "Er… I could check…"

"No. You know what?" I down the rest of my coffee in a couple of gulps, set the mug aside, and reach out to grab the syringe from his hand. "This is ridiculous," I say, climbing out of bed and getting to my feet. Trent looks away as he realizes I'm clad only in a gossamer nightgown, but I'm too full of righteous indignity to care. All of the important bits are covered, anyway. "There's no reason why Lord Sebastian can't get his own blood," I say. *Especially* after we spent yesterday evening together.

Trent's eyes widen. "I'm not so sure he—"

"At *least* while Ellen is away," I continue, ignoring him. I'm not going to stop and doubt myself; I have to ride this wave of anger as far as it will take me. I grab my toast off the breakfast tray, finish it in a few savage chomps, and stride toward the door. Trent trails after me, looking like he wants to argue but can't quite find the words. I whirl to face him in the hallway, and he nearly plows right into me before catching himself. "Where is he?" I demand.

Any remaining intent to argue withers in the face of my determination. "Library," Trent says in a small voice.

"Of course he is." Always with the damn library. Like his books are *so* preferential to my company. I march down the hallway, still in my nightgown, the wooden floors cold against my bare feet. At some point Trent stops following—probably afraid to be complicit in my behavior—but I don't pause to knock at the library door before entering.

Sebastian sits frozen in the same chair as last time, book in lap. For a moment, we just stare at one another. "What is it?" he asks. He slides a bookmark between the pages he's reading, sets the book aside, and stands. "What's wrong?"

I take a deep breath, pausing to collect myself and steady the rapid thumping of my heart.

Now that I'm here, in only my thin nightgown, I'm beginning to realize that this may be an ill-advised move. But I'm here, so I thrust out the syringe in his direction. He glances at it, and then up at me again, one eyebrow arching. "Ellen isn't in today," I say.

"I'm aware," he says. "I sent Trent."

I frown. I'm about to tell him there's no way I'm letting an untrained boy jab a needle into my vein, but I don't want to get Trent in trouble. So instead, I ask, "Why don't you do it yourself?"

He grimaces. "Amelia," he says, as though I'm being unreasonable. "I'd rather not."

I flush. "Why?" I demand. "You did it yourself at the ball. I know you're capable."

His eyes flash. "It's not a matter of capability."

Perhaps it's unwise, but I feel victorious summoning up any kind of emotion from those icy depths, so I press onward.

"Then what?" I ask. "Do you not want it?" I flash back to the reactions of all the vampires who drank from me. "Are you even drinking the vials that Ellen takes?"

"Of course I am drinking them," he snaps.

"Then what's the issue?" Maybe he's bluffing, trying to spare my feelings. Either way, I feel a sudden, urgent need to know. I step toward him, holding out the syringe in one hand and the bare wrist of the other. "Have it fresh."

For a couple of moments we're frozen like that, eyes locked. Then he shakes his head, sits, and reopens his book.

"I will wait until Ellen returns," he says. "You may leave. Enjoy your day off." He barely looks at me.

I straighten up with an indignant huff, ready to tell him off for the rudeness before taking my leave—but then I notice the slight tremble in his hands, the way his throat bobs as he swallows. I hesitate. "But you need to drink. Don't you?" Benjamin told me that most vampires feed every day in small amounts, and I know that Sebastian has not been taking enough from me to warrant a day off.

He looks at me then. His eyes are very dark, and I notice his fangs are out as his gaze drops to the curve of my neck. Suddenly, I don't see a man who is indifferent to me, but a man trying very hard to keep a lid on his self-restraint. But *why?* I reach up and—hardly able to believe my daring—brush my hair behind my shoulder to reveal the pale, unbroken skin there.

"If you really want me to leave, say it again and I will," I say.

Sebastian swallows again and stays silent. I approach him, step by step, giving him ample opportunity to tell me to go if that's what he wants, but he doesn't say a word. Just looks at me with those dark, dark eyes.

It encourages me to be even bolder. I set the syringe on a side table and hold my breath as I lower myself onto the edge of his armchair, close enough that one of my knees rests against one of his. I reach over to take the book from his lap and slide his bookmark into it before setting it aside with the syringe.

"You don't have to do this," Sebastian says, but it sounds half-hearted and thick with his fangs out.

I swallow. My heart pounds in my ears. "I want to," I say, and then, smiling shyly, hold my wrist up to him.

"You don't know what you're asking," he says, but the low grumble of reproach in his voice has less of an effect when he's unabashedly staring at my veins.

"I do," I say. "I know my blood isn't exactly to your liking, but you don't have to starve yourself."

His eyes were wandering back to my neck again, but he pauses, a furrow forming between his dark brows. "What?"

I flush. Is he going to make me say it again? Apparently so, because he's staring at me like he has no idea what I just said. "I mean, you're not subtle about it. You can barely tolerate my presence, you only drink from a syringe— So, I don't know." I'm rambling, but I can't stop, my words only coming faster and higher as I work myself up. "It's *fine*. I get it, I appreciate you taking me in like this either way, but—"

He lifts a hand, and I cut off the chaotic train of thoughts spilling out of my mouth.

"Amelia," he says, "why would I have taken you on as my valentine if I disliked your blood?"

I shrug. "Pity?"

He huffs out a hoarse little sound. It takes me a moment to recognize it as a laugh. I stare at his mouth without meaning to, shocked that it's capable of making such a noise.

"Flattering, but no, I am not quite so magnanimous," he says. For a moment he pauses, as if gathering his thoughts, and then he finally says, "Amelia, I do not find your blood repugnant. That's not why I've been avoiding you, taking such care with your safety. It's… quite the opposite." I blink at him, startled, and he clears his throat and continues more softly. "I do it because I find the taste of you irresistible."

I stare at him as the words sink in. The corner of my mouth creeps upward. *Irresistible.* I thought I had resigned myself to my blood being the opposite, but… God, it feels good to hear. Especially when I'm sitting so close to him, and I can see that his eyes are almost black with desire. Even though I know it's not *me* he's desiring, not really, just the blood running through my veins… it's still enough to spark heat in my lower body. I push my shoulders back, arching my back and tilting my head to expose my neck fully to him.

"Then stop trying to resist," I tell him, looking down and sideways to meet his gaze.

One of his large hands grips my waist and pulls me so I'm seated on the armchair between his legs, my back to his chest. Before I have time to be shocked, his mouth is against my neck. But his fangs don't pierce the skin. "You don't understand," he murmurs. "I don't know if I can hold myself back."

"I trust you," I say. I lean against him, ready for the bite, but he grabs my hand and lifts my wrist to his lips instead.

I gasp—both at the sensation of his fangs piercing my skin, and the feeling of the hard length straining against his tailored pants, now pressed firmly against my ass. Sebastian lets out a muffled moan against my skin as he drinks from me.

He really does like the taste of me. I grin, knowing he can't see it with me facing away from him. But my eyes soon flutter shut and I have to bite back my own moan of pleasure. It's been so long since I've been bitten. It feels better than I remember… and his obvious arousal feels good, too.

I can't help myself, it feels too good and is far too tempting; I roll my hips against him. He lets out another moan in response, and his arm snakes around my waist to pull me even closer. So I do it again, and again, rocking on his lap in a steady rhythm and imagining he's inside me instead of trapped within his trousers. Still, with my nightgown riding up around my waist, only those pants and my lacy underwear remain between us, and the friction feels fucking incredible.

Then I feel cold fingers sliding between my legs, and it feels even better. I gasp and shift, trying to turn to look at him, but his hold on my wrist keeps me firmly in place as his other hand squeezes my thigh before moving higher. His fingers brush over the front of my panties, making me whimper—and then he pushes my underwear to the side.

"Sebastian," I gasp, and he grips me tighter, still drinking from me in slow sips, like he's savoring me. Once his cold fingers slide against me, finding me already wet and ready, I give up on trying to escape and arch back against him. But I continue rolling my hips, rubbing my ass against his hardness. His fingers find the same rhythm as he strokes my clit. My eyes flutter shut as I lose myself in the pleasure, going light-headed as a liquid heat builds inside of me. It's been so goddamn long, I am so desperate to be touched, and his fingers feel fucking magical. I don't even need them inside of me; his light, careful touch soon brings me to the edge.

"Don't stop," I whisper. "I'm close, yes, just like that—"

He keeps his rhythm and his pressure just as they are, so that delicious heat slowly reaches its peak and then rolls through my body. I gasp and shudder and grind against his hand, riding the waves of my orgasm until I go limp against him.

It takes me a few moments to realize he's no longer drinking my blood. I'm not sure when he stopped, when the pleasure shifted from his fangs to his fingers. I'm feeling pleasantly fuzzy from the blood loss and the much-needed orgasm, and it feels like I could doze off on his lap.

But Sebastian has other ideas. He picks me up with all the ease of lifting a doll and sets me gently back on the chair he was previously occupying. He pricks his finger on a fang and heals the puncture marks on my wrist. I look up with heavy lids and reach for him, ready to undo his belt and try to give him the same pleasure he gave to me. But he turns his back on me and rushes out the door, leaving me alone

Chapter Sixteen

When the door to the library opens again, I sit up, thinking for a confused moment that Sebastian has turned around and come back. Instead, it's Ellen peering in at me. I frown, rubbing my eyes. Then the events of the night rush back, and I swallow hard and tug my nightgown down.

I can only imagine what a rumpled harlot I must look like, but Ellen's eyes are focused on my wrist as I approach. The puncture wounds are gone, but there's still a smear of dried blood. I resist the urge to cover it. This is my job, after all, and getting intimate with one's patron is par for the course, from my understanding.

I'm pretty sure most valentines don't get dumped in an armchair and abandoned after their fun… but maybe that's just the romantic in me. It's not like I was promised a *relationship* out of this, so I guess I shouldn't be surprised by him not treating it as one.

Still, I refuse to be embarrassed. Or to think too hard about my concern that Sebastian is using me, just like Declan did. Only pain lies that way.

"Hi," I chirp instead, forcing cheer. "You're here."

"Yes," Ellen says, hesitantly entering the library once I've made myself semi-decent. "Sorry for my absence earlier this evening. I saw that you barely touched your breakfast and skipped tea, so I wanted to make sure you're alright…"

I guess we're just going to ignore the fact I'm sleeping in Sebastian's favorite armchair in the library. Has she been searching the house for me? Or did Sebastian tell her where to find me and why? God, I'm not sure which option is more embarrassing.

"Thank you," I say, and stretch out in the chair in my best attempt to act normal. "I'll take it here."

When she sets the tray on the small table beside me, I notice that it not only has a fresh cup of coffee and my usual breakfast, but a side I don't recognize and a few pills.

I have a sinking feeling those are the same type that Benjamin always pushed on me, but I ask anyway. "What's this?"

"A spinach and prosciutto salad, and some extra supplements," she says without pause. "Bridget was told that you may have given more blood than usual this evening, and recommended this for recovery."

"Oh, lovely," I grumble, picking up my toast and tearing off a piece with more violence than necessary. I chew angrily and then eye Ellen. So Sebastian *definitely* clued the staff in about biting me, but… "Did our *lord* leave any messages for me, by chance?"

Her brow furrows. "He did not. Were you expecting one?"

I sigh, cram the rest of my toast into my mouth, and shake my head.

* * *

I spend the rest of the night trying to scrub off my mistakes in the tub and resting in bed. I almost want to decline dinner, but Ellen might have a breakdown over it; she's already dropped by twice to try to force extra food on me. When I show up in the dining room, Sebastian's seat is empty, and it remains so.

I guess this is how things are going to be, then. We're going to go back to ignoring each other like he didn't drink from my wrist or admit my blood makes him horny *or* give me a mind-blowing orgasm. Whatever. Fine with me. Everything is back to normal. My lonely, lonely normal.

And this time, when I climb into bed with my laptop, the words start flowing.

I have no plan, just a fire in my chest that demands to be expressed. After months of being stopped up, the words finally erupt from me like a dam's been broken. I never thought of myself as a nonfiction writer. I never thought my life was interesting enough. But what emerges on the screen is more of a diary entry than anything else.

I write about my experience at the Valentine's Day Ball, and my offer of patronage, and pulling up to the gate to the estate for the first time. I write about wandering the halls at night like a ghost, how painful it was to think Sebastian didn't want my blood, and how much more painful it is to realize he *only* wants my blood.

When I finally stop, my fingers and eyes are aching. I blink, look at the window, and realize that the sun is up. This is more daylight than I've seen since I arrived here; usually I get barely a glance at the sunrise before slipping into bed. I'm exhausted as I set the laptop aside and slide under my silk sheets. Writing has drained me—but it also leaves me feeling less alone, somehow.

I fall asleep with more words running through my head, written on the inside of my eyelids, whispering through my dreams. And I feel, for the first time in a very long while, that I have an awful lot to say, and it might be worth reading.

* * *

The next evening, I wake up and prepare for the usual routine. But when Ellen knocks on my door and enters, she comes bearing only the breakfast tray, and not the usual syringe.

"No blood today?" I ask, nibbling at the edge of a buttery mini quiche.

She shakes her head. "Before you ask, he didn't explain. You'll have to ask him yourself when you next see him."

I roll my eyes. "Right. Assuming he ever decides to stop avoiding me."

She bites her lip. It looks like she wants to say something, so I sip my coffee and wait, letting the silence simmer until she's ready. "He's been avoiding everyone," she says finally. "It was such a nice change having him at dinner, but now..."

It's as close to a critique of Sebastian as I've heard from anyone in the household. I sip my coffee again, trying to think of how to respond. Before I can, she asks, "Did something happen between you two?"

My mind flashes to my ass on his lap, his teeth on my wrist, his fingers against my clit. I nearly choke on my drink. "No," I say. "Well, yes, but..." I stumble over my words in my haste. Part of me is tempted to talk to her just so I have someone to vent to, but it doesn't feel appropriate to tell one of his employees. "I don't know. It's complicated."

"Right. Well…" She takes a breath, pushing her hair behind her ear. "If anyone can draw him out of this solitude, it's you."

I almost laugh. It's a ridiculous thought, that I could have any influence on the man. Just getting him to spend time with me is like pulling teeth. I had to ask him for the simple act of joining us at dinner, and again to give me a tour of the grounds, and once more to take my blood himself. I'm not going to embarrass myself by groveling to him *again,* begging for his attention. He's made it clear he doesn't want to give it to me. I believe him now when he says he enjoys the taste of my blood—it's hard to deny after our encounter in the library—but that only makes his refusal of me today feel like even more of a snub.

"Look, I appreciate that you and the rest of the staff treat me like I'm some sort of… lady of the house or whatever," I say, "but I'm not. This is just a job to me. And Sebastian is just my employer, the same as he is to you. I'm not going to try to convince him to socialize. He can stay holed up in the library all he wants."

Ellen looks taken aback. She blinks at me and then nods, her expression shuttering. "I understand," she says. "I won't bring it up again."

Guilt hits me as soon as she speaks in that formal tone. I must have sounded pretty harsh, and she doesn't deserve it. It's not her that I'm mad at. "Wait, Ellen, I didn't mean…"

"No, please. I overstepped. I apologize," she says, and is out the door before I can stop her.

I spend the next hour marinating in my guilt and loneliness and annoyance at Sebastian. I post some passive-aggressive song lyrics I'm not proud about on my social media, and take a bath. When I emerge, a message from Alexander waits on my phone.

Everything alright?

I bite my lip, staring at the screen. I shouldn't respond. But my room feels lonelier than ever right now. I've even managed to drive Ellen away.

I need someone to talk to… but I won't stoop to talking badly about Sebastian. *Just bored*, I type.

Shall I entertain you?

I tap my finger against my phone. He's toeing the line of flirtation again… but I'm probably overthinking it. He's a hot vampire with a busy social life, not some desperate incel who's going to send me a dick pic the second I show interest. He knows Sebastian is my patron, anyway. His interest in me is obvious, but he struck me as too much of a gentleman to truly overstep. Still, I try to play it safe: *How would you do that?*

A few minutes pass, and I fear he's lost interest already. But then, to my surprise, a video pops up in response. When I open it, my heart beats double at the sight of his face. Then he brings a violin into the camera's view and begins to play.

My jaw drops. Even through my tinny phone speaker, and to my untrained ears, the sound is gorgeous. Slow and sweet and sad. And the look on his face as he plays, his eyes closed and his mouth moving as he focuses, is almost more beautiful.

I text the second it's done: *WOW. Not what I expected. That was amazing!! Thank you for the show!* Insert several clapping emojis.

My pleasure. I hope I've made your night less dull.

He has. But soon, I find myself turning to my laptop instead. Nothing is quite as satisfying as pouring all of my loneliness and anger and shame out onto the page.

I can't talk to anyone about the way that I'm feeling. Alexander is off-limits. Sebastian is avoiding me again. The staff is kind, but I can't badmouth their beloved employer in front of them. My sister still doesn't know that I'm a valentine; I haven't even managed to admit that Declan and I broke up. I keep telling myself I'll tell her everything in person when she moves out to California in a few months, but every time I lie to her, I dig my hole deeper.

I have always found solace in words, and right now, the empty page is the only person I can tell about everything I'm experiencing. So I pour it all out, regurgitating my feelings in a way that feels almost violent.

It gives me an outlet for all of the things I can't say. But pouring these words onto the page isn't the same as feeling *heard*, and it doesn't help with my loneliness.

It makes me think about the valentine gossip columns and TV shows, the "tell-all" memoirs that never seem to have moments where anyone feels like I do right now. For so long, I read those stories as an escape from my day-to-day life. Now it's *become* my day-to-day life, and it isn't anything like what I thought it would be. But there have to be other valentines out there who feel like this.

I'm hit with a sudden, reckless need to tell somebody, anybody, the truth. I know I could potentially save this material and publish it later, probably snag a book deal that kicks off the writing career I've always dreamed of... but I'm not sure that's what I want to be known for. And it won't give me the acknowledgment I'm yearning for right now.

So on a whim, I quickly read through what I've written, scrub out any identifying details about me or Sebastian, and search out a popular blogging site. I designate myself as

Confessions of an Anonymous Valentine and upload a few posts detailing my experiences. I spend some time lurking on similar blogs and social media pages and post links to my own work in an effort to make some connections. I hadn't thought about making friends with fellow valentines online, but it does have a certain appeal. There *must* be others like me, who aren't living the high life that all of the famous valentines seem to be enjoying.

Once it starts to get hard to keep my eyes open, and the sun is rising, I shut my laptop, crawl into bed, and quickly forget all about the confessional blog I threw onto the internet.

Chapter Seventeen

The next evening, I wake feeling refreshed. Ellen shows up without a syringe or an explanation for why Sebastian no longer wants my blood.

I have to get out of my room before I go insane. I get ready for the day and slip down to the parlor, hoping to catch someone around for tea.

But I'm too early. Tea isn't set out yet. The only one here is Barnabas.

At least he still likes me. His tail starts thumping the moment he spots me, and his ears perk up. It makes me wonder if Sebastian has been avoiding Barny, too. Does he feel as neglected as I do? The thought makes me feel so sad that I grab his leash from its spot near the front door before I realize what I'm doing. When he sees it, Barnabas wiggles around with such excitement that I can't possibly change my mind. It'll be good for me, too, I decide. Languishing in my bed isn't helping.

"Okay," I say, clipping the leash on to his collar. "Just a quick walk, buddy."

The weather is overcast, bitterly cold, and miserably damp, with fog settling over the estate and rendering the grounds gloomier than usual. Still, Barnabas is eager to forge ahead, and so I allow myself to be pulled along. But if I thought some time outside would be good for me, I'm proven wrong. Soon my shoes are caked in mud, my socks are soggy, and my hair is frizzing. The cold wind bites through my coat, and the clouds are darkening overhead, promising worse weather to come.

"Alright, Barny, I've had about enough of this," I say, trying to turn around. But he digs his feet in, straining forward. My shoes slip in the mud. I curse as my feet slide out from under me; my ankle twists as I try to catch myself, and I tumble to the ground, the leash slipping from my hand. Barnabas bounds off into the fog.

"Barny!" I scramble to my feet. It takes a couple of tries; the mud keeps bringing me down, and my left ankle hurts like hell when I put my weight on it. Still, I lurch forward, searching the fog for a spotted menace with a wagging tail. There's no sign or sound of him.

"Shit." I teeter, unsure of what to do. Maybe I should go back to the house for help; surely Tobias and Trent know the grounds better and would have an easier time finding Barnabas. The grounds are gated, so he can't get into too much trouble… but then I think of the gates opening and a car driving through the fog, unable to see Barny until it's too late, and my stomach drops like a stone. I would never be able to forgive myself if something happened. I can't take that risk.

Caked in cold mud, with pain throbbing in my ankle, I limp forward into the fog. I don't know where I'm going, and soon I've lost any sense of where I am. I wander aimlessly, calling out for Barnabas, but no response follows. The fog becomes suffocating. It's like it enters my lungs with every breath. Still, I trudge onward.

When I hear a bark from the fog, I jolt to a stop, relief flooding me. "Barnabas! Barny! Here, boy!" I call.

For a moment, there's nothing. Then my lovely, spotted boy comes trotting out of the fog, leash dragging through the mud behind him. But instead of being his usually wiggly self, he stands stiff beside me, tail straight up, and growls toward the fog. I've never heard him make a sound like that before, or seen his fur standing on end.

"Barny? What is it?" I carefully crouch down to take his leash in hand. "It's okay, buddy."

But as I tug the leash, Barnabas stays where he is, still snarling fearsomely. I frown, tug again, but he only digs his heels in.

Unease slithers over my skin, leaving goose bumps in its wake. I stare into the fog. There's nothing. Nothing visible to me, at least. But I swear I feel eyes on me.

I stand still until the moment passes. After another minute, Barnabas lets his lips fall back over his teeth, and his posture relaxes. He glances back at me and wags his tail, as if to say, *Didn't I do a good job?*

"Yes, you were very fierce," I say, running a hand over his damp fur. "I think it's about time to head home now."

Yet once again, as I try to pull the leash, he refuses. Instead, he whines and points his nose in a different direction.

I sigh. Maybe he knows something I don't. Or maybe he's just being stubborn. Either way, I don't want to risk another leash-dropping fiasco, so I follow him into the fog.

After a couple minutes of him trotting along without a care in the world, me wincing with every step, Barnabas comes to an abrupt stop, his ears perked up and his eyes locked on something. I stop as well and follow his gaze to a gravestone ahead.

I suck in a breath. The stone stands alone beneath the drooping limbs of a weeping willow. It looks old, but the bouquet of roses sitting at its base is fresh and new. It feels like I'm approaching something I wasn't meant to find… but with curiosity driving me and Barnabas keeping me company, I move forward to get a closer look.

Etta Langley, the headstone reads. Below, etched into the gray stone, is an inscription: *Eternally beloved.*

Something about the scene makes my heart ache. Gravestones are always sad, but this one, alone beneath the willow… it feels painfully lonely. Who would be buried all the way out here by themself? And the fresh flowers… those speak of a lingering pain, not an old loss.

A drop of water hits my head. And then another. I look up, dismayed, to realize the dense clouds have broken. Within a few moments, it's pouring. Barnabas shakes himself off and ducks under the willow tree for shelter, and I follow him, crouching against the trunk.

The earlier incident with Barny has left me spooked, and the last thing I want is to be stuck here beside a grave. But the pain in my ankle is only getting worse, rain is pounding, and I don't know the way back to the house. So after a moment, I sigh, lower myself to a cross-legged position on the ground, and settle in to wait for the weather to clear.

Chapter Eighteen

An hour passes, maybe two, and the rain shows no sign of letting up. I'm shivering and wet. Barnabas lays curled up beside me with his head in my lap. He keeps looking up at me with his big brown eyes like he's asking me to do something about this horrid situation, and it only makes me feel worse.

"I'm sorry, Barny," I whisper, running my fingers through his wet fur. I realize he's shivering, too, and a fresh wave of guilt hits me. I unbutton my coat and pull him up into my lap. He nuzzles closer to my warmth, sticking his cold nose into the side of my neck. It only makes me colder and wetter, but I hope I can share some of my body heat with him.

I've resolved to wait here till morning when I hear something through the rain. I squint against the sheet of water, wondering if I imagined it.

"Amelia!"

No, that was real. Definitely real. I cup my numb hands around my mouth and yell back, "I'm here!"

Shockingly fast, a form dressed in head-to-toe black emerges from the rain and joins us under the protective branches of the weeping willow. I stare, half-delirious and startled and clutching Barnabas. The last person I expected to see was Sebastian himself. Barny lets out an excited whine at the sight of him, but he doesn't move from his spot on my lap.

"Amelia," Sebastian says again. "What are you *doing* out here? What in the world were you thinking, coming out in this weather?"

"Just," I say, teeth chattering, "a little. Chilly."

Sebastian mutters something unintelligible and unbuttons his coat. "Take yours off," he says. "It's wet."

I nod, too tired and cold to argue. When my stiff fingers fumble with my buttons, he reaches over and helps me. He pulls the coat off and wraps me in his own. He doesn't have any body heat to offer, of course, but it's still nice and dry and smells like him, and I wrap it around myself and Barny.

"Here Trent!" Sebastian shouts over his shoulder. He lifts Barnabas off my lap with one arm and helps me to my feet with the other.

The moment I'm up, my ankle gives. I cry out; I had almost forgotten the injury, since my body's gone numb.

Sebastian catches me, his eyes widening. "You're hurt."

"Twisted my ankle," I say, leaning on him for support.

A moment later, Trent ducks in from the rain. "Oh, thank God," he says, his eyes flicking from me to Barny.

"Get Barnabas back to the house," Sebastian says, his eyes never leaving me as he hands Barny over to Trent.

"Yes, sir." Trent pulls Barny into his coat, cradled safely in his arms.

"I'm fine," I say belatedly. "I'm just—" I cut off in a squeak as Sebastian scoops me off my feet. He holds me in his arms, bridal-style, like I weigh nothing at all. I want to protest but his arms are strong, his coat so blessedly dry around me, and it's instinctive to just burrow my face into his chest and let myself be carried.

With Sebastian's long strides and knowledge of the grounds, it only takes ten minutes or so to get back to the house, but he doesn't set me down when we get there. He carries me through the entryway without pausing to take off his shoes.

Trent comes close behind with an extremely muddy Barnabas. "I'll take care of him, Lord Sebastian," he says.

"Thank you, Trent." Sebastian carries me through to the drawing room and the fire waiting there. He sinks down in front of it, lowering me to a seat on the rug in front of the fireplace. I shut my eyes, enjoying the warmth on my skin, but then they fly open again as I think of my filthy shoes.

"I'm getting mud all over," I protest. "I should take a bath—"

"No. That would be too much of a shock for your body. You need to warm up slowly."

He starts to stand, and I reach out and grab his arm before I can second-guess myself.

"Please don't go."

I think I might be delirious, because I didn't mean to say that out loud. But I'm too cold and dizzy to care how pathetic I sound right now. Something about the way he carried me here made me ache to be taken care of, even though I'm sure he's furious with me.

"I was just going to get you a change of clothes," he says. But he lowers himself back to his knees on the rug, and I gratefully lean back against him. "A blanket, then. But you need to get out of those."

I nod but make no move to undress. I'm not sure my stiff limbs are capable of it yet.

Sebastian leans over to grab a nice fuzzy throw from an

armchair. Then he pulls his borrowed coat off my shoulders and sets it aside. A moment's hesitation, and he reaches for the hem of my soaked sweater. I lift my arms to assist him, and he carefully peels it off me. I'm left only in a bra, but I can't bring myself to be self-conscious right now. Anyway, he's still kneeling at my back, so he can't be getting much of a view.

"You can take that off, too," I mumble, since I don't feel like fumbling with it with my numb fingers.

Sebastian hesitates. Then his fingers find their way to the clasp of my bra. He undoes it, and I shrug it off and let it fall to my lap. A moment later, he wraps the blanket around my shoulders.

I expect him to leave it at that, but instead he grabs me by the waist and slowly but oh so easily spins me around on the rug to face him.

"Which ankle is the one that hurts?" he asks. Not quite able to form words, I tilt my chin at my left foot.

He takes that mud-caked sneaker—my poor, yellow shoes may never recover—and sets it on his knee without a care for the dirt smearing on his nice pants. He undoes my laces, slips off the shoe with utmost care, and scrutinizes my swollen ankle.

I can't help it; I stare at him, my awareness gradually sharpening as warmth seeps into my bones. I pull the blanket tighter around my shoulders, although he never lifts his eyes from my ankle. His expression is creased with concentration as he gently feels along the bone.

It doesn't make any sense. I can't wrap my head around the way he carried me back to the house, the way he's treating me so softly, after ignoring me for days.

"I suspect it's just a sprain," he says, lowering my bare foot to the rug. "But I'll call the doctor tomorrow to have a look at it."

"Can't you just give me some of your blood?" I ask, remembering the way he closed my puncture marks after he bit me.

He shakes his head. "You'd have to ingest it for an injury like this, and I'd rather avoid that," he says. "If this were a serious injury, it'd be one thing, but for a mild sprain…"

I frown. "What's wrong with ingesting it?"

"It can be addictive, for one," he says. "And it also creates a temporary bond." When I give him a quizzical look, he continues, "It's akin to the bond between a fledgling vampire and their sire. I'd be able to sense your location and emotions, and influence you to an extent."

"Oh." The thought is enough to make me blush. Definitely best to avoid that so I won't pester him with all of my wild mood swings and unsavory thoughts. "Well, yes, okay, let's not do that. It's not bad, anyway. I'll be fine. I'm sure a doctor isn't necessary, either."

He slowly raises his eyes to meet mine. "I say it is."

The intensity in his gaze makes heat flood my face. Now that my mind is finally clearing up, the reality of what happened today sinks in.

"You came looking for me," I whisper.

"I wasn't sure what to think when I realized you weren't in your room." He lifts my other sneaker into his lap and begins to attend to those laces as well. "And when I asked around, I heard that you had missed dinner." He removes the shoe, peels off the sock, sets my foot beside the other while I sit still. "I wondered if perhaps you had… left. But then I realized

Barnabas was missing."

"I just wanted to take him on a walk," I say, sheepish.

"In the rain." His lips purse. "Of all the imbecilic—"

"It wasn't raining when I left!"

He sighs. It's especially dramatic because I know the man doesn't even need to breathe. He reaches up to touch my ankle, just below where my jeans are plastered to my skin. "Can you remove these yourself?"

"I could." A beat. "But you're doing such a good job of it."

He blinks, his eyes shifting up to meet mine. When they do, I crack a small smile.

Something almost like relief floods his expression. "You certainly seem to be feeling better," he says. He shifts forward, his hand sliding over my jeans from my ankle to my knee, to the inside of my thigh. I suck in a sharp breath, but he's all businesslike as his hands move to the button of my jeans and my zipper. Almost like he's… teasing me?

Then he tugs my jeans down my legs, and any hint of sexiness is quickly lost as my wet pants stick to my equally wet skin. I try to wriggle to help him out, which only makes it feel more ridiculous. He sends me tumbling on my ass with one firm yank, and I collapse into helpless giggles as he finally pulls the pants free.

"My God," he mutters dourly, which only makes me laugh more. I look up at him from where I'm sprawled on the rug before the fire, wrapped in a blanket with my hair still soaked and wild, and catch a glimmer of what I dare say is amusement in his dark eyes. He sets my pile of wet clothes and shoes aside and tugs me up so I'm sitting on his lap in front of the fireplace. He wraps his arms around my almost-naked but blanket-cocooned body.

I wish I had a reason to get him under the blanket with me, but unfortunately, I can't use the excuse of body heat when he's a vampire. Instead, I just rest my face in the crook of his neck and breathe in the smell of him.

Whenever he's out of sight—which is most of the time—it's easy to convince myself that Sebastian hates me, that he's using me for my blood or taking care of me out of pity. That he's some callous asshole. But when he's here, holding me so tenderly like this, I feel *dangerously* fond of this infuriating man.

"You're lucky you weren't hurt worse," he murmurs into my damp curls. I think I feel the faintest brush of his lips against my hair, but it could be my imagination.

"How long were you out searching in the rain?" I ask.

"Not long, thankfully," he says. "I thought that if you were with Barnabas, he would lead you to…" A pause, a swallow. "On the path of our weekly walk."

To the grave, I realize, flashing back to that lonely headstone beneath the willow trees. *Eternally beloved.* The fresh roses. He walks there every week? I almost ask about it, about *her*, but I stop myself. As curious as I am, I can't bring myself to ruin this rare moment alone with Sebastian.

Plus, his arms are so strong around me, and the fire is so lovely and warm. Slowly, my frozen skin and chilled bones thaw. As the cold seeps out, exhaustion creeps in. Before I know it, my head is drooping onto Sebastian's shoulder, and my eyes are drifting shut.

The last thought that occurs to me, before I fall asleep, is that I never asked Sebastian why he was looking for me in my room in the first place.

Chapter Nineteen

I wake in my own bed to the smell of coffee. A breakfast tray rests on my nightstand. I must have slept through Ellen delivering it, though thankfully the coffee is still warm. I drink a third of it in one big gulp, and then nearly choke on it in surprise when I realize there's a sealed letter underneath.

Who would send me a letter? Benjamin, maybe. As soon as I think of him, I feel a pang of guilt for not keeping in touch with him more. But as I tear the envelope open, I read the short message in seconds and realize it's not from Benjamin at all.

"He *would* deliver a letter in his own house," I mutter, but I can't stop myself from grinning as I scan the short message again.

To my Valentine,
I would like to request your presence at tea. 12:00.
Sebastian

If anyone else had written this, I would assume they hated me and/or were planning on giving me a stern talking-to. But this is Sebastian. I'm beginning to understand that words aren't his strong suit. And just the fact he sent me a letter has to be significant.

Especially because he requested tea. The other staff don't usually meet for tea, so I assume it will just be the two of us. I had to practically beg to get him to dine with me in a room full of people. This has to be progress, especially due to how he took care of me last night. It still makes my stomach flutter to think about the way he carried me, his careful touch as he undid my sneakers, his slender fingers unclasping my bra...

I down the rest of my coffee and scramble out of bed only to almost collapse as my ankle gives out. *Shit.* I almost forgot about that, but now that I'm looking, I see that it's still hideously swollen and angry-red. Still, I limp to my drawer and search for my sexiest lace set to wear to tea. Just in case.

* * *

After a long, warm bath, several changes of outfit, and careful consideration for my hair and makeup, I still find myself ready an hour early. Sitting and waiting seems impossible when I'm nearly bursting with nerves.

To keep myself busy, I grab my laptop and type up another entry to my diary-slash-blog. The more I write, the easier it gets. I'm finding my groove now, and it feels so good to pour out my thoughts and feelings rather than leaving them to rattle endlessly around my brain. Only after writing my slightly altered story of being stranded in the rain and rescued by Sebastian do I think to click over and check out how my online blog is doing so far.

I'm surprised at the amount of views and comments that have trickled in on my first couple of posts. It's not blowing up the internet or anything, but people are reading it. Some have *very* strong opinions. There are valentine wannabes telling me how spoiled I am for complaining about my life when I have the best job in the universe, while others inform me I'm going to hell for my "unholy profession." People on both ends of the spectrum go nuts about valentines, and of course there are also plenty of users declaring it "fake news" or "obviously a creative writing prompt by a twelve-year-old." But I scroll through the fights in the comments, resist the urge to fling out some poop emojis in response, and laugh it off.

The personal messages have far more of an impact on me. There are heartfelt emails from other valentines—also anonymous—thanking me for telling my story and sharing their confessions.

Sometimes I feel like I'm nothing more than a toy to him, one confesses. *I know he'll replace me one day with a younger, fresher human.* I wince in sympathy.

My patron promised she'd turn me, but I'm beginning to think it was a lie, another says. I shudder; at least I don't have to worry about *that*.

Sometimes I think giving blood is an unhealthy addiction. Now, that one I can relate to...

Each message makes my chest ache. People are baring their hearts and souls to me, freed by the promise of anonymity and someone on the other side who understands what it feels like. I answer as many messages as I can manage without making myself late for my tea with Sebastian, post my next blog update, and shut my laptop.

* * *

I'm wearing my favorite dress, all bloodred lace with the lipstick to match, and aware of the scandalous lingerie beneath. When I step into the parlor, my eyes find Sebastian sitting and waiting for me, and my heart surges.

Then I see the stranger sitting beside him, and it drops straight down to my stomach.

"Amelia," Sebastian says, looking up from the tea he's pouring. "This—" He pauses as he sees me, eyes widening as he takes in my outfit, and spills some tea. He clears his throat and averts his gaze, and I suddenly feel horribly embarrassed. He must be embarrassed *for* me, dressed like this for what is clearly not the romantic tea I was expecting. "This is Dr. Bailey," Sebastian says, recovering but still not looking at me. "She's here to take a look at you… at your ankle."

"How do you do?" Dr. Bailey is an elegant older woman, kindly and without a hint of judgment, but that doesn't stop me from being mortified. My mouth seems to be glued shut, so I just hobble through an awkward curtsy and take a seat at the table. Sebastian slides over a cup of tea and a small plate of food, still without meeting my eyes. Seeing the food, including the types of iron boosters I usually take for blood giving, also just reminds me that he hasn't asked for any of my blood in days.

I thought I felt a spark between us yesterday, but now I'm back to doubting everything again. This is torture.

"May I take a look?" the doctor asks.

"Of course." I shed my slipper to prop my foot up on an ottoman, and Bailey scoots over to examine me with warm, careful hands. I try not to think about Sebastian's cold fingers on my skin last night, and busy myself with my tea and biscuits, murmuring my answers to each question about tenderness and pain as she presses on and moves my ankle to test it.

"I believe it's a mild sprain," Dr. Bailey says eventually. "It'll be swollen and tender for another day or two, so I recommend you rest as much as possible. You can use ice and ibuprofen to manage the pain and inflammation. I expect you'll be back on your feet soon, but if the pain continues, feel free to call me again."

I nod along, feeling a spark of mingled relief and new embarrassment. I never would've called in a doctor for such a mild issue. Years without health insurance made me pretty self-sufficient about these things. "Thanks very much," I say. "Sorry you had to waste your time coming all the way out here."

"It's not a waste." She smiles at me, finishes her tea, and shortly afterward bids us farewell to head back into town.

The room is silent once it's just me and Sebastian. I dunk a cookie into my tea and swirl it around to avoid looking at him.

"You shouldn't bother getting all dressed up like that while you're injured," Sebastian says.

My cookie crumbles in my suddenly tight grip. "Sorry?" I ask, glowering at him.

He looks taken aback at my expression. "I only… What I meant is… I want you to rest, is all." A pause. "You look… it's a nice dress."

"Hm." It would be more convincing if he didn't sound like he was reciting sums, all stiff and awkward like the compliment is uncomfortable on his tongue. Deciding I don't particularly care about impressing Sebastian right now, I lick the crumbs of the lost cookie off my finger. His eyes follow the motion, and he swallows.

"I'm afraid I'm doing this all wrong," he says. "I hadn't thought you'd be injured when I invited you to tea."

I stare at him, curious enough that I forget my lingering irritation. "You mean you didn't invite me here just for the doctor?"

"No," he says. "I wrote the invitation yesterday. I was coming to your room to deliver it when I found that you were missing."

"Oh…" I sit back in my chair and fold my arms over my chest. "What did you want to talk to me about?"

His mouth works for a few seconds before he manages to produce any words. Then his expression drops to my injured ankle, and he shakes his head. "It doesn't matter now," he says. "You should focus on resting."

So cold. As if the intimate moment never happened last night. I frown down at my tea, and a moment later he gets up, eager to excuse myself.

Another thought occurs to me as I think again about that walk last night… and the grave I found, with the fresh roses. "Sebastian?"

He pauses. "Yes?"

I lift my eyes to meet his. "Who was Etta Langley?"

I'm looking right at him, so I see his facial expression freeze, then shutter, every hint of emotion hidden as suddenly as though he's turned off a switch. He hesitates, and then says, "Never ask me that again."

Then he turns and leaves me stunned and stung.

Chapter Twenty

After tossing and turning all night, I wash, dress, and limp down to the parlor on my still-tender ankle. Ellen finds me waiting at the table before the sun is down, bleary-eyed and rumpled.

"Ah, there you are." She sets down my breakfast tray. "No blood today. Lord Sebastian said you're recovering from an injury."

"M-hm…" I take my coffee. "By the way. Do you know what Sebastian's surname was before he was turned into a vampire?"

"Beaumont," she answers.

So whoever was in that grave wasn't a relative. "Do you know who Etta Langley is?" After all, Sebastian told me not to ask *him* again. He didn't tell me not to ask anyone else.

But Ellen shakes her head. "Should I?"

"Hm." I sip my coffee and glance up at her. "That's weird, because she's buried on the grounds."

Her eyes widen. She turns away before I can read her expression. "Oh… well. Whoever she was, must've been before my time."

She rushes out before I can ask anything more, and my

suspicion heightens. It was possible she was an old relative of Sebastian's, or a staff member who passed away… but then, why not tell me?

I eat my breakfast, throw on a few more layers of clothing, and limp determinedly down to the kitchen.

Bridget waves a spatula at me. "Get out of here! I swear your mere presence is enough to make things start burning."

"First of all, ouch!" I press a hand to my chest in mock-woundedness. "Second of all, who's Etta Langley?"

The question is unexpected enough to make her pause. "Etta? Sounds familiar…"

I perk up. "Really?" The gravestone didn't have a date, so perhaps the older staff members knew her.

Bridget frowns thoughtfully and pulls a cookbook from a stack on the counter. She shuffles through it before stopping. "Is this what you mean?"

I take the book—an older, yellow cookbook with clear 1950s flair—and look at the recipe within. *Lemon Chiffon Pie*, the top of the page reads. Beside it, someone has scrawled with pen: *Etta's favorite!*

"Hmm…" I hand the book back. It's not much information, but it's proof that someone named Etta was here, once. "Nothing other than that?"

Bridget shakes her head. "I don't think so. But the name sounds familiar. Now get out and let me work!"

I leave her in peace and head out onto the grounds. The grave and that book both seemed old… so if anyone on the staff knows anything about Etta, it's bound to be the one who's worked here the longest.

I find Tobias trimming the bushes outside, his work precise and crisp despite his gnarled hands. He doesn't look up as I walk over.

"Who's Etta Langley?" I ask. "Why is she buried on the grounds?"

He pauses and then resumes his work. "Sounds like a question for Lord Sebastian."

I scowl, placing my hands on my hips. Of course Tobias is forever loyal to his boss… and Sebastian, as per usual, is nowhere to be found. I try to think of another approach. "Do any roses grow on the grounds?"

"No."

I don't get more out of him than that, but at least it gives me a new lead. There were fresh roses on that grave, just like the one that always sits on my nightstand… and if they don't grow here, they must be delivered.

As Sebastian rarely has need of a driver, Vincent isn't here daily. It takes a few more days—full of more unsuccessful digging, and Sebastian's empty chair at dinner—before I find him bringing in the weekly haul of groceries.

"Did you bring the roses?" I ask, oh-so-innocently.

The older man blinks at me. "Of course," he says. "A dozen, just like always."

He points out the bouquet waiting alongside the groceries. One dozen roses, every week… one for me, and the rest for Etta's grave.

I pick up the flowers, breathing in the smell, and remembering doing the same when I first arrived and found that rose on my nightstand.

Something about that pricks my memory. I leave the flowers with Vincent and return to my bedroom, looking around. It takes me only a moment to realize what I was thinking of—the mirror on my vanity with a frame of carved roses.

I trace a finger along it. I remember thinking, when I first arrived, that this seemed like a valentine's room. But everyone on the staff claimed Sebastian had never had another valentine... except for Tobias, who dodged the question. Damn that old man for being so determined to keep Sebastian's secret.

But there's one other person who might now. I take out my phone and text Benjamin: *Did Sebastian have a valentine before me?*

Not that I know of, he answers. *Why?*

I bite my lip. *Just curious.* Would Benjamin lie to me? I don't *think* so... but he's a courtless vampire. He might not know the truth. *Are there any records of that sort of thing?*

Yes, but not public ones... especially not for human access.

I tap my finger against my phone. I might not have been the best student, but I remember enough of Benjamin's lessons to guess which vampire courts might have such records. The Celeste court preserves history, which would leave me out of luck if I intended to pry into one of their own vampires... but secrets? Secrets belong to Solomon court.

My fingers hover over my phone for a moment before I begin to type.

Alexander? If I asked you something, would you keep it between us?

Of course. Anything.

Did Sebastian have a valentine before me?

I stare at the screen, waiting for a response. Bubbles indicate that he's typing, but it takes a while for the answer to come. A long while.

Yes, her name was Etta, if I recall correctly. About 75 years past. A charming woman, absolutely lovely.

My stomach drops. I wasn't sure if he'd answer the question, and certainly wasn't prepared for the possibility that he *knew her personally.* I'm struck with a sudden urge to fling the phone away from me and try to forget this, but I can't stop myself from asking the follow-up question. *What happened to her?*

This answer comes much more quickly than the last. *You'd have to ask him. All I know is that one day she was gone.*

Chapter Twenty-One

I skip dinner that night and pick at breakfast the next morning, mumbling answers to Ellen's worried questions. I can barely bring myself to look her in the eye. Does she know the truth? Does everybody?

I can't stop thinking of Alexander's last message. *All I know is that one day she was gone.* When I started probing into Etta, it was mostly just me being nosy. But now… now I'm wondering if I should be afraid. It would be easy for someone to disappear out here, I realize. Nobody even knows where I am, except for Benjamin and the staff.

And all of them are willing to hide Sebastian's secrets.

I *need* to know the truth. And if nobody is willing to tell me, I suppose I'll have to do some snooping.

I spend my evening exploring my room, searching through every inch in the hopes of finding something hidden. I find an old silver hairbrush in a drawer in the bathroom, and a dress I don't recognize in a chest in the closet—further proof that a woman was in this room before me, but not much in the way of information.

So I venture out to the hallway, resisting the urge to tiptoe; I know Sebastian will be able to hear my heartbeat even if my footsteps don't announce me. The rest of the staff should be gone for the evening. While I'm debating about where to begin in my search, I pass in front of a window and feel eyes on me.

I freeze and then slowly step backward to peer out through the glass. I catch a glimpse of a tall, lean figure in the tree line—but then I blink, and he's gone.

I can't believe Sebastian would lurk around outside to avoid me. But… it gives me an opportunity. Since Sebastian is out, I'm the only one here. I have the entire house to myself. I hesitate for only a moment before rushing to the library and struggling with the heavy door.

Sebastian's usual chair sits empty, a book resting on the end table beside it. I open it, wondering if it will provide any insights   but it's in Latin, because of fucking course it is. I huff, set it aside, and search for anything else personal but find nothing.

Next door is the music room, and it doesn't hold much except an old grand piano. Then the drawing room with a stone fireplace and carved mantle. Neither of them seem promising.

The next door, one at the end of the hallway that I've never been inside before, is locked.

Sebastian's bedroom? The temptation is too great. I fumble with my up-done hair and yank out a bobby pin.

I've never tried anything like this before, but I've seen it in movies. Surely movies wouldn't lie to me, right? And anyway, I'm desperate at this point. I unfold the bobby pin so I have a flat metal piece, strip off the rubber knob with my teeth, and insert one end into the lock. Then I fumble around with it, face scrunched in concentration.

"Amelia?"

I shriek, nearly jumping out of my skin, and the bobby pin snaps in half. I hurriedly hide the makeshift lockpick in a fist behind my back as I whirl to face Sebastian, barely noticing the prick of a sharp, broken piece of metal in my thumb.

Sebastian is staring at me, his shoulders braced. "What in god's name are you doing?" he asks. "You can't go in there, it's…" He reaches for me—and then he goes still. I glance at his hand where it squeezes my arm and then up at his face. His eyes are so dark, they're nearly black. His lips are slightly parted, and his fangs are out. He looks like a stranger, unrecognizable from the man who carried me through the cold a few days ago.

Blood trickles down the injured finger I'm hiding behind my back, and I shiver with realization. My dread doubles as I recall, again, that we're alone in the house… and that Sebastian did not feed this morning. Or yesterday morning. Or the one before.

Sebastian has never hurt me. He has always been achingly polite and gentle, even when he was cantankerous. But there's something animalistic in his gaze right now, and I remember all of Benjamin's lessons about how vampires use manners to cover up their true, violent natures.

And I realize that perhaps I should've been more afraid when I started probing into the mysterious disappearance of his former valentine.

"Sebastian," I whisper, and try to pull my arm from his grip. His cold fingers tighten until they nearly hurt.

He's so strong and so *fast*. I can't believe he got from the trees to this hallway so quickly without me even hearing the crash of the front door or the creak of the stairs.

In one quick motion, he drags my hurt hand out from behind my back and pins my wrist to the door behind me. I cry out, more from surprise than pain, and struggle as his eyes zero in on the drop of blood where I pricked myself. He leans in and licks the droplet off my finger, slow and almost sensual, and groans.

"God," he whispers. "The taste of you."

I can't lie—it would be hot if I weren't scared out of my goddamn mind. And if he didn't look so unlike himself right now. "Sebastian," I whisper. "You're scaring me."

His eyes are blank. His mouth ghosts over my fingertips and down to my wrist, where his fangs graze the delicate skin just over my pulse point. My heart is hammering in my chest; I'm sure he can feel it through my skin.

"Sebastian," I whimper again.

He opens his mouth.

"Sebastian, *stop!*" My voice cracks in desperation as I shout at him. My free hand presses against his chest in vain—I might as well be shoving a brick wall.

But he stops. Blinks. Recognition flickers behind his eyes, and then they focus on me. A moment later, he releases me and stumbles back as though I've burned him, horror etched on his face.

"Go," he rasps. "Slowly. Don't run, or I'll... I can't control myself, I..."

I back away, breathing hard, too afraid to turn my gaze away. But he stays in place, hands braced against the wall, until I make it into my bedroom. I slam the door behind me and lock it. Then I back away, trembling, certain that the flimsy piece of wood will do nothing if Sebastian decides to pursue me.

But he doesn't. I know because a minute later I hear the front door slam so hard, the entire house seems to shake. When I dart over to the window to peer out, I see a car pulling out and racing down the road away from the estate, leaving me alone.

Chapter Twenty-Two

If I thought my life was lonely before, the next few days prove that I have newer depths to sink to. The staff avoid my eyes. There is no word about when—if?—Sebastian will return from his hasty departure. I'm not sure I want him to.

I consider reaching out to Benjamin to ask for his advice, but I'm not sure what I'll tell him. He warned me that vampires could be dangerous, after all. Maybe this sort of thing happens all the time. And it's not like Sebastian actually hurt me. He could have if he wanted to. He could've bled me dry and buried me on the grounds, and the staff probably would've just accepted his excuses.

That makes me think of Etta again, and I feel physically ill. Still, I can't bring myself to reach out to Benjamin with what he'd doubtlessly see as an official complaint.

Normally, I'd call Maisy to ask her advice, but she still has no idea I'm a valentine. Lying to her has grown exhausting, so I've been dodging her calls lately. Isolating myself even further.

When my phone buzzes one night, I assume it's her. But instead I glance at the screen and find a message from

Alexander. *Haven't heard from you in a minute. Everything okay?*

I bury my phone under my pillow and toss and turn through another restless day.

* * *

Ellen bursts into my room earlier than normal the next morning, looking frazzled. "Amelia? You have a visitor."

"A what?" I sit up, rubbing my eyes and certain I heard her wrong.

"Someone is here to see you."

But who could it possibly be? Nobody knows where I am. Unless… someone figured out the truth. My heart sinks as I imagine Maisy coming to confront me for lying to her, or Declan showing up. Probably with a gaggle of torch-wielding business bros ready to call me a blood bag whore, or something similar.

I'm aware that my anxiety is placing ridiculous scenarios in my head, but still. Who could possibly be here, at Sebastian's middle-of-nowhere estate, for *me*?

I dress quickly with some help from Ellen and rush to the stairs. I pause at the top, looking down the staircase to see a familiar, gorgeous blond man waiting at the bottom with his hands clasped behind his back.

I gasp. "Alexander?"

He looks up at me and smiles. "Amelia. I hope you'll forgive the early-night intrusion."

My thoughts are in a scramble. Why is he here? How is he

here? I guess it makes more sense than anyone else I know showing up. Vampires are probably aware of where the others reside. Surely this isn't nearly as weird as it seemed to me at first blush. *I'm* the one making it weird, standing here gawking at him and being horrifically rude.

I hurry down the stairs when I realize, nearly tripping over my dress. "Of course, I just— Wow! You're here." He looks at me oddly, and I realize I'm still being rude. I hurriedly drop into a curtsy. "I mean, Lord Alexander de Solomon. Um, welcome. Can I offer... can we offer... anything?" I look frantically at Ellen, who is standing at the top of the stairs.

She straightens. "Right! Coffee? Tea?"

"Tea would be lovely," Alexander says, smiling. "Thank you."

* * *

The long dining room table feels even more ridiculous when it's just two of us sitting across from each other. Ellen drops off the tea set and places a vial of blood in front of Alexander.

"I'm sorry, we have only chilled blood in stock, nothing fresh," she says.

"That's perfectly fine," he says, but his eyes dart quickly to my neck. I resist the urge to cover it with my hair. I'm well aware that vampires think fresh warm blood tastes best, but I also know it's inappropriate for me to offer my blood to anyone other than my patron. Even when said patron is being a shit.

"I hope it's alright that I dropped in," Alexander says, stirring the blood into his tea. "But I was in the area... well. A couple of hours away from the area, to be fair, but I wanted to check in on you."

"Oh," I say, surprised. "That's sweet of you." I suppose I did ask him about Sebastian's previous valentine and then dropped off the face of the planet… but it feels inappropriate discussing my relationship with Sebastian with him. "I'm fine, really. But thank you."

He looks around the room, eyes lingering on the old grandfather clock. "I can see how one could get bored here," he says. "It's quite remote. And old-fashioned. I guess some vampires are like that."

I bite back the urge to defend the place. It's not like he's saying anything insulting.

"And I take it Sebastian is not present?"

"Um, no. He's away on business." The lie comes smoothly.

"But this is supposed to be the honeymoon period for you two," he says with a concerned look. "I can't imagine leaving a brand-new valentine alone in a place like this. If you had accepted me as your patron, I would be spending every night with you. Taking you to all of the best parties, showing you off as much as possible…"

It takes a moment for the words to sink in. I stare at him. "What do you mean? I only received an offer of patronage from Sebastian."

Alexander frowns—and then anger breaks like a storm across his expression, sudden and startling before his face shifts into regret. "I knew your chaperone disliked me, but I didn't think he'd go so far."

Neither did I. I stare into my cooling mug of tea and try to wrap my head around the idea. Why would Benjamin hide an offer of patronage from Alexander? Even if he believed

Sebastian was a better match for me, I should've had a choice in the matter.

"I suppose I should have known," Alexander says. "A man like Sebastian de Celeste has ways of getting what he wants. Power, money, influence…" He shakes his head, a strand of fair hair falling across his forehead. "I'm nobody compared to him."

He looks so demoralized that I reach across the table and squeeze his hand. "I'm sorry," I say. "I never would have tossed your offer aside based on that. I don't know why Benjamin lied to me."

Alexander looks up at me, his eyes arresting as they latch on mine. "Would you have chosen me, if you had known?"

"I…" I suddenly remember that we're in Sebastian's house, at Sebastian's table. That I am Sebastian's valentine. I slowly retract my hand. "I guess it doesn't matter. I'm Sebastian's valentine for the next few months."

Alexander's brow furrows. "More than that, surely?"

I shake my head. "Our contract was for six months."

"How… unusual."

I shrug and look down at my lap. "He's an unusual man."

The grandfather clock ticks seconds of silence past. Then Alexander shifts in his seat, leaning forward in his chair. "Listen," he says. "Far be it from me to speak ill of the man in his own house, but… I had concerns when I heard you were matched with him. I must confess that's why I came here. When you stopped posting online and didn't answer my message, I was worried."

My stomach rolls with discomfort. I don't want to talk badly about Sebastian, but Alexander gives me pause. "What do you mean, worried?"

"Worried about your safety," he says. "They say Sebastian was a beast in the years of the court wars. And the valentine you asked about… well, there were rumors."

I try to hold myself back from asking, but this may be my only chance to find out the truth. "What rumors?"

"Nothing of substance, but… there was talk of arguments between them. Jealousy. People said she fled this estate in the middle of the day when she knew he couldn't follow."

A chill seeps through me as I remember the grave. If she left, why would she be buried here? I remember, too, that black hunger in Sebastian's eyes, which nearly drove him to hurt me.

I attributed those fresh flowers on Etta's grave to lingering fondness… but what if, instead, it's lingering guilt?

Still, for reasons I can't name, I'm reluctant to voice my suspicions aloud. Our conversation runs dry after that, and soon Alexander excuses himself. I walk him to the door and he pauses to take my hand, placing a princely kiss on my knuckles.

"Please call me if you're in LA again," he says, his eyes lingering on mine. "Or if you ever need help."

* * *

I'm grateful that Sebastian is gone so I don't have to face him with these suspicions yet. Part of me thinks it's absurd that Sebastian could've killed his last valentine. He's not always been kind, but he's never harmed me. Yet… he almost did when his hunger overtook him. If he had been a younger vampire, or a hungrier one, who knows what would have happened?

And although my gut tells me to trust him… I've been wrong before, with Declan. I can't trust my instincts.

The thoughts whirl and whirl around my head. I spend time around the staff as much as possible, grateful for human company and reluctant to be alone in the suddenly unnerving house. The creaks I was starting to grow fond of now make me jump. The beautiful windows leave my skin crawling with the sense I'm being watched.

One night, a box is waiting for me on my bed when I return to my room. I unfurl the beautiful golden ribbon and open it to find a stunning set of jewelry waiting for me. A necklace, earrings, and matching bracelets, all subtle but utterly beautiful, shimmering like liquid moonlight as I lift them in my hands. A note underneath catches my eye.

Sterling silver, it reads, underlined twice. Realization dawns on me as I think back to my lessons with Benjamin. Silver is a weakness of vampires; it burns their skin to the touch.

There's no note about who sent it, but I can assume. Alexander mentioned that he was worried for my safety. Touched by the gesture, I upload a selfie of me wearing the necklace on social media. Alexander likes it almost immediately.

I set the jewelry on my nightstand and fall asleep thinking how good it is to have someone looking after me for once.

Chapter Twenty-Three

A week slips past, and then another. The weather warms and my nerves gradually calm down. I take the time to care for myself, vent on my blog, and chat with the staff at dinner. A couple more mysterious gifts arrive—a bottle of red wine from the year I was born, a book of poetry by Catullus. I try not to worry about what Sebastian would think if he knew I was receiving gifts from another vampire. I try not to think about that grave out on the estate grounds, either.

And then, one day, Ellen comes into my room bearing a breakfast try and a handwritten note inviting me to tea.

I run my finger over the paper. "Sebastian is back?"

She nods. "He arrived this evening."

"Hm." It's encouraging that he wants to see me immediately upon his return, rather than skulking around in the library and ignoring me for days. I suppose I owe it to him to hear him out, at least. "Please tell him I'll be there."

* * *

Despite everything that's happened between us, Sebastian is no less devastating to look at. He appears far more put together than he was during that encounter in the hallway, severe in a black button-up shirt, not a single inky strand of hair out of place. He sits straight-backed in his chair, hands folded in his lap, and barely moves as I walk in and take a seat across from him.

Ellen and Bridget set out tea for us both and breakfast for me. Once they leave, an uncomfortable silence blankets the dining room. I can't bring myself to eat when my stomach is in knots. I toy with the silver bracelet I decided to wear.

Sebastian glances at it, and then at me. He clears his throat. "You've been well, I hope?"

I shoot an incredulous look across the table and fold my arms. That's how he means to begin this conversation?

He grimaces and runs a hand through his hair. "Right. That was a foolish question. I… what I meant to say is, I apologize for what happened before I left. My hunger got the best of me, which is my own fault." He stares down into his tea rather than looking at me. "The night you were hurt… I had intended to ask if I could begin to drink from you directly. But then you were injured, and I didn't want to ask it of you, and… I waited longer than I should've, knowing the effect your blood has on me. It was a stupid error." He raises his eyes to me. "I should never have put you at risk like that, nor made you doubt that you're safe."

I've been practicing this conversation in my head for days. I pictured myself being angry or cold. Threatening to tell the world what he did, making him beg for my forgiveness. Confronting him about Etta. But I never imagined him apologizing so willingly, and despite my better instincts, I find myself softening. "Thank you for saying that," I say. "I... accept your apology. As long as it doesn't happen again."

"It won't," he says, in a firm tone that brooks no argument.

I nod, and then it's back to awkward silence. I pick at a scone just to have something to occupy my hands. I try not to think about the fact that Sebastian is sitting where Alexander did, not so long ago, and how easily the conversation flowed then.

"Ellen mentioned that you had a visitor while I was away," Sebastian says, as if reading my thoughts. His tone is neutral. "A vampire visitor."

My pulse rises. I need to keep reminding myself that Ellen and the staff are loyal to Sebastian, not to me. I'm hesitant to admit the truth about Alexander, especially after the suspicions he raised about Sebastian.

"Benjamin came to check in on me," I lie.

Sebastian pauses, his brow furrowing. He looks again at the silver bracelet on my wrist. "I assume you told him about what happened." It's impossible to read his tone. Would he be angry if I did? Guilty?

I could claim that I did tell him. Maybe it would make me safer, if Sebastian thought suspicion would fall upon him if something happened to me. But as I look into his dark eyes, I can't quite bring myself to voice the lie. "No," I say instead. "I didn't think it was any of his business."

Sebastian looks away. I'm surprised that he seems troubled rather than relieved. "You should have told him," he says. "He would have considered it a breach of our contract. Taken you away. He should have, after I lost control like that."

Is that what Sebastian thinks I want? ...*Is* that what I want? I hesitate and then reach over the table, giving Sebastian plenty of time to pull away before I take his hand. Again, I'm uncomfortably aware of parallels between this conversation and the one with Alexander, but I try to push the thought away. "I won't deny that you frightened me," I say. "But you didn't bite me. You didn't hurt me. You didn't lose control." He looks up at me, and I'm surprised to see agony written all over his face. Maybe I'm a fool, but when I look into his eyes, I can't bring myself to believe Sebastian would hurt me. I squeeze his hand. "Like I said, as long as it doesn't happen again..."

"It won't. We'll return to using the syringe. It was foolish to attempt otherwise." He pulls his hand away from mine.

It's stupid to be disappointed. Even though it feels like taking a step back, he's doing this for my safety. I always took his use of the syringe as a snub, but now I think he's been trying to keep me safe from the beginning. I was the one who pushed for more. I crossed a boundary when I asked him to drink from me, and again when I asked about Etta. Maybe I'll never know what happened with her, but... maybe it's not my place to know. As long as I believe he won't hurt me—and I do —then maybe it's none of my business what happened here a century ago.

Perhaps I've been asking too much of Sebastian. This is, after all, a contracted relationship. He does not owe me anything beyond what's laid out there, and it was stupid to hope for otherwise.

* * *

With Sebastian back at the estate, my life settles back into routine. Ellen takes my blood via syringe every evening; Sebastian's place at the dining table sits empty every night. I avoid the library and keep to myself. I spend most nights alone in my room. Sometimes I read—I'm slowly making my way through the book of poetry that Alexander sent, which is surprisingly good—but mostly I write in my blog. It's the only place I can be honest.

Who am I supposed to talk to, anyway? I still can't talk to Maisy about any of this. It feels awkward chatting to Alexander with the truth about his offer of patronage hanging over us. I no longer trust Benjamin, either, after finding out he lied to me about it, so I only respond to his check-ins with brief, bland answers. I don't feel comfortable with the staff either, knowing that they concealed facts about Etta from me.

I can tell that they're trying to make it up to me. When I excuse my lack of talkativeness as trouble sleeping, fresh pillows are waiting at my door the next morning. When I decline dessert—practically unheard of—that next night, Bridget makes the chocolate cake I so enjoyed at a previous dinner. When I explain my distance from Ellen by the fact that I've been busy writing, a set of buttery-soft leather notebooks and fancy pens arrives with my breakfast tray the next morning.

But despite their efforts, it's impossible for me to unlearn the truth now that I've figured it out. The staff are not my friends, and this place is not my home. This is a job, and for my sanity, I need to treat it as such.

One day, Maisy texts me: *Two more months till move-in!* And I realize, with a shock, that it's true. It's June now—and August will not only mean Maisy moving to LA, but the end of my contract with Sebastian.

I try to convince myself that all I feel is relief.

* * *

One day, the monotony of my day-to-day routine is broken by the arrival of a letter with my breakfast tray:

To my Valentine,
  Please join me for tea. 12:00.
  Sebastian

I stare at it, remembering the delirious hope I felt last time I received a note like this. This time, I won't be so foolish.

Still, my traitorous heart is pounding at the thought of seeing Sebastian face-to-face for the first time in weeks. I can't resist the urge to put on one of my favorite dresses, a lacy pink thing that enhances my curves. I hesitate before leaving my silver jewelry on the vanity table.

Sebastian is waiting alone in the dining room. I startle when he stands as I walk in—but he only moves to pull out my chair for me. I sink into it with a perplexed glance up at him.

"Good evening, Amelia," he says as he takes the seat across from me. As if it hasn't been weeks since we've spoken.

"Good evening, Sebastian," I say, matching his polite tone. I refuse to let myself soften over one invitation to tea. Even though… goddamn it, the man looks *fine* when he wears that white linen shirt.

I fold my hands in my lap and harden my heart. "Is there

something you wanted to discuss?"

"Yes. Well..." He reaches into his pocket and sets a creamy envelope on the table between us. "I... I understand if you would rather not be in my company for a while. But I arranged... That is, I thought perhaps..."

It's funny, watching such a dangerous man become utterly tongue-tied. I spare him by picking up the envelope and pulling out the letter within. My eyes widen as I scan it. "An invitation to a ball? With the Celeste Court?"

Sebastian nods. "There is no obligation, of course. But I was hoping you would—"

"Yes," I say, before I can think better of it. Things may be awkward between us, but I've been dying for a chance to get out of this house. I can't deny an opportunity to socialize now.

And, after all, events are included in my contract.

* * *

Of course, mere hours after I accept the invitation, I descend into an agonizing spiral of self-doubt. The man has spent months ignoring me... so why invite me to a ball now, when our contract is more than halfway over? Does he feel obligated because he's realized he's kept me cooped up here? Should I have politely declined to save him the trouble of interacting with me for a night?

In the weeks that follow, Sebastian's behavior becomes increasingly bizarre. He begins to show up at dinner—not every night, but occasionally. And twice, he actually strikes up a conversation with me. The first time, he asks me, completely unprompted, how I feel about poetry. I stare at him for an uncomfortable amount of time before stuttering out something barely intelligible. The second time, he asks if I'd like to take a walk with him and Barnabas. Panicking, I tell him I have an upset stomach and flee the dinner table.

When Bridget knocks on the door with a bowl of chicken soup and some medicine a couple of hours later, I feel even more confused. Is all this because of the staff? Could they be pressuring Sebastian to be kind to me? But no, none of them seem like they would speak up to him in such a manner.

What, then, is the point of this?

And then I realize: our contract. Surely Sebastian has realized it will be ending in a couple of months. He's made it clear that he doesn't care for my companionship… but he's also made it clear that he cares for my blood. Does he intend to woo me in the eleventh hour for the sake of keeping me as a blood source?

When I think of living with this loneliness for another six months, or a year, it fills my chest with aching dread. If that's what Sebastian is trying to do… I can't let it work. I won't. My poor battered heart can't take it.

* * *

On the evening of the Celeste ball, Ellen helps me get ready.

"Lord Sebastian has not attended a Celeste ball in years," she says as she pins up my hair. "Thank God he has you to drag him out of this place now and again."

I stare at my reflection in a gorgeous crimson dress. The

top is a lace-up corset, the skirt flowing down to my ankles. It's gorgeous, just like my perfectly applied hair and makeup, but when I stare at my reflection, all I can see are my stray curls, my lips chapped from my nervous biting, the fine lines at the corners of my eyes. All of the reasons I will never be enough.

"Is something wrong?" Ellen asks, and I realize I've forgotten to throw on my fake smile. I can't seem to summon it now.

"I'm just nervous, I think," I say, brushing my hands down over my sides. I've gained some weight since I stopped working on my feet all the time and started eating so decadently here, and I'm suddenly self-conscious about the way the dress highlights the new fullness in my bust and hips.

"You? Nervous?" Ellen asks, sounding shocked.

I lift a brow at her. "Of course I am. This is my first ball as Sebastian's valentine."

Her face reddens. "Well, yes, that makes sense. It's just..." She shrugs. "It's hard to imagine you being nervous about anything. I—everyone on the staff—we're always in awe of your confidence."

I almost laugh before I realize she's serious. Then I have to pause to think about how I've been acting since I arrived here. The way I've shown up to dinner dressed in luxurious dresses, how I've confronted Sebastian and made demands of him... I suppose I can see why she might think that. I'm not sure how to feel about it. On the one hand, I'm glad she doesn't seem to see the insecurities that lie at the heart of me; on the other, it's sad to realize how little she understands me.

As I make my way down the staircase to the foyer, I find that the rest of the staff has gathered to see us off. They all stare at me and, for the first time, I realize how I must look from their eyes. I notice how Trent blushes and stares with open admiration as he holds Barnabas by the collar to stop him from jumping on me. Our driver, Vincent, sweeps his hat off his head and hastily moves to grab my coat. Ellen is beaming. Even Bridget is outside of her beloved kitchen for once to see me off, and cranky old Tobias gives me a nod of what might be approval and cracks the tiniest smile.

Of course, the second I think too hard about being perceived, I forget how to walk in these heels. One of them catches on my dress and my balance wavers, and I think with horror that I'm about to tumble head over heels and completely ruin the staff's image of me forever—

A cold hand seizes my elbow and pulls me upright. I turn, open-mouthed, to find Sebastian at my side.

The chill of his fingers seeps through the silky fabric of my dress. His dark eyes bore into mine. He is perfection in a charcoal suit. I'm close enough to marvel at his face all over again. He's practically carved from marble, all devastating cheekbones and dark eyes I can drown in, so handsome it's hard to imagine any future where he doesn't make my heart race.

He studies me in return. I notice him taking in the silver jewelry set I chose to wear tonight. If he disapproves, he doesn't say. He simply steadies me and offers his arm. I hesitate before I take it, and we descend the rest of the staircase together.

Sebastian keeps his expression stoic and his eyes ahead as I say goodbye to each member of the staff, and then he takes me out to the waiting car. Vincent opens the door, and Sebastian gestures for me to slide in first before joining me.

The moment the door is closed behind us, the silence is

stifling. I fiddle with my silver bracelet. I wasn't sure if it would be rude to wear to this event, but…

Well. Given how careful Sebastian has been lately, his insistence on using only the syringe to take my blood, I feel confident that he wouldn't hurt me on purpose. Whoever Etta is, I don't think he hurt her on purpose either. But I'm still too afraid to ask for the full story, and I don't intend to take any chances.

Sebastian sits with his hands in his lap and looks out the window while I try not to stare at him. But it's impossible to miss the way he clasps his hands tightly on his lap, the set of his shoulders and jaw. He looks gorgeous, and miserable.

Because of course he is. He hates these events. He must resent being forced to take me out and parade me around; I'm sure he'd rather keep me cooped up in the estate. He must feel obligated, or guilty. Just trying to fulfill our contract in the hopes he can have more of my blood, like I suspected already.

But I shake away those thoughts. I'm just getting in my own head again, and that's the last thing I need before going into my first public event with Sebastian. I try to remember what Ellen said about me, calling me *confident*, and summon up that version of myself to show to the public. The *valentine* version of Amelia. I can wear her like a mask, just like the fake customer service smile I used in my last job.

These are vampires I'm dealing with, after all. If they smell blood, I'll be nothing but prey to them.

Chapter Twenty-Four

The Celeste ball isn't what I expected.

Gone is the gold filigree and dripping decadence of the Valentine's Day Ball. There are no blood cards or sparkling cocktails or lovers passionately entwined on the couches. Instead, this place has a sort of subdued old-money charm that is even more intimidating. Art is displayed around the room: huge paintings hung on the wall, marble sculptures on pedestals, and ancient-looking books displayed behind glass.

Sebastian and I enter to the soft sounds of a solitary harpist, not loud enough to overwhelm the quiet murmur of conversation. Which means it's easy to notice that it stops as we enter the room.

I cling to Sebastian's arm as he walks with his eyes straight ahead and his expression as impassionate as stone. My heart is pounding in my ears and only seems to beat faster when I think of how Sebastian and every other vampire in the room must be aware of it. I dig my fingers into his bicep without meaning to. He places one of his hands over mine, a feather-light graze of his fingertips along my knuckles. I'm surprised how much it eases my nerves. I think back on what Ellen said about how rarely he attends events and wonder, for the first time, if he might be nervous too.

Sebastian leads us to a circle of conversation at the foot of a marble statue. Some of the others nod at us—or rather, at Sebastian—politely, but otherwise there's no attempt to bring us in. Sebastian doesn't try to introduce me, either.

I can barely follow the flow of conversation, but I'm content to stand quietly and let my eyes roam over the room. I eye the harpist in the corner, and then the couples twirling around the dance floor. There are only a few of them, far less than at the busy Valentine's Day ball. It makes me remember, with a jolt, that dance I shared with Alexander. I feel a guilty sort of nostalgia over it. How different would my life have been if I had known he offered to be my patron? I've never danced with Sebastian.

I wait for a lull in the conversation before tugging on his sleeve to get his attention.

"Shall we dance?" I ask, smiling up at him.

He shifts, eyes sliding away from mine. "I'm not much of a dancer, I'm afraid."

My smile fades, and I suppress a sigh. "Alright."

Back to listening to a conversation I can barely understand. I can tell from Sebastian's intent expression that he's following it, but he doesn't try to step in. He just stands here and listens in silence… which makes me wonder why he brought me here. He doesn't want to dance, nor even to introduce me. Am I just here to look pretty on his arm?

Stick to the contract, I remind myself. I don't know why I keep expecting anything more than that.

I excuse myself to the bathroom, and when I return, my eyes catch on a group of humans situated around one table. I drift that way instead of heading back to Sebastian and the others.

"—Hasn't painted a thing since he's been turned," one man is saying. "Honestly, what a disappointment for the Vulpe Court."

I follow the table's eyes to a vampire who sits alone under one of the paintings. He glances at me, and I have a quick impression of sad blue eyes in a striking face before I look away.

"Ahh, someone new," one woman says, drawing my attention back to the humans. The others turn to me as well, their conversation halting. "You must be Lord Sebastian's valentine."

I swallow self-consciousness as I extend a hand. "I am. Amelia Burton."

"Farah Badawi." The brown-skinned woman is older than most valentines I've met, though still undoubtedly beautiful, with piercing dark eyes and thick brown waves of hair. "I'd say I've heard a lot about you, but I haven't. Everyone's been curious about who finally captured Lord Sebastian de Celeste's cold heart."

"I wouldn't say I have his heart," I say, releasing her hand. And then, remembering I'm trying to channel confidence, I add, "Yet."

"Are you sure about that? Because he's staring at you across the room right now like some lovestruck teenager," she says with a smirk.

I blush and resist the urge to look as I take a seat. I can't tell whether she's messing with me.

As the rest of the table starts giving introductions, nerves overwhelm me again. Farah is a museum curator; another woman introduces herself as having a PhD in vampire history, which I didn't even know was a thing. I recognize another man as a well-known writer of vampire biographies. They are all scholars and otherwise accomplished individuals, as I guess I should've expected from the Celeste valentines. By the time the spotlight falls on me, I feel thoroughly inadequate.

"My name is Amelia Burton," I say, fingers twisting together in my lap. "I'm… a writer." It tastes like a lie on my tongue, even though it isn't.

"Oh, what have you published?" the biographer asks.

I flush. "Nothing yet." And that makes me aware that even with my nearly infinite free time in the estate, I haven't managed to write anything other than my silly blog.

"Well, I'm certain you have plenty of material now," he says.

"I… hm? What do you mean?"

"Well, you are living with Lord Sebastian, after all. I have no doubt that his life provides *fascinating* subject matter." He leans forward. "I must admit I'm jealous. He's declined me for an interview. *Twice*." A fact he sounds positively affronted about.

I hesitate, unsure how to tell them that I know next to nothing about the man I'm living with.

"Well, he's a private person," I say.

"I'll say," the man huffs. "I've barely managed to get more than a couple of words out of him at a time. And that's when he even deigns to grace us with his presence."

"Oh, hush," Farah scolds. "He's a two-hundred-year-old war hero. Of course he has better things to do than talk to you."

That prompts a guilty smattering of laughter that I don't join in. Instead, I bite back an urge to defend Sebastian. It's true that he can be cold and distant, but I've never thought of it as being because of any sense of superiority. Instead it's… well…

My eyes find him across the room. I watch as he stands in the circle of vampires with his arms folded over his chest, silent even as the conversation flows around him. I study his expression, and think, unbidden, of my shock when Ellen called me *confident*. How it felt like she didn't see me at all, but only made assumptions.

I've made plenty of assumptions when it comes to Sebastian as well. I tend to think I understand what goes on beneath his mask… but what if I'm as off-base as Ellen? What if it isn't an aversion to me that holds him back, or an iciness that makes him reserved. What if he's just…

Just what, exactly? I think of Ellen's statement that he barely leaves the estate, corroborated by the conversation among the valentines here, and a new theory finally comes to me. What if Sebastian is… shy?

"As I said," I tell the other valentines, my eyes still lingering on Sebastian, "he's a private man."

The conversation moves on while I reflect on my new theory about Sebastian. It feels like a shift in world view. I've thought, this entire time, that he was being cold on purpose. I've been so puzzled by his behavior, but if he is just introverted—perhaps even anxious—it explains some of it. It's hard for me to imagine him as shy beneath that stern expression and flawless face, but I suppose the same was true of how Ellen saw me.

Knowing this doesn't excuse his behavior toward me. I still deserve better treatment and communication. But it helps me understand him better.

"—Anonymous Confessions of a Valentine," Farah says, and I'm drawn back to the conversation.

"What?" I ask, a knee-jerk reaction, assuming I didn't hear

correctly.

"Oh, have you read it as well?" she asks, holding up her phone.

"Who *hasn't*?" the biographer asked, rolling his eyes as he sips his scotch. "Even Jonah Montgomery was gossiping about it at the last Camelia party."

I think of that beautiful, haughty man stretched across Viktoria's lap at the Valentine's Day Ball reading *my* blog and feel light-headed.

"Of course he did," someone else interjects. "He's chronically addicted to sensationalism. Which is all that drivel is. I wouldn't be surprised if he wrote it himself for a publicity stunt."

Oh, God. My stomach is dropping to the floor. I try to think of an excuse to leave this conversation, but I'm terrified it will only make me look suspicious. I already admitted I'm a writer...

"I don't believe Jonah can string together that many sentences. Especially since I would *not* call it drivel," Farah says, frowning. "I quite liked it, actually. It was... honest. Raw. People of our line of work so rarely get to tell our stories." She shoots a cutting look at the biographer. "They're usually more interested in romanticizing *vampires'* stories."

"I believe in capturing beauty," he says, shrugging.

"Even if that beauty is a lie?"

"Well..."

As the conversation drifts off into a debate about realism versus escapism, I excuse myself from the table. They barely seem to notice me leaving. I walk over to Sebastian, noticing that he has an almost pained expression on his face, and thinking again about my newfound hypothesis about his social anxiety.

"Excuse me?" I lay a hand on Sebastian's arm, and everyone in the circle turns to look at me, even though I'm trying to be unobtrusive. I put on my most winning smile and look up into Sebastian's eyes. "Pardon the interruption, but… someone mentioned this place has the most beautiful library, and I was wondering if you might take me to see it?"

Some of the tension in Sebastian's shoulders relaxes, only visible because I'm looking for it. "Of course," he says, and excuses himself from the conversation. As I expected, nobody seems surprised or offended that I might want to see the library. At a Celeste party, it's the perfect excuse for us to wander away from the crowd.

"I apologize," Sebastian says as he leads me out of the ballroom and down a hallway.

I glance up at him. "For what?"

"I was afraid you would be bored at an event like this," he says, his eyes still ahead. "But it is the only sort of thing I am invited to, other than the Valentine's Day Ball."

I almost laugh. "Sebastian, I didn't pull you away because I was bored. I pulled you away because you looked like you were in physical pain trying to carry on that conversation."

He blinks, finally looking down at me. "…Oh," he says. "Well. Yes. They were eager to reminisce about the war, which is not a topic I'm fond of."

"And you are not particularly fond of conversation in general."

He pauses. "I am rather rusty at it, I admit."

He sounds almost embarrassed. It's enough to make me squeeze his arm in solidarity. "Well, I have it on good authority that you *are* fond of libraries."

He cracks a rare smile, but it flickers out just as quickly as it appears. "You don't have to remove yourself from the party for me. I know the estate is not exactly rife with social opportunities, and I want you to—"

"Sebastian." I squeeze his arm and cut him off before he can wind himself up any further. I wait for him to look at me, and then I give him a genuine smile. "There is no one here I would rather spend time with than you." We come to a stop outside of the huge double doors that must lead to the library, and I lean in on my tiptoes and mock whisper, "And it just so happens that I really *do* want to see the library."

Sebastian's library at the estate was already a shock. I think I'm at least somewhat prepared for what I'll see as Sebastian pushes open the heavy wooden double doors to reveal this one. And yet—my breath still catches in my throat as I step inside. There are multiple stories to this room, each with its own small balcony. A winding staircase leads up to the top. On each level, polished wooden bookshelves reach so high that I would need a ladder to reach the top. And they have one—one of those rolling ladders that I thought only existed in movies.

And the *books*. There are more of them than I thought existed. I see ancient leather-bound tomes, and fresh-looking new editions; titles in different languages, different alphabets I don't recognize. An overwhelming amount of knowledge.

I spin in a slow circle, my eyes wide as I try to take in all of it at once. It's dizzying, looking at the sheer amount of books. I have a rabid impulse to just start grabbing them and flee, countered by the paralyzing knowledge that I could spend the rest of my life here and still not have time to read them all.

"Wow," I breathe.

"Indeed." Sebastian's voice draws my attention to him. I catch him staring at my face before his eyes shift—almost guiltily—away.

Shy, I remind myself. Not ashamed of me, not revolted by me, just… shy. I reach out to touch his hand. He jerks, eyes darting back to me, but doesn't pull away from my touch.

"Have you been here before?" I ask.

"Yes. Whenever I get a chance, I slip away from the crowd to come here."

I smile. "Somehow, I'm not surprised." I twine my fingers with his, his skin cold against me. "I hardly know where to look. Will you show me some of your favorites?"

He glances down at our entangled fingers and back up at my face. His jaw works for a moment. "I doubt you'll find my favorites to be of interest."

"Try me."

Holding my hand, he leads me into the tall shelves.

Truthfully, the books he shows me are not ones I would have paid attention to on my own, but it is fascinating to listen to him talk about them. He shows me outdated medical textbooks in Latin, Greek poetry, volumes and volumes of leatherbound books about the Victorian Language of Flowers. I have never heard him talk so much at once, and his voice has me swooning. So does the sight of him handling the books. The featherlight touch of his long fingers as he cradles the old texts, the way he slides his thumb lovingly along the spine before he places a book back on the shelf.

"Are these all vampire authors?" I ask only when his words trail off, because I have no desire to interrupt him.

"Mostly mortals, actually," he says. "The majority of vampire knowledge is stored in the Solomon Court's vaults, away from the public eye. It's… an important point on which our courts have always disagreed. Had they absorbed us in the last war, as they tried to, I suspect we would have lost a great deal of this knowledge."

I hesitate. He's never spoken about the war before; that conversation earlier must have put it in his mind. Part of me is desperately curious, but it doesn't seem like a good time to pry into his past. "You value human perspectives so much?"

"Oh, yes. I have always found mortals to be superior writers. Something about their awareness of time, of death, drives them to be better creators. Perhaps the sense of time running out." He glances at the shelves and runs the tip of one finger along the spines. "Some would disagree, of course. But I have always been most interested in preserving human work. Especially the histories."

"Huh." I tilt my head. "I would've thought a human view of history would seem short-sighted to your kind."

"Perhaps that's what gives it value," he says. "Vampires always view events from the outside, thinking themselves above it all. There's such a sense of *hubris* about it…" He glances at me and stops. "Pardon me. I'm ranting."

I smile, run my thumb over his hand. "I like listening to you talk."

He clears his throat and hesitates before asking, "But… what about you? You're a writer as well, are you not?"

I blink, startled. "I don't think we've ever talked about my writing."

He averts his eyes. "Ah… no. I suppose not. But Ellen mentioned it."

"Oh. Well…" Now I'm flushing. "I've always called myself a writer, but honestly I haven't written in a long time." Aside from the blog. But that's such a silly thing, and not something I want to mention to Sebastian at all, especially now that I know other valentines are talking about it. I should probably go home and delete it the second I get a chance.

"Why not?"

"I…" I wind a strand of hair around my finger, trying to think of a decent answer. "I was just… too busy, I suppose. I know it's a stupid excuse, but when I was with my ex, between working and chores, I just…" I trail off, embarrassed at trying to explain how I let my passion fall to the wayside for a failed relationship.

"It's not," he says. When I stop, I note that flicker of awkwardness in him again, but he continues. "It's not a poor excuse. I think, with humans having lifespans as limited as they are, it is an incredible endeavor to take the time to write at all. Even with all of my endless hours, I myself have no talent for it, only a talent for preserving it. So I… I admire it. Greatly."

A shy smile creeps onto my face. "You haven't even read my writing," I say. "It could be awful. It could be like… like all those sordid vampire romances I won't name."

"And as widely derided as they may be, those books captured the hearts and imaginations of millions," he counters. "They are a testament to the power of fiction. I would respect you for it."

A slow heat begins in my belly, floods up into my chest, warms my face. When I look at Sebastian, I see that his eyes are locked on mine. I feel, for perhaps the first time, that he is looking at me and truly seeing me. Seeing me in a way that even Declan didn't over our years together. Dec never cared about my writing, never asked a single question about what I might want to work on if I had the chance.

I realize, too, how close Sebastian and I are standing. Our hands are still clasped. His eyes drop to my lips, and he doesn't look away even when he catches me looking.

My heartbeat quickens. Is it ridiculous that I'm thinking about this? I've been telling myself that tonight is all about our contract, that I'm just fulfilling my duties… but valentines have unofficial duties, too, if you believe the gossip. And I've been sorely slacking on that side of the job.

Before I can second-guess myself, I press up on my tiptoes, slowly lean in, and press my lips against his. It is a shock to realize that despite our previous intimacy, this is the first time we've kissed. When I imagined kissing vampires, I did not quite think about the details: the chill of his skin, the bump of fangs behind his lips.

The kiss is chaste at first, but it feels wildly intimate. The tenderness in his touch, the reverent quiet of the library, the moment we just shared, something makes this feel different. It makes it feel *real*, and my thoughts are too muddled for me to tell myself otherwise. Sebastian lifts the hand that isn't clasping mine to grasp the back of my neck, and I tilt my head, opening my mouth against his as he deepens the kiss.

I wrap my arms around his neck. His grip on my waist tightens in response. It's been so long since I've had any sort of intimacy. Even that all-too-brief encounter in the library was months ago now, and I am *hungry* for it. I press myself closer and let out a needy little sound against his lips.

But as he begins to slide a hand under my dress, I grab his wrist, and he stops.

"I apologize," he says. "I shouldn't have…"

He trails off as I lower myself to my knees on the floorboards in front of him. I drink in the way his eyes change, his pupils blowing wide, as I slowly undo his belt buckle.

"I think it's unfair," I say, "that you gave me an orgasm and I've hardly been allowed to touch you."

He swallows. "You're under no obligation—"

"Unfair to me, I mean." I pull his belt free, set it aside, and undo the button of his trousers. "I want this, Sebastian." I drag the zipper down and pull his pants down to his ankles. He remains staring at me, his expression almost desperate. "So… may I?" I pause, fingers dipping into the waistband of his black briefs, and look up at him. I bite my bottom lip. "Please?"

He nods, at a loss for words, his eyes never leaving my face.

I pull his briefs down and gasp as his already hard length springs free. It is… *impressive.* I wrap my fist around him and slide it up and down, marveling at the weight of him in my palm. It's almost unfair, how perfect he is.

"You have a beautiful cock," I whisper. I remove my hand from him and lean in to drag the flat of my tongue up the bottom of his shaft slowly, slowly, all the way from base to tip.

Sebastian lets out a low, almost pained groan. I glance up to see his head leaning back against the shelves, his eyes shut and his lips parted. It gives me such a thrill to see how I affect him.

I love giving blow jobs, though with Declan it became more of a chore than anything. He was always silent, usually wouldn't even warn me when he was about to finish in my mouth. No fun at all. I can already tell that Sebastian is going to be much more receptive to my efforts, and it makes excitement zip through my body.

I lick him again, dragging it out even further this time. Then

CHAPTER TWENTY-FOUR

I get a wicked idea.

"Grab one of those books," I say.

He opens his eyes, faintly dazed. "Huh?"

I run my tongue over my lips. "I want you to read to me while I suck your cock, Sebastian."

He stares at me for a moment. Then he fumbles on the shelf behind him and grabs a book. He glances down at me while I wait, my lips hovering just beyond his tip. Then he opens the book and starts to read.

In goddamn Latin. Of course. But… it's actually pretty hot, hearing the way the foreign words glide off his tongue. And it reminds me a little of the readings at church when I was growing up, making this feel extra naughty.

I wrap my lips around the head of his cock and take him into my mouth.

"*Fuck*," Sebastian moans, the stream of Latin cutting off. I don't think I've ever heard him curse before, and hearing that filthy word from his perfect lips, because of *me*, sends heat rippling all the way through my body. But I still stop moving as he stops reading. He stares at me, then seems to remember, and begins to read again.

I take him into my mouth and hum in appreciation as I slide my lips down his shaft, taking him deeper. He's so thick, I can barely fit my mouth around him, but I welcome the challenge. I bob up and down on his length while he reads to me, his voice breathy and rough and occasionally punctuated by a groan.

He's struggling to maintain control. I want to make him lose it. I push myself until I choke, flooding my mouth with thick saliva.

"Amelia," he gasps. His hand grasps at my hair and then lets go.

I pull my mouth off him and let my breath ghost across the head of his cock.

"You can grab my hair," I murmur, looking up at him. "Be a little rough with me if you want." I smile. "I like it." And then I suction my lips around his cock again. His fingers grab a fistful of my hair without needing further encouragement.

But he's still holding back, I can tell. Treating me like a delicate thing. I increase my pace, suck him deeper, push myself until I gag again. I keep going until his cock is wet and messy and he can't read a full sentence anymore.

"Fuck," he whispers again, and tosses the book aside. His hips jolt forward, driving himself deeper. I open as wide as I can and stay still, letting him set the pace now. And he does, driving into me in shallow but frantic thrusts. "God, that mouth of yours, I—" He cuts off in an incoherent groan and his grip on my hair tightens. "I'm going to cum."

I moan my agreement around his length and reach up to grip his thighs, digging my nails into his skin. He groans one last time, pushing my head down, and then I feel him pulse and spill warmth into my mouth. I suck it all down, every last drop, and wait for his grip on my head to go limp before I pull free.

I lick my lips, staring up at him. Our eyes meet, and I see wonder on his face. He helps me to my feet and kisses me. Slow and sensual as his tongue slides against mine, tasting himself. He runs his fingers through my messy hair, smooths my rumpled dress over my hips.

For a few minutes, everything seems perfect. But then he breaks the kiss, glances at the door, and says, "We should go."

I blink. "Back to the party?" I wipe my lips, realizing that my lipstick must be a mess. "Sure, I can just go to the bathroom and clean up…"

He gives me a shocked look. "God, no, not back to the party. We should go back to the estate."

"…Oh." I glance at the door and then back at him. "I feel like we just got here. You barely even introduced me to anyone."

"Well, I can't now," he says, as if it should be obvious.

Heat creeps up my face, and I step back to let him re-dress himself. I become aware of the stiffness in my legs, the discomfort where my knees rested on the floorboards. It was fun in the moment, but now I feel dirty. Ashamed.

"We can't be the only ones who have disappeared from the party for a quick blow job before," I say, trying to be lighthearted, but my voice comes out tight.

"Yes, perhaps, but never *me*," he says.

My stomach drops. "Right," I say. The thought that he might be ashamed of me makes me want to shrivel up and die, but I plaster on a smile and let him lead me out of the library and through a back door, away from the sounds of music and conversation.

Chapter Twenty-Five

The ride back to the estate is somehow even more awkward than the ride to the ball was. I take a corner seat in the back of the limo, arms wrapped around myself, gnawing at my lower lip and staring out the window. I hate how exposed I feel in my dress, and how my lips are still swollen from that blow job in the library.

Sebastian sits across from me, stock-still and silent. I can't stop thinking about whether he's ashamed of what we did—what *I* did—and whether I ruined whatever night he had planned for us with my impulsiveness. All of the other Celeste valentines were so impressive, so smart; of course Sebastian would be embarrassed to have the fake writer more interested in being on her knees.

After the silence stretches out and begins to weigh on me too heavily, I blurt, "I'm sorry."

Sebastian turns to me, eyebrows drawing together. "For what?"

"For ruining the ball. I'm sure that wasn't the experience you had in mind for tonight."

He looks even more baffled. "I…" He pauses, seeming to gather his thoughts. "Amelia, I only attended this ball because

I thought it would please *you.*"

As I suspected. It makes me feel even worse. "You did it for me," I say, and am horrified to find tears welling in my eyes. "And I ruined it... We had to rush out the back door like a couple of guilty teenagers, and—"

In the blink of an eye, Sebastian is suddenly sitting beside me, one cold hand lifting to wipe my eyes. "Amelia," he says softly. "You did not ruin anything. Look, it's nearly... what time is it, anyway?"

I pull my phone out of my pocket and show him.

"Midnight already? I'm quite certain that's a record for how long I've stayed at one of these awful things."

I wipe my eyes. "Ten to midnight, technically," I say, sniffling. "I set my clock ten minutes fast so I won't be late all the time."

Incredibly, he smiles at that. "Even so. A record."

"Really? But..." I shake my head, not sure what to say.

He cups my face, his touch gentle. "I'm sorry if it wasn't everything *you* wanted it to be, but I must confess, that's the best time I've ever had at a Celeste ball."

I blink at him through the blur of tears. "Really?"

"Yes. They're positively exhausting. A bunch of intellectual peacocking and exaggerated war stories." He studies my face. "Did you have a good night?"

"Well..." I lean into his touch, manage a watery smile. "I liked the library part..."

His lips twitch upward. "As did I."

"Then why did you want to rush out like you were ashamed?"

"Oh. That." He shifts so he can put an arm around me, and I lean into his touch, relishing the rare affection. "I didn't want the gossip and the judgment. They're a heinously critical bunch. I couldn't stand the thought of them judging you, spreading nonsense. I don't know what I would've done. But I..."

He shakes his head. "I shouldn't care so much, I know. That's my issue, and I should not have put it upon you as well." He leans in and presses his lips to my forehead. "I apologize."

I'm embarrassed at how quickly I melt at his affection. But it's so rare for him to hold me like this, to speak plainly so I don't have to wonder what he's thinking. It makes me think that maybe we're finally making progress. That he's opening up to me.

And yet still, I am troubled. It feels like every step forward for us comes at the expense of my heart. He is only kind to me after I've been hurt.

And tonight has reminded me that despite the mixed signals and the neglect and everything else, I am starting to fall for Sebastian. I know he doesn't owe me a relationship. Our contract doesn't guarantee anything of the kind, but... I don't think I can spend time like this with him without wanting it. Maybe I'm just not cut out for this line of work. My heart is sore from being tossed around like this. I'm not sure how much more it can handle. How much more I am willing to handle.

But for now... for now it feels good to nuzzle against him.

"What did you read to me?" I ask, yawning. "In the library?"

"That was Catullus 5 in the original Latin."

I smile, eyes drifting shut. "The ode to Lesbia," I say. "I like that one."

Where is it I know that poem from? I'm too tired to remember. Too comfortable resting against Sebastian's side. As I doze off, I feel cold lips press against my temple.

Yet when I wake up in my bed at the estate alone, I am not

even surprised.

*   *   *

"Lord Sebastian wanted me to tell you that he'll be away again for a few days," Ellen tells me over breakfast. "So there's no need to give blood."

I purse my lips, spreading whipped butter on a flaky scone. Of course he is. He always retreats after getting close to me. And of *course* it's Ellen delivering this news instead of him. I didn't even get a note this time.

This man is infuriating. I'm finally beginning to understand him better, but that doesn't make it any easier to deal with. Especially not when he leaves me alone with my thoughts again.

Even though it went well, what happened at the ball has me more confused than ever. This time I'm not going to sit around and wait for Sebastian to return. I need some distance to get my head on straight. And I need some outside advice before I make any important decisions.

I'm tired of doing this alone. But in a stroke of good luck, my sister is meant to move into her new apartment this weekend, so I have a good excuse to go help her get things set up. I'll force myself to finally tell her everything while I'm there... and set up the guest bedroom. My contract is almost over, after all.

"I think I'm going to leave as well," I say, as lightly as I can manage. "Could you arrange transportation for me to LA?"

Ellen gives me a wide-eyed look, and I falter.

"Surely I'm allowed to, yes?" I ask, suddenly uncertain. I thought maybe I could pull off a casual trip without making it a big deal. "I want to see my sister, is all. She's moving away from our hometown for the first time."

"Oh, I, yes. Of course. I'll arrange it, don't worry. I thought…" She takes a deep breath and wipes at her eyes; I'm shocked to see tears gathering there. "Oh, dear, I'm sorry. I thought you might mean that you were leaving permanently. And I thought, Lord Sebastian— all of us—" She pauses while I grapple with a surge of guilt. "Well, I've grown quite fond of you."

"Aw, Ellen." I plaster on a smile and extend a hand, which she grips and squeezes. "You've been such a kindness through all of this. And I—" I want to tell her I'm not leaving, but I'm not sure if it's a lie yet. "It's just a long overdue visit with my sister," I say, which is not quite the truth but not a bald-faced lie either. No matter what happens, I plan to come back and say my goodbyes before officially giving my resignation. I'm not that much of a coward.

I keep telling myself that once Ellen leaves, and I pack my bag with guilt gnawing at my stomach.

Chapter Twenty-Six

I step out of the airport and wrinkle my nose at the blast of heat and smog. Ahh, Los Angeles. I can't say I missed it much.

When I text Maisy to suggest brunch, I get a bunch of question marks in return. *It's seven p.m.,* she says, and I get a jolt as I remember not everybody is on vampire time.

You know what I meant, I type back, biting the inside of my cheek.

Just come over, you absolute weirdo, she says. *You haven't even seen the apartment yet!*

I was hoping to have this conversation in public, in case she decides she hates me and never wants to see me again, but I can't explain that, so I agree. I wave off her offer to pick me up, insisting I'll take a cab and there's no need for her to brave the horrors of LAX. I need all the time I can get to prepare for this conversation.

As much as I'd prefer not to soil my reunion with my sister, I know it's time to fess up. I'm not sure I can stand being there and lying to her face in person, and I know the longer the lies go on, the harder it will get to tell the truth. Better to pull off the band-aid now. Especially because I could use her advice.

My guts are doing nervous somersaults the whole ride to the apartment. I try to force myself to take in my surroundings rather than dwell in my thoughts, but the concrete and graffiti of LA is only more depressing after my months away at the gorgeous, green estate. At least the apartment complex I chose for Maisy is nice. Safe. A gated community with manicured lawns and all. It's nothing compared to Sebastian's home, of course—*oh, God, stop thinking about it*—but still, for LA? It's great.

And when the door opens and I see my little sister, I break into a grin. She squeals and throws her arms around my neck, nearly bowling me over.

"Oh my God, Amelia, I've missed you so much!"

I hug her back just as tightly. "You, too." I haven't seen her since Thanksgiving two years ago, which was such a disaster that I finally decided to cut off my parents for good. Maisy looks familiar and so different at the same time. So absurdly grown up. "Your hair!" I exclaim, pulling back to see it better. The last time I saw her, she had her long, natural brown waves; now it's cut and dyed into a chic blond bob.

"You like?"

"I love it." I beam, tugging at a strand. "You look ready for college, though I can hardly believe it."

"You look different too." She looks up at me, studying my face.

I make a face. "I know. I'm getting old."

"No, that's not it," she says, shaking me gently by the shoulders. "You seem… I don't know. More confident. Your skin is glowing, and your hair looks amazing… This new job must be treating you well, huh?"

My elation about seeing her shrivels back into anxiety. I

take a deep breath. "Well, yeah, actually. About that… I, um…"

"Wait, wait." Maisy grabs my hand and half drags me into the apartment. "Let me show you around first!"

I follow her, grateful for a reason to stall.

The inside of the apartment is nice, like the outside. A neat little two-bedroom with a decent-sized kitchen and a cozy living room area. It even has air conditioning. I make approving noises as she shows me the tour. Honestly, it's way better than the places I've lived over the years of struggle with Declan; she's not going to be battling cockroaches like I was at her age. There's plenty of room for me to stay here once my contract is up, too.

Maisy chatters as she shows me around. "It came pre-furnished, but I haven't had a chance to decorate yet, so don't judge!" She brings me to the guest room last. "This room is like, extra boring. But you're probably the main person who's gonna be staying here, so maybe you can decorate it? Some of those vampire posters you were never allowed to have at home?"

I laugh guiltily. "Yeah…"

"Oh, *oh*, speaking of! I *have* to ask. Have you been reading that valentine blog?"

I didn't think I could possibly get more nervous, but now my stomach is launching into a full gymnastics routine. "Blog?"

"*Confessions of an Anonymous Valentine?*" She seems to mistake my frozen panic for ignorance, because she says, "Oh my God, you *have* to read it, it's *so* your thing. Remember how we used to pore through the gossip mags for all that stuff? And all the vampire books you'd hide under your bed so Mom and Dad wouldn't confiscate them?" She giggles, digging her phone out of her purse, still oblivious to my horrified silence.

"It went viral a couple of days ago, and—"

"It *what*?" I grab the phone out of her hand before she can pull it up and stare at my blog page. Oh, God, she's right. I don't have my email for this account linked to my phone, only my laptop, and I haven't checked it since before the Celeste ball. "Holy shit." I press my hand to my mouth, trying to fight back panic.

"It's wild, isn't it?" Maisy asks, still grinning. "I've read it all. Like, at least three times. It's addicting. I can't believe she hasn't updated in a week! And she still hasn't revealed the truth about the previous valentine who went missing!"

Oh, no. *Oh, noooo.* If I thought it was going to be hard fessing up before, I can't imagine how I can possibly tell her the truth now. She's read the gory details—how it turns me on being bitten, things I had never imagined telling anyone I know personally...

"But, no, okay, sorry for interrupting," Maisy says, waving her hands. "I've hardly been able to reach you lately! There's so much I want to talk about that I'm just, like, word vomiting. But your job! You were about to tell me about your job!"

I stutter. "Well... uh... now that you mention it..."

I'm interrupted by the doorbell ringing. We look at each other.

"Oh," Maisy says. "Right. He's a little early, but I was gonna surprise you."

I stare at her. "Surprise me?" My stomach rumbles with the reminder that I've barely eaten without Ellen to look after me today. "Please say you mean with a food delivery?"

"Nope! Though we should order a pizza!" She's all smiles as she skips over to the door. "But for now... your surprise!"

She opens the door.

For some reason, I turn expecting to see Sebastian. I think that maybe Maisy managed to figure out the truth without me, and this is all one big prank and I won't have to explain at all.

Then Declan walks into the apartment.

Chapter Twenty-Seven

While I stand frozen, Maisy wraps Declan in a hug. He gives her an awkward one-armed embrace, looking over my sister's shoulder at me. When our eyes meet, cold panic floods my chest.

"What the hell are you doing here?" I don't mean to say it out loud, but the words slip out anyway.

"I knew you've been out of town with work, and I didn't want you to feel like you had to choose between spending time with me and Dec, so I reached out to him. And he suggested making it a surprise, so…" my sister starts. Then she turns, sees my face, and pauses. "Is everything okay?"

I stare at Declan, waiting for him to answer. My sister's reasoning explains why he was invited, but not why he showed up.

At least he has the good grace to look embarrassed. He shuffles, flushing. "I wanted to see you, but I didn't think you'd agree to meet me if you knew."

"Wait." Maisy looks back and forth between us, horror dawning on her face. "What's going on? Did I fuck up, Amelia?"

"No. You're alright." I close my eyes, take a deep breath.

Declan being here is going to make this harder, but that's fine. It's *fine*. I just need to start telling the truth and then the words will flow, I'm sure of it. "I'm the one who fucked up. I haven't been honest with you, Maisy, I'm sorry. Declan and I broke up a few months ago."

"Six months," Declan says. "Next week will be six months."

Shit. He's right. I lost track of time, but it is awfully close to that, isn't it? Which means my contract with Sebastian…

I yank my thoughts back to the present as Maisy's eyes go wide.

"Oh… oh, no, Amelia, I'm sorry, I had no idea." She looks between me and Declan, who is still fucking standing here for some reason. "Was it because you had to travel for your new job?"

"You got a new job?" Declan asks, giving me a puzzled look.

"Yes, I did, but not the job you think, and that's not why we…" I pause, leveling a look at Declan. "Hold on, first of all, you need to get the fuck out of here."

"Wait." Declan takes a step toward me, giving me that puppy-dog look that has worked far too many times in the past. "I need to say something first."

"You really don't," I say through gritted teeth, rubbing the bridge of my nose.

"I made a mistake," he continues. "I didn't mean any of those things I said, and you left so quickly, it—"

"And what about the other girl?" I snap, unable to take that self-pitying tone of his, like he's the victim here. "Did you mean *that*?"

Maisy gasps, then slaps a hand across her mouth.

"That… that was…" He stutters, looking uncomfortable. "It's over, I swear."

I roll my eyes. "Let me guess, she dumped you and that's why you're here."

He stares at me. I get the sense this is not how he thought the conversation would go. Because of course it isn't. He expected me to be a doormat, like I have been many times over the years.

Maisy slides over to my side and takes my hand in a show of support. "You heard her, Dec. Leave."

"But it isn't *fair*," he says, his voice taking on a definite whine. It makes my ovaries shrivel just remembering that I used to have sex with him. "Just hear me out, Amelia. I still love you. I realized how much I needed you when you were gone. It's always been us, and I don't want that to end over one mistake."

"*One* mistake?" I ask, taking a step forward. "Declan, you took advantage of me for years. You let me support you through school when you had no intent of returning the favor. You bailed on me last minute and were willing to let me and my sister pay the price for it. And even before that, things were..." I wave a hand. "Fine. They were always just *fine* because I thought that was the best I could get. But now..." My thoughts drag me unwillingly toward memories of Sebastian. His dark eyes, his stubble under my fingertips, his lips against mine, his hand between my legs— I pull my mind away, but still, it helps me find the words I want to say. "I deserve better, Declan. I always have. We are *done*."

"Amelia?"

For a moment, I think my vivid memories summoned the voice from the depths of my mind. But no. No, the truth is much worse. As I turn slowly—along with my sister, and Declan—I see Sebastian standing just outside of the still-open apartment door.

CHAPTER TWENTY-SEVEN

Chapter Twenty-Eight

I think I'm in shock. It's hard to make sense of Sebastian standing in an LA apartment complex, dressed in one of his usual mouth-watering suits. I've never seen him outside of a vampire ball or his own estate before, and it's like a man photoshopped into a painting he doesn't belong in.

"Sebastian?" I turn toward him, away from Declan and my sister. "What are you doing here?" I pause. "How did you know where to find me?"

"Ellen told me that you left, and this was the address we had on file for you," he says. "I'm sorry, I realize this is inappropriate, but I was afraid that you weren't going to come back, and…" He takes a step toward me. His eyes flit around, almost as panicked as I feel, but then his gaze lands on me and steadies. "I wanted to apologize."

I blink. Blink again. I still can't seem to wrap my head around the fact this is actually happening.

"For leaving without warning," he continues when I don't speak. He takes another step forward. I can see tension in the line of his shoulders, and I know how much effort it must take for him to be doing this in front of strangers, considering his reserved nature. It melts my heart, despite his atrocious timing. "It was a foolish, selfish thing to do. When I was told you planned on leaving the estate, I thought… I wasn't sure what to think. So I came looking for you to make sure you know…" He trails off as he finally seems to register that Maisy and Declan are both staring at him wide-eyed. He glances from them to me. "I'm… I'm sorry. I'm interrupting, aren't I? Could we step outside…?"

"Absolutely not," my sister butts in before I can get a word out. She steps forward, grabs my arm with one hand. "Amelia! Aren't you going to introduce me?" Her fingers are trembling. She must have never been around a vampire before; I almost forgot the effect they have on humans. Still, she whispers, "Please tell me this is your new, hot boss-slash-boyfriend."

"This is my sister, Maisy," I say. "Maisy, this is my…" I shake my head. "This is, um. Sebastian."

"How do you do?" Sebastian says with a formal little nod. "Lord Sebastian de Celeste."

Maisy lets out a strangled sound like a kettle releasing steam. "You're a… a…"

"A *vampire*?" Declan's disgusted words remind me that he is, for reasons beyond my comprehension, *still fucking here*. He puffs out his sad little man chest and takes a step toward Sebastian, though his hands are trembling at his sides. "Is *this* your new job, then, Amelia? You've become one of those bloodbags?" he asks, giving me a sideways glance. His lip curls. "Really? I didn't know you were serious about that vampire kink bullshit."

Heat flares in my face. I open my mouth, but before I can speak, Sebastian steps forward and places himself between me and Declan. He tilts his head to look down at my ex, his expression cold and imperious, summoning up the full force of his aristocratic nature. "And you are?" he asks in a low, dangerous voice I've never heard from him.

"I'm her boyfriend," Declan says.

Sebastian's icy mask falters.

"He is *not!*" I finally manage to find my voice and step forward, placing a hand on Sebastian's arm. "He's my ex, Sebastian. He's nothing to me." I glower at Declan. "And I've been telling him to get. The. Fuck. Out!"

Declan grits his teeth, turning red. I recognize that face, the one he makes before he's about to say something cruel, and brace myself. "Fine," he says. "If you want to whore yourself out to some undead freak—"

Sometimes I forget how quickly vampires can move. But in the small pause Declan makes to take a breath, Sebastian is on him. Cold white hands seize him by the front of his jacket and yank him off the floor while Dec lets out a yelp of fear.

"I believe the lady has made herself clear," Sebastian says, the sibilants hissing out around his fangs. He marches Declan toward the door while my ex struggles in vain. "It is time for you to leave. And if you ever speak to my valentine again in such a manner—if you ever approach her *at all* without her explicit permission—we will have a problem." He sets him down and gives him the tiniest shove, which sends Declan sprawling on his ass on the sidewalk. Sebastian is so strong, he must be exerting an enormous amount of restraint to not do more than that.

And still, as Declan scrambles to his feet with a green tinge to his skin, I note with glee that there's a wet spot spreading down the front of his pants. He turns without a word and flees toward the parking lot.

Sebastian brushes off his sleeves as if ridding himself of any last traces of Declan and turns to face me and Maisy. By the time he does, his fangs have retracted and he is once again the image of a perfect gentleman. "I apologize about that display. I hope I didn't overstep."

"Oh, *don't* apologize," Maisy says, recovering faster than I can. She grins at him. "Please say you're staying? I can tell we have a lot to talk about."

Sebastian looks uncertainly at me.

I finally manage to start breathing again and form a coherent sentence. "Yes, please," I say. I nod at Sebastian and then smile weakly at Maisy. "I have a lot of explaining to do. But maybe, um… can we go get something to eat first?"

* * *

It's unbelievably strange, crowding around a diner table with Maisy and Sebastian. Sebastian still looks out of place, and too big for the tiny chair he's seated in. He sits with his back rigid against the seat and his legs held stiffly together, like he's trying to take up as little space as possible. Maisy can't stop staring at him, and then at me, like she's trying to make this make sense.

The wait staff also doesn't seem to know what to do about having a vampire as a patron. The waiter attends to me and my sister with an anxious zeal and apologizes at least three times to Sebastian about not having anything vampire friendly on the menu. Sebastian, of course, is the picture of perfect poise and politeness, assuring the young man that it's fine, thank you, and he's already eaten, and he didn't mean to cause a fuss. Still, the waiter's hands tremble every time he comes to refill our water or bring food for me and Maisy.

I inhale my waffles and do my best to explain what happened between bites. I'm mostly talking to my sister, telling her about the breakup with Declan and my lies, but every so often my eyes drift over to Sebastian and I notice him listening intently, his dark eyes never leaving my face. All of this is news to him as well, I realize with a guilty twist of my stomach. Maisy doesn't know anything about Sebastian; Sebastian doesn't know anything about Declan and the circumstances of how I became his valentine. Nobody around me has received the full truth about my life. There's something cathartic about finally laying it all out; I hadn't realized how exhausting and lonely it was to not be able to tell anyone about everything going on.

But when I finish, the silence falling over the table makes me anxious. I gulp some water and push the remains of my waffles around my syrup-sticky plate.

"Oh my god." Maisy sits with her face in her hands. "That is… nuts. Absolutely nuts." She slowly lifts her head and gives me a hurt look. "You could've told me. You *should've* told me."

"I know," I say, my shoulders slumping. "I'm sorry. I just… I didn't want you to worry. I knew you were already probably freaking out about moving away from Mom and Dad's, and then…" I shake my head. "The longer it went on, the harder it got to tell you. But I came out here to admit everything."

"So this has been your new job the whole time," she says. "You've been lying to me about everything. For *months*. Months, Amelia?" To my horror, I see her eyes starting to well up with tears. "Everything about the writing retreat… the big project you were working on… that was all fake."

"Most of it," I say. I take another gulp of water and a deep breath. If I'm fessing up to the truth, I might as well say the whole truth. "I… have been writing a little." I steal a guilty look at Sebastian. This is news to him too. But I guess it's about time for me to come clean. "Some, um, nonfiction. You know that blog, the one you mentioned earlier…"

"No. Fucking. Way," she breathes. *Anonymous Confessions of a Valentine?*"

Sebastian looks sharply at me. His expressions have been muted during my explanation, but now I see a flicker of shock. "What's this?"

"Yeah…" I gnaw at my bottom lip. "I… I've been so isolated, not being able to talk to anyone about what's going on in my life. It started as a personal thing, a way to vent about my day-to-day life, but it sort of… blew up."

"Then… you…" My sister's expression changes as she blinks. "Oh, God. Christ. But then…" She turns abruptly to Sebastian, and her face solidifies into anger. "You asshole!"

Sebastian stares at her, and then at me. "Amelia?" he asks, clearly at a loss.

"No, you look at me, not at her!" Maisy leans forward, jabbing a finger into his chest with a boldness that makes my breath catch. "How dare you treat my sister like that. She's not some *thing* you can use for blood and sex and then leave—"

"You… wrote all that about me?" Sebastian asks, sounding winded. "Publicly?" He looks straight at me instead of the girl poking him in the chest, and his expression is so deeply wounded that it feels like my chest is going to cave in.

"It's not like that," I say. I know my sister with her over-the-top reactions, and I know she's lashing out right now because she's hurt and confused by all of this, but Sebastian doesn't.

"Maisy, please stop, let me explain—"

"No, *he's* the one that needs to explain! What is wrong with you, man? Talk about emotionally constipated," Maisy says. "You've got a real, live woman who clearly *adores* you, and—" She pauses, finger hovering in the air, and then recoils in sudden fear. "Wait, oh my god, you're... you..." She leans closer to me and clutches my arm. "All of that stuff about Etta..."

I suck in a breath. *No, no, no.* I open my mouth to apologize, to plead, to explain myself, but before I can do any of that, Sebastian abruptly pushes his chair out and climbs to his feet. His expression is stricken.

Maisy finally seems to realize that she may have overstepped. "I—sorry," she says, looking between me and Sebastian and shrinking down in her chair. "I'm sure it wasn't how it seemed I know you didn't, like, *kill* your last valentine, or..."

I shut my eyes.

"Yes," Sebastian says after a moment. "I did."

Cold shock douses me. My eyes fly open. "Sebastian—"

Again, I forget how fast a vampire can be. By the time I get to my feet and reach for him, he's already out the door in a blur of motion, leaving me grasping at nothing but air. I gape after him, and then back at Maisy, still staring at the table with her mouth half-open. After a moment, I, too, rush out the door in a panic.

Chapter Twenty-Nine

At first I'm chasing Sebastian, but of course, that's in vain. He's gone before I'm even out the door. After that, I'm just running.

I don't even know where I'm going. Just *away*. Away from Sebastian, from Maisy, from all of it. I run until there's a stitch in my side. I sink down to a crouch with my head in my hands. No matter how far I go, I know I'll never escape the memory of that conversation. I already know it's a situation that will replay in my mind for years. *The diner encounter that ruined my most important relationships and then my entire life.*

I want to disappear. I can't stop thinking about the betrayed look on Maisy's face, and then on Sebastian's. Remembering everything I wrote in that blog. I'm certain he's going to read it now, and the thought makes me sick to my stomach. I'd delete it, but I know it's already too late for that; screenshots exist all over the internet.

And… Etta. Sebastian admitted that he killed her.

I can't see a way back from this. Even though I can't face her right now, my sister will probably forgive me for lying eventually because she's, well, my sister. And I'll forgive her for possibly ruining my job for the same reason.

But Sebastian… I doubt he will ever get over the fact that I blasted him online like that. Or that I'll ever overcome the fact that he killed his previous valentine. If you asked me yesterday, I'd say I wasn't invested in my relationship with him. There have already been so many ups and downs, and he's constantly keeping me at arm's length, so how can this work?

But today… today he came looking for me. He finally broke down those barriers and tried to reach out… only to find betrayal and lies. When I think of being ripped away from him, it *hurts*.

And now I'm here, utterly alone, in LA. I lean back against a graffiti-strewn building, cars blaring past, and try to think. I have enough money in my account right now that I could easily grab a cab to a hotel room, or wherever I want. I'm not as trapped as I used to be, but it feels like it.

I can't stand to be alone right now, while I'm still reeling from all of this. But who can I reach out to? I'm not ready to face Sebastian. Maisy hates me. Benjamin… I once thought I could trust him, but I've barely spoken to him in months now, and after he lied to me about Alexander…

Alexander.

I think about cold lips pressing to the back of my hand. *Call me if you're ever in LA.* Contacting him feels like another betrayal to Sebastian, but… I need someone. Someone who hasn't lied to me, who I haven't lied to. That list is shockingly short right now. I take a deep breath, wipe my eyes, and pull my phone out of my purse.

* * *

Alexander arrives faster than I would've thought possible in LA. traffic. He pulls up to the curb in a flashy black sports car. I'm sure I look like a mess as I get into the passenger seat, mascara streaked down my face and my nose still stuffed up, but he doesn't say anything about it, other than, "I'm glad you called." He doesn't ask me anything either, other than, "Are you hurt?"

When I shake my head, he drives. Soon, we arrive at a gated apartment building, and he leads me through the fanciest lobby I've ever seen, up an elevator, and to an utterly gorgeous high-rise. But as I look at the all-white, modern design and the stunning windows with a view of the city around us, all I can think is that it feels nothing like home.

A fresh lump rises in my throat as I realize that's how I've come to think of the manor. *Home.* Sebastian's estate may be quiet and isolated and a little bit spooky sometimes, but to tell the truth, I love even its eeriness.

Or... *loved.* I doubt I'll ever see the place again.

I get choked up all over again at that, and Alexander leads me to one of his stark white leather couches. Soon, I have a cup of tea in my hands and a blanket over my shoulders, and he sits on the couch beside me and waits patiently for me to speak.

"Thank you for picking me up," I say, trying to wipe snot off my face before he notices.

"Of course," he says. "I'll always come when you call." He studies me with his pale eyes. "Though it hurts to see you like this. Is there anything I can do? Do you want to talk about it?"

I hesitate. Part of me wants to vent, but it feels inappropriate, talking about Sebastian to another man. Another *vampire.* A Solomon vampire, nonetheless. For a moment, fresh uncertainty churns my stomach… but I'm already here, and Alexander is being kind.

Still, I won't stoop to sharing private details about Sebastian. I shake my head. "Not right now. But being here is helpful. Really, I appreciate it."

He nods. "I'll give you some time alone, then. Please make yourself comfortable. The kitchen is stocked for guests, and you're welcome to the bathroom down the hall. I'll be in my office."

* * *

Alone in Alexander's living room, I brace myself to face my blog. I didn't bring my laptop on the trip, so I log in on my phone. My stomach drops as I see the sheer number of notifications waiting for me. Likes and comments and messages, news outlets asking for interviews, and more. It's overwhelming just to think about, so I drop my phone again, shuddering, and decide to deal with that later.

A shower leaves me feeling better, though I spend the whole time trying not to miss the claw-footed tub from my room in Sebastian's estate. By the time I'm done, I'm feeling guilty. I'm not sure what I was thinking, coming here. Alexander has been sweet to me, but this is the last thing I need right now.

As I fix my hair and makeup, I resolve to thank Alexander and excuse myself. But when I look for my phone to start making travel arrangements, I'm surprised to find it's not on the couch where I left it.

Just then, Alexander comes out of the kitchen with two

cocktails—one of them stained red. He holds the other out to me.

"Oh… thank you," I say, taking it and having a sip. It's delicious, fizzy and sweet.

"You're welcome." He sits on the other end of the couch I'm still occupying and has a swig of his own drink. "Oh, by the way—you left this on the counter." He pulls my phone out of his pocket and hands it to me.

I frown as I take it. The counter? When was I in the kitchen? God, I can be forgetful sometimes. "Thanks." I sip my drink as I open an app to search for flights.

"We should go out tonight," Alexander says.

I nearly choke on my drink. "Huh?"

"I've been dying for a chance to show you what you're missing." Before I can dig too deeply into that statement, he gestures towards the lit-up skyline outside of the window. "The LA vampire scene is incredible, and you've been locked up in that mountain manse for far too long."

"That's… generous of you," I say, my mind whirring as I try to think of a way to let him down gently. I sip my drink to stall. "It's a sweet thought. But I don't think I'll make good company tonight. Another time?"

Alexander leans forward, reaching out to take my hand. I awkwardly sip my drink some more, refusing the urge to snatch my fingers away from him. This drink must be stronger than I thought… I already feel the beginnings of a buzz. It's a relief to have my brain go fuzzy around the edges and my anxious thoughts slow down, so I keep sipping.

"Please," Alexander says, his pale eyes intense as they lock onto mine. "All I ask is one hour of your time. If you're not having a good time after that, I'll take you to wherever you wish to spend the night. I promise."

I have no desire to go anywhere with him or do anything other than curl up in bed. Preferably my bed at Sebastian's place. But… with the beginnings of tipsiness blurring my mind, I can't seem to think of a polite way to turn him down. He did save me today, and grant me the use of his apartment. What could be the harm in one hour?

The more I turn it over in my head, the more it seems like a reasonable idea.

"Okay," I say.

When he smiles, I catch a glimpse of fangs.

* * *

As we approach the nightclub, I feel the music just as much as I hear it—a steady throb of bass vibrating me down to my bones. I stumble over the curb and lean on Alexander for support. *Shit.* I only had one drink, and already I'm making a fool of myself. This is bad.

But Alexander holds me upright, his eyes bright with amusement. "This may not be the kind of party you're used to," he murmurs into my ear, the chill of his breath making me shiver. "But I do believe you'll enjoy it." He pulls back and grins at me. "A Solomon party is hard to forget."

There's a line around the block. Mostly humans, from what I can see. And rather than the finery I've seen at the Celeste gala and Valentine's Day ball, it's all ripped fishnets, messy hair, and black eyeliner.

"I think I'm overdressed," I murmur. I assumed this would

be more in line with the other vampire events I've attended, and Alexander loaned me a nice pink dress for the occasion, so I assumed everyone would be dressed this way.

"No, you're dressed like a valentine," Alexander says. He's dressed closer to how I am, in a button-up shirt and tailored slacks, so at least I don't feel totally out of place. "They wish they could be you, darling. Don't mind them." Then he turns his head and mutters something that sounds like *desperate* and *bloodbags*, but I can't be sure I hear him correctly.

Maybe he's right about the jealousy. Everyone glowers at us as Alexander walks to the front of the line, and I bite back the urge to apologize to them. Alexander doesn't even need to say anything to the gigantic bouncer—the man steps aside to let us pass.

We descend a flight of stairs, toward a neon sign that announces *Rouge* in scarlet letters. I've heard about this place. Once, I dreamed about coming here and meeting a handsome vampire who would sweep me away from everything.

Sebastian's face flashes through my mind, but it's difficult to hold on to the thought of him.

With each step lower, the bass sinks deeper under my skin, until I swear my heartbeat is throbbing in time to it. I grip Alexander's arm more tightly, suddenly afraid of what I've gotten myself into.

At the bottom of the staircase, we step into another world. A windowless underground one, with black walls and pulsing red lights, fog machines and dancers in cages. The floor is crowded with bodies gyrating and grinding together, no more than silhouettes in the dim lighting. On the couches pushed against the wall beyond them, more silhouettes are entwined. Vampires are feeding openly—maybe more than just feeding, judging from the way their bodies move…

I'm gawking without meaning to. Alexander tugs me along, navigating the chaotic scene with the ease of familiarity. "Stay close to me," he says, practically shouting to be heard above the music. He doesn't have to tell me twice; I cling to him, terrified about being lost in the crowd. I am dizzy from that drink, and the smell of sweet smoke heavy in the air, and the overwhelming crush of bodies around us as Alexander heads toward the bar.

Alcohol seems like the last thing I need, but my mouth is dry and my hands are shaky, so I take the drink he hands me anyway, and drink when he encourages me to. It's so sweet. Deceptively sweet, probably, like the one he made for me in his apartment. I sip it as I look around. Every time I do, I catch more details under the red lights. In the middle of the dance floor, I spot a man with his teeth buried in a woman's neck and his hand up her dress. On one of the couches, a man is bound at the wrists and ankles while two vampires take turns biting him.

The vibe here is intense—all black clothing and blood, sex and barely restrained violence. Everything seems consensual, but something about it feels off. Or maybe it's just not for me.

It's astonishing to remember that I once would've been into things like this, craving that rush and attention. If I had been Alexander's valentine, I'm sure I would've been down. But now… now I think of the quiet estate on the mountain, the crackle of the fireplace, the leather-and-ink smell of the library. I miss it. I miss home. I miss Sebastian.

And as my chest aches at the thought of him, I finally admit to myself that I'm not ready to give up on what we have yet. I need to try to make things right. Which means I really shouldn't be here.

I'm just going to finish my drink and tell Alexander I'd like to leave. But as I'm about to take my final sip, his cold fingers close around my wrist and he tugs me toward the dance floor. My protests are lost in the thumping music, and once we're in the crowd, I'm boxed in on all sides. I fight back panic as Alexander yanks me against him, his hands on my hips. My head is spinning.

I pull away, and thankfully, Alexander finally gets the picture and helps me off the dance floor. I only realize when I'm out of the crowd that we've made it over to the couches the vampires are using to feed. It stinks of blood and sex. I sink onto the first available couch anyway, trying to catch my breath, and Alexander is at my side in an instant.

"Are you having a good time yet?" he asks, his hand on my knee. "Or am I going to have to try harder?"

His hand slides higher. I reach to push it away as politely as I can, but he suddenly pulls me onto his lap with all of the ease of lifting a rag doll. I feel queasy with the knowledge of how strong and fast he is. My heart is thumping. I hope he's just misreading my signals, but if he doesn't… if he wants to hurt me…

"I can't believe I still haven't had a taste of you," he murmurs as I freeze. One hand cradles my spinning head and tilts it to the side, exposing my neck to him. "But I know it's going to be worth all of the restraint I've shown…"

"Stop," I say weakly as I feel his mouth graze my neck. "I don't want—"

"Alexander?"

Alexander freezes, the tips of his fangs against my skin, as a figure approaches from the crowd. And then another. I slip from his arms while he's distracted, pushing myself to the other side of the couch.

I recognize the two vampires approaching us from the night of the Valentine's Day Ball. Dante and Dominic, with their piercings and tattoos. The ones who almost fed on me before Sebastian scared them off.

Alexander doesn't look particularly happy to see them. "Hello, little fledglings."

"Sire," says Dominic, the one with dark hair and piercings. He dips into an over-the-top bow.

Alexander's lip curls over his fangs. "What do you want?"

"A word." Dominic steps closer, leaning over and lowering his voice till I can't hear it above the music.

Sire. Fledglings. Those are coven terms, I remember with a queasy flip of my stomach. Alexander is the one who turned these two into vampires. Which means I doubt I'll find allies in them.

But Alexander is distracted, so I take the chance to push myself from the couch on wobbly legs, teetering on my heels. I glance from Alexander to the staircase on the other side of the room, and my heart sinks. I'll never make it through the crowd on my own. Still, I have to try.

I take a step forward, and a body is suddenly in front of me. Looking up, I see the silent, tattooed Dante staring down at me, and my despair grows. But then he shifts so he's blocking me from Alexander and inclines his head. I follow his gesture to see a small neon sign behind the couches: *Exit.*

It must be a fire escape. Another way out. I glance at Dante again, and he jerks his head more insistently.

I don't know why he's helping me, but I'm not going to ignore the chance... or the clear warning. This whole time, I had still been telling myself that maybe Alexander misunderstood what I wanted, but now I'm not so sure. I swallow and creep toward the exit sign, step by slow step, until I'm out of Alexander's line of sight. Then I open the door and—

"Leaving already?"

I freeze at Alexander's smooth voice and then slowly turn to face him. Of course he's right behind me. It was stupid to think I could sneak away from someone with his senses.

"The night is still young, Amelia," he says, his eyes boring into mine. "Stay a while longer."

I hesitate. It sounds so reasonable when he says it like that, but… no. No. What the hell am I thinking? I shouldn't be here in the first place.

"No, I don't think so," I say. "It's time to go."

Alexander's face hardens. As I turn to leave, his hand darts out and catches my wrist.

"I *insist* you stay," he says with a fanged smile.

I freeze. I'm all too aware of the sharpness in those fangs, the strength in his grip. There's no way I can get away from him by fighting or running. And while other vampires are starting to look our way—including Alexander's two fledglings—none of them seem eager to step in to help me.

I'm on my own… and I'm not even wearing my silver, since I didn't expect to encounter any vampires in LA. I remember Benjamin's lessons. He once insisted that *manners* would keep me safe, but I have something more than that to protect me now.

"Let go of me," I say. "You are well aware that I am under contract with Sebastian de Celeste."

More heads turn our way at the name. Alexander's smile

falters. Even in the chaos of the club, people are watching us with interest. I know the Celeste name won't gain me any friends here, but I hope that it will instill some wary respect.

I may not know much about vampire history, but I know that Celeste won the war.

"I am Amelia Burton, a valentine under the protection of the Celeste Court," I say, "and I will be leaving now."

I pull my wrist away—and after a glance at the other vampires watching, Alexander lets go of me.

Then I make a break for it.

There's a staircase on the other side of the door, and a blessed taste of fresh air. As fresh as LA gets, anyway. I suck in a greedy gulp of it before I stumble up and onto the street. I run until I can't feel the bass in my skin anymore, and duck into a twenty-four-seven coffee shop.

Once I stop shaking, I fumble to get my phone out of my purse. The screen blurs in my vision; it takes me two attempts to call the contact I'm looking for. "Hey," I say when it finally goes through, my voice coming out slurred and shaky. "I know you hate me right now, but…"

Chapter Thirty

Maisy drives me back to her apartment in silence. She came when I called her because she's my sister, but it's obvious that she's still wounded by the fact I lied to her too. And I'm still angry that she jeopardized my position as a valentine.

When the car rolls to a stop, I stay in my seat with my eyes shut. My drunkenness has already transitioned into a hangover, leaving my head pounding and my stomach churning. I don't want to move.

My sister takes off her seat belt. "Let's get you into bed."

"Just leave me here to rot," I grumble.

"You want me to drag you? Because I will."

I sigh. "What happened to the sweet little sister I remember?"

"I dunno, what happened to the older sister who told me the truth?"

I sigh, unclick my seat belt, and open the car door.

I'm silent as I follow Maisy inside and to the guest room. She opens the door and takes a deep breath. I brace myself for more arguing. We might as well have one of those knock-down-drag-out sisterly fights to top off the night.

Then she whirls around and throws her arms around me in a fierce embrace. I hug her back, chomping down on my suddenly wobbly lower lip and telling myself not to cry.

"Thank you," she says, her face pressed against my shoulder. "I… I saw what this place costs. I never would've been able to afford it without you. And I know you never would've been able to afford it without your… without becoming a valentine." She pulls back and looks up at me, her eyes watering in a way that almost makes my own spill over. "But… please tell me you didn't do that for me. That you didn't put up with Sebastian for me and that's why all of this happened and you couldn't tell me and—"

I pull her in for another hug, murmuring comfort against her hair to stop the outpouring of panicked words. "No, Maisy, no. Honestly, I…" I swallow, fighting a surge of fresh pain as I think of Sebastian's dark eyes, his long cold fingers twined with mine. "I did it for the money to support both of us, yes, but there were a lot of things I could've done for that. I chose that path because I wanted to. And it was such a roller coaster with Sebastian, but…" My voice trembles. "I… I really, really liked him. I wouldn't have stayed with him if I didn't."

We stay embracing for several seconds. Then she finally pulls back, tucking her hair behind her ear.

"I'm still mad that you didn't tell me the truth," she says.

"Well, I'm still mad that you brought up my hot boss-slash-romantic-interest's dead ex."

"That's fair." She bites her lip. "I'm sorry."

"Yeah. Me too."

"Now…" A hint of mischief creeps into her expression. "Can I get some of the juicy details you've been withholding?"

I laugh tearily. "Please tell me you have some wine?"

"I don't think you need any more wine," she says, giving me a once-over. "But how about some ice cream?"

* * *

We both change into cozy pajamas and spend the night sitting on the couch, sharing cartons of ice cream while I pour out everything I've been bottling up for the last few months. I start with the breakup with Declan, which causes her to block his number and social media profiles while swearing profusely. Then I tell her about my training with Benjamin, the Valentine's Day Ball, my first meeting with Sebastian. I leave Alexander out of it; I'm still confused and anxious about what happened tonight, and the story is complicated enough without him.

Maisy listens with rapt attention. Then I get into arriving at Sebastian's estate, and the confusing and frustrating push and pull of our relationship, while she sighs and shakes her head and groans.

She still gives plenty of the over-the-top reactions I expect from her. But... she isn't completely freaking out. I'm beginning to realize she's grown more than I realized, and she doesn't need to be taken care of in the way I thought. Which only makes me feel more foolish about hiding everything from her.

Once it's all out in the open, I slump back on the couch, emotionally drained. I stare at the ceiling and think, again, of Sebastian's face when I mentioned the blog.

Maisy is quiet for several moments, digging for the last

chunks of cookie dough in an ice cream carton. "So… what are you going to do?"

I scrub a hand across my face and sigh. "I don't know. What can I do? I don't know if he even *wants* more, maybe it's just in my head. Or…"

"Amelia." She waits until I lift my hand and peek over at her to get the full brunt of her look of disapproval. "Don't do that."

"Do what?"

"Sabotage yourself." She licks her spoon clean and sets it aside on the coffee table. "If you think this relationship is worth saving, then you have to fight for it."

It's a hard truth, but she has a point. Sebastian has been hot and cold with me… but he has his scars from the past, and I get that. And I'm not innocent, either. I put our personal business on the internet for all to see, knowing it would be his worst nightmare. I scrubbed enough details that no one knows it was us, but that's a fragile excuse. I should have told him either way. I had a perfect opportunity during our talk in the library, but I hid the truth instead.

But I wasn't the only one. "Still… you heard him. He admitted he killed his previous valentine. Is it stupid of me to even consider being with him after that?"

Maisy frowns. "I don't know… That was such a long time ago, and it seems strange given everything else you said about him. I have a feeling we don't have the whole story, and I think you owe it to yourself to get it."

I smile. "When did you become the mature one?" I should've been asking her for advice this whole time, not thinking of her as some fragile thing in need of protection. "I know you're right, I need to do… something. But I'm not sure what." I put my ice cream carton down and rub at the bridge of my nose.

"Well, you're not going to fix it tonight," Maisy says. "You're welcome to spend as much time as you need here, obviously. But if you want my advice… don't let Sebastian slip away. Not without at least *trying* to make things work."

***

Days pass. I don't hear from Sebastian. I *do* get a few texts from Alexander, but I block his number.

Maisy and I spend time together, shopping for apartment decorations and books for the school year. I wander USC's campus with her and bring her to my favorite local donut shop. As she licks chocolate frosting off her fingers, she declares that she officially forgives me.

So that's one down. But Maisy is the easy one. She's my sister, my family. She practically has to forgive me. Sebastian may never find it in himself to do the same.

And God, I miss him. I miss the fragile, tender connection we were finally starting to figure out. I also miss Ellen, and the estate, and my life as a valentine… but mostly, I miss Sebastian. That little quirk to his lips when he's almost-but-not-quite smiling, his solemn dark eyes, his quiet kindness…

He is also aggravating and distant and difficult. There was so much that was wrong with our relationship. We were so bad at communicating. But still, somewhere along the way, I made the devastating mistake of falling for him. I've never been more aware of that than now, when I'm realizing I may never have a chance to say goodbye. I do intend to reach out to him, but I'm carefully considering what I want to say. I don't have much time left before our contract is up, so I need to do this right.

When I'm not spending time with Maisy, I curl up in bed with my laptop, trying to think about that inevitable conversation, and checking on my blog. The amount of comments and messages I've received are mind-boggling. Most of the public comments are begging for an update that I'm not ready to give yet. The personal messages, though, are much more touching. Many of them are from fellow valentines, thanking me for telling my story and offering their own confessions.

I had planned on taking the blog down, but those messages change my mind. I regret airing Sebastian's private life without his permission... but I can't regret sharing my own feelings, especially knowing that they resonated with so many people. And when I read through what I wrote again, I'm confident that no one will be able to guess his identity. There are no mentions of his estate's location, the court he belongs to, or anything that could out him. And judging from the messages I received, feeling like one is competing with a past, long-dead valentine is more common than I would've thought.

I don't know if Sebastian would feel the same when he reads it. *If* he reads it. Maybe he'll just judge it based off what my sister said and assume the worst. That thought makes my stomach flip.

I have to clear things up. But will he be willing to listen? I want to give him more time, and space if he needs it...

But we don't have time. This weekend will mark six months since I became Sebastian's valentine. That means our contract will be over. If we're ever going to have a discussion, it needs to be before then.

I think about posting it all on the blog, but I can't be sure he's even reading it, and I know he would hate that sort of public gesture. Sebastian is private; he'd want this handled privately. If he's hurting, he'll retreat back to the estate. He's probably holed up in his library right now with the door locked, avoiding everyone.

I'm the one who's sought him out so many times before. But the other day, he came for me. That was an enormous leap of faith for him. So now it's my turn. I'll go to him one more time to see if what we have is worth fixing. One last try, for both of us.

Chapter Thirty-One

My heart is pounding as the car pulls up to the estate. It is just as haunting and beautiful as it was the first time I saw it; I don't think the view will ever stop taking my breath away.

Part of me hopes I'll see Sebastian's silhouette waiting in the window. But the windows are dark. Nobody is waiting for me in the lobby when I walk in, either.

I knew it was going to be on me to approach Sebastian. This doesn't change anything, though it is odd that not even Ellen or Barnabas are here to greet me. I turn to Vincent as he carries my bag in behind me. "Do you know where Sebastian might be?"

He scratches his head. "Not sure, miss. He gave everyone the weekend off, said he'd be away."

My stomach drops. "Oh, *shit*," I say. I thought I was playing it safe by coming here the day before our contract ends, but if he's not here… "I, uh—wait here for a minute, will you? I might be running out again."

Then I race upstairs, hoping to find him lurking in the library, having dismissed the staff for some solitude.

But he's not there. No one is. The house is empty. I can

feel it in the air even before I check the rooms to make sure Sebastian isn't hiding away somewhere. It doesn't make any sense. Retreating into privacy is Sebastian's signature move, the only thing that's predictable about him. Where else would he go?

I enter my own room last. I pause in the doorway and then slowly approach the bed, where a dress is laid out for me. A *yellow* dress, perfectly matching my favorite yellow sneakers, which I'm wearing right now.

It's so unlike everything else in my new wardrobe. It's also so *me*. I pick it up, running my fingers over the buttery-smooth fabric, my chest aching.

A card waits beneath it.

Dear Amelia,
I would like to formally invite you to the Camelia Summer Ball.
August 15th
Sebastian

Tomorrow. The day our contract ends. As I set the card down, I notice two pins waiting beneath it, both in the shape of anatomical hearts. Valentine pins. One is black, to designate a valentine with a patron; the other is white, indicating a valentine searching for a match.

My heart is pounding. Why would he leave both? And did he set out this invitation for me before or after he found out about the blog and rushed off? Where is he now? Would he plan on going to the ball without me? God damn this man and his atrocious communication skills. God damn his refusal to use a cell phone, too.

As I'm spiraling into panic, my phone buzzes. I pick it up to see a text message from Benjamin: *Call when you get a chance. We need to discuss your contract.*

My stomach lurches.

There are only two options: I can stay here and hope that Sebastian comes home. Or I can go to the ball and hope that he's there.

I stare down at the pins. One white, one black. Two choices. What will Sebastian do?

I close my eyes and force myself to breathe. I've spent so long trying to figure Sebastian out, only to be proven wrong time and time again. I can't predict his actions or his feelings.

So I focus on a different question. What do *I* want?

This relationship with Sebastian has been hurdle after hurdle. At the end of the day, even with perfect communication, we may simply be too different for this to ever work in the long run. We both have an easy out with the end of our contract coming up. Maybe that's Sebastian's intent, to hide somewhere until the contract runs out.

But again, I'm not thinking about that. I'm thinking about what I want, for myself and my future.

…And maybe, just maybe, that's what Sebastian is thinking about too. As soon as the thought occurs, something snaps into place in my mind. I open my eyes and pick up the dress he chose for me.

Chapter Thirty-Two

It's nearly midnight when I make it to the ball.

This one is held at the same mansion as the Valentine's Day Ball, and it is just as dazzling. All glittering crystal and startling beauty, goblets of blood and wine, bite marks on necks and flashes of fangs. But this time, as I stand at the top of the stairwell and look down on it all, I don't feel dizzy or overwhelmed. My heart pounds, but it's with excitement rather than fear. I feel confident, even without Benjamin hovering at my side as my chaperone. I take a deep breath and adjust my bodice. I know my worth and I know my assets, and I am not afraid to show it off in this curve-hugging yellow gown. The color stands out in a sea of valentines dressed in red and pink. So do the sneakers I'm wearing with it.

Six months ago, I would've been self-conscious. But now, I feel confident. In control. This is my world now, and nobody is going to make me doubt my place in it.

I am aware of eyes on me as I descend the staircase, and I keep my chin high. The room is all glitter and gold, perfect vampires and valentines on their arms—and I belong among them.

I spot the familiar, tall form of Viktoria de Camelia, elegant as she swoops around the dance floor, leading her painfully handsome poster-boy valentine Jonah in a waltz. An unexpected pain jolts through my chest at the sight. A burst of jealousy. They look so thoroughly enamored with each other, a perfect pairing.

Can Sebastian and I ever be like that? I don't know. But then I remember all of the anonymous messages I received on my blog and realize that maybe even these two are not as perfect as they seem on the surface. For all I know, they're a mess behind closed doors. I can't compare the private details of my relationship with my surface-level understanding of theirs.

Besides, I'm beginning to realize that relationships aren't just about how you're suited to one another. They're about putting in work. Making concessions for the needs of the other person.

I fiddle with the pin on my dress as I search the room for Sebastian. He's not on the dance floor, not that I expected him to be. He's not near the bartender or the buffet tables, either, nor on the chaises where vampires are feeding on valentines eager for their attention. More shockingly, he's not in the library, either. I step outside, feeling frazzled and wondering if I've made an enormous mistake in thinking he'd be here.

My eyes wander to the open back doors.

Of course. The garden. If he's waiting for me, that's where he will be—the place we first met.

My sneakers are far more effective for walking on grass than my heels were that night. I wander into the hedge maze, searching for the bench that Sebastian and I sat on during our first meeting.

Before I can find it, a prickle on the back of my neck tells me I'm being watched.

"You're here."

The familiar voice sends a shiver down my spine. I turn to see Alexander, imposing in a pure white suit, with hunger in his pale eyes.

I freeze, unsure how to handle this. "I am…"

"I had hoped you would be," he says, his gaze drifting down to my cleavage. "You left so abruptly after our lovely night out."

I resist the urge to pull my dress up. I felt empowered when I first put it on, but now the cool air against my skin makes me feel vulnerable. Instead, I reach up to fiddle with the black heart pin that marks me as having a patron, drawing his attention there. "I'm here with Sebastian. My *patron*."

He meets my eyes again and his smile widens. Sharpens. There's a flash of fangs, barely visible. "I don't see him."

My heartbeat picks up. He's looking at me like a piece of meat, and I'm suddenly aware that I'm here based on a guess. I thought Sebastian would come because he expects me to be here. But maybe I was wrong. Maybe he's already back at the estate, wondering where I've gone—or maybe he doesn't even care.

Maybe I'm here alone, without a patron or a chaperone, or even a crowd to witness us, like we had in the nightclub. I take a small step backward, and Alexander takes one forward, his eyes burning into me.

Benjamin warned me that a valentine without a contract is vulnerable. I do have a contract with Sebastian… until midnight. But I have no idea what time it is. Nor do I think the vampires would truly care to investigate too deeply to find out whether I died at 11:45 or slightly later. I could be in real danger.

A blink, and suddenly Alexander is gone. I step back again and meet the hard wall of his muscular chest behind me.

"Don't be afraid," he murmurs into my ear.

I yelp and lurch forward, but he yanks me back against him.

"What are you scared of, little valentine?" he asks. "If you're here with a patron, there's nothing to worry about, so…"

Fear makes my mouth go dry and my chest tighten. I have nowhere to run, nowhere to turn to, no one to save me.

But I do have my silver jewelry.

I twist in Alexander's grip, rip the thin silver chain off my neck, and shove it into his face with all of the force I can muster. His flesh sizzles at the contact, and he shrieks in pain and fury, stumbling back and clawing at his skin.

I turn and run. He's between me and the mansion, so I have no choice but to flee deeper into the gardens. But as I lose myself in the hedge maze, there is no one here to help me. There is no one at all. I pull my phone out of my pocket, dialing Benjamin's number—

But Alexander appears again from the shadows, teeth bared, an ugly slash of red marking the spot my necklace touched him. He grabs my wrist and twists until I cry out with pain and my phone falls into the grass.

"You *bitch*," he snarls. There's nothing human in his expression now, it's all violence and fangs as he shoves me to the ground and pins me beneath him. I try to fling my necklace at him, but he keeps my wrist in an iron grip. "You could've made this easy," he spits. "You could've come willingly. That would have been revenge enough. He took Etta from me, so I'll take you from him. But now?" It only takes one of his pale hands to wrap around my throat. "I suppose I'll have to settle for killing you."

His thumb digs into my skin as I writhe and choke. His expression is impassive, the way he grips me almost casual.

"It should be easy enough to frame him," he muses aloud. "After I expose the identity behind your blog." He grins at me. "It was stupid of you to leave your phone lying around my apartment when you had so much incriminating information on there. All I have to say is that you found the truth about Etta, and he killed you just like he killed her."

I kick and struggle in vain. My vision goes dark around the edges.

But then the pressure disappears from around my throat. I suck in a desperate gasp of air. For a moment, I think I've been saved, but I see Alexander leaning down toward my neck, his fangs out. "Still, I think I deserve a taste after all of that hard work," he murmurs. "I have to know if it's true. If you taste just like her..."

I feel the prick of fangs and try to scream, but it comes out as a hoarse croak. I squeeze my eyes shut.

Then, in an instant, the weight on top of me is gone. I gasp for air, vision rushing back, and roll over onto my side. A tall figure steps up beside me, glaring at Alexander where he's been thrown against a bench.

"Keep your hands off my valentine," Sebastian snarls.

Chapter Thirty-Three

Heart in my throat, I raise to my knees on the grass.

Sebastian looks far from his usual polished, reserved self. There is a look of pure murder in his eyes as he watches Alexander pull himself to his feet. With his eyes dark and his fangs out, he looks almost like a stranger. He lets out a low hiss that I've never heard him make before, a feral noise.

Alexander bares his fangs. "You have no claim to her, *Sebastian.*"

The vitriol in the way he spits the name makes me realize, with a dawning horror, that I am in the middle of something I do not understand. I have been this entire time.

Sebastian is still, his eyes locked on the vampire challenging him. "That is where you are wrong, Alexander," he says, his voice frighteningly quiet. "She is under contract with me until midnight."

Alexander grabs my phone from the grass and shows Sebastian the time: *12:05.* "As I said," he spits. "You have. No. Claim."

Sebastian shrugs off his coat and leans down to tuck it around my shoulders. He straightens up and rolls up his sleeves. "Again, you are incorrect," he says. "She sets her clock ten minutes fast."

I gape at him. He... remembered that? Then I turn to Alexander, who is staring in disbelief. He takes out his phone to verify it, and for a moment, something like fear flickers across his face.

"Fine," Alexander says. "I can wait."

"But I cannot," says Sebastian, his voice very cold. "You've harmed my valentine. I demand redress."

Alexander lifts his shoulders in a theatrical shrug. "Have your court take it up with mine, then."

"You mistake me." Sebastian cracks his neck and rolls his shoulders back. "I am old-fashioned. I'll take my right of trial by combat. Now."

Alexander stares at him for a moment. And then he laughs, taking off his own coat and tossing it carelessly aside. "Fine," he says. "It's your funeral."

He launches himself at Sebastian without another word. He's a blur of movement, and I cry out and press a hand to my mouth, but before I can comprehend what's happened, Sebastian is holding Alexander by the wrist. He twists Alexander's arm behind his back, but then Alexander snarls and breaks free.

The following exchange of blows is dizzyingly fast and eerily silent. I catch only snippets: Sebastian with his hand around Alexander's throat; Alexander with his fangs in Sebastian's shoulder; both of them struggling in a tangle of limbs on the ground. It is fast and dirty and feral. The opposite of everything vampires pretend to be at these balls.

My head spins as I try to keep up. All I can do is climb to my feet, stumble out of their way, and hope that Sebastian has the upper hand. I should probably run, but I can't bring myself to do it. I can't leave before I know if Sebastian is okay.

All at once, it stops.

Alexander is face down on the grass. Sebastian has a knee on his spine and a hand on the back of his neck, holding him prone.

"Yield," Sebastian says. Dark, viscous blood drips from the wound on his shoulder where Alexander's teeth found skin. His hair is askew, his clothes rumpled and torn. I've never seen him so thoroughly uncomposed—but he won.

Alexander struggles, spits words that are muffled by a mouthful of grass.

Sebastian presses his knee harder. "*Yield*," he says.

Alexander's spine pops, and he shrieks. "I yield," he says, barely audible.

Sebastian releases him, stands, and brushes himself off. I'm tense, wondering if this bout will bring out the frightening side of him I saw when he almost bit me that night at the estate. Yet the violence disappears from him the moment he turns to me.

"Are you hurt?" he asks, his eyes falling to where Alexander gripped me by the neck earlier. I can feel the bruises forming, but I shake my head.

"I'm fine," I say hoarsely. "But your shoulder—"

"It's nothing." He can't seem to look away from my face. He tucks my hair behind my ear with a care that is more shocking after the power and violence I just witnessed. "Amelia..."

A blur of motion out of the corner of my eye is the only warning I get. Cold fingers clamp around my ankle hard enough to make me cry out and buckle. I look down to see Alexander crawling with a mad glint in his eyes, fangs sliding out as his mouth comes for my leg—

And then Sebastian reaches down, grabs him by the neck, and rips Alexander's head clean off his body. I stare, mouth open, as it rolls to a stop near one of the hedges.

Sebastian clears his throat.

"Apologies," he says. "I was hoping to spare you that sight."

"That's, um…" I can't seem to look away from the severed head. "Quite… alright…"

Sebastian places a finger on my chin and tilts my face until I'm looking at him. I keep waiting for fear to hit me after the sheer power I just witnessed his hands being capable of. He just killed someone. He admitted he killed his previous valentine too. But I find nothing but gentleness in his eyes when he looks at me. I feel nothing but safety in his touch. He just ripped off another vampire's head… for *me*.

Is it fucked up to find that romantic? Probably. But I find myself tearing up anyway.

"Oh, God," I say, sniffling. "This is going to cause a whole mess for you, isn't it? The Solomon Court… and Celeste… and the war…"

Amazingly, Sebastian cracks a smile. "*That's* what you're worried about?" He pulls me toward him. I bury my face in his neck and wrap my arms around him, and he holds me like I'm a precious thing while I cry. "It's alright, darling," he murmurs against my hair, and I nearly melt at the endearment from his lips. "This is a clear-cut case of vampire law. It won't be any trouble."

Despite his assurances, now that the floodgates have opened, I can't seem to close them again. There's so much that I've been bottling up. He strokes my hair while I blubber half-coherent confessions and apologies about my first meeting with Alexander, and my night out with him, and his visit to the house.

He pulls back to look at me. Shock flickers across his face, and then anger. "He was *at the estate?* How?"

"I… I don't know? I swear I never told him where I was. I thought that maybe it was public knowledge…?" But Sebastian is shaking his head.

"That doesn't make sense," Sebastian murmurs. "Hardly anyone knows where I make my home. Certainly not Alexander de Solomon. If you didn't tell him, then…" He pauses, realization breaking across his face. "You said you had a drink with him at the Valentine's Day Ball."

"Yes?"

A muscle twitches in Sebastian's jaw as he clenches it. He looks even angrier than before. "He must have dosed you with his blood and used it to track you there."

I press a hand to my mouth. "Oh, God." If he followed me after the Valentine's Day Ball… Now I'm remembering the times I thought I was being watched over the last several months. Barnabas snarling at something in the fog. The dark figure I saw in the tree line, which I assumed was Sebastian…

And if he dosed me during that first meeting, he must have done so again when I went to his apartment.

Seeing my panic, Sebastian pulls me against him and kisses my forehead. "It's alright," he says. "You're safe now. And I'm sorry I failed to protect you before."

My eyes start welling up again. "You don't hate me?"

He wipes away my tears. "Alexander manipulated you from the start," he says. "I know how he operates. And… I only made it easier for him by keeping you at arm's length." I shake my head, ready to argue, but he continues before I can. "I know that you have a lot of questions, Amelia, and I think it's time for me to give you the answers you deserve."

But then he tenses and pushes me behind him as he turns to face the entrance to the hedge maze. I had almost forgotten that there's an entire party and several dozen vampires not far from here. When I see Dominic and Dante, Alexander's fledglings, approaching us, my stomach sinks.

The two Solomon vampires both stop abruptly as they see Alexander's body—and, several feet away, his head.

"He's dead," Dominic murmurs. "I felt it, but… I couldn't believe…" He stares at his sire's head, dazed. At his side, Dante stares at us instead, his shoulders squared and his expression guarded.

"You killed him," Dante says to Sebastian.

Sebastian lifts his head high and nods. "He laid his hands upon my valentine," he says. "I challenged him to combat. He accepted, he lost, and he refused to yield."

Dante looks at him, and then at me. I'm sure he remembers that night out at the vampire nightclub, and I'm braced for him to accuse me of being at fault somehow—but he only nods. His face is unreadable, but I remember the way he urged me to get away from Alexander at Rouge. I wonder how much loyalty he really felt for his sire. After a moment, he turns and puts an arm around Dominic's shoulders.

"Let's leave them to it," Sebastian whispers to me, once it's clear neither of them intends to confront us. He leads me out of the hedge maze and to a bench in a quiet corner of the gardens, barely touched upon by the light and music of the ball.

"This is not precisely how I intended for this night to go," Sebastian says.

I croak out a laugh from my still-sore throat. "No? What did you intend?"

He takes both of my hands in his. "Well, I was going to start by telling you about Etta."

The grave. The flowers. The suspicions I voiced on my blog, the accusation my sister threw at him…

And the admission he made. He said he killed her.

I hesitate. "I know it was a long time ago…" I say, torn. I know I'm not entitled to all of his secrets, but if there's any hope for us continuing this, I do think I need to know.

He shakes his head and gently squeezes my hands. "I would like to tell you," he says. "I would like you to understand."

I nod, any further words dying in my throat. Truth be told, I'm afraid that hearing what he has to say will break my heart. But neither of us can hide from the truth.

"As you've likely guessed, Etta was my former valentine," he says. "It has been almost seventy-five years since I became her patron." He pauses, but I wait in silence, knowing he's only trying to organize his thoughts. "She was my first valentine. I had always sworn I would never take one on. Companionship does not come easily to me. But her blood was… singularly appealing." He glances sideways at me, and I look away, my face heating when I realize what he's hinting at. Her blood was *like mine*.

That makes me think of what Alexander said to me about me tasting *"just like her."* And his words about Etta.

"My tastes are… particular, and unusual. I had never found blood that sated me like hers. I could not resist it, and so I took her on as my valentine, even though I knew…" Sebastian grimaces, shakes his head. "I knew the danger of growing close to a mortal. The terrible price of loving one. Yet still

I fell, helplessly, foolishly. I could not help myself. She tore down the walls I had constructed around myself like they were no more than paper mâché. She stuck in my heart like a thorn." He smiles, and it has a bitter tinge. "And then she… asked me to change her. To make her a vampire so that we could be together forever."

I blink, so startled that for a moment I forget my own emotional ties to this story, my horrible jealous heart pounding in my chest. I remember the clause in our contract that made it crystal clear I didn't intend to ask him the same thing. "And what did you say?"

"I said no." His voice has never been so quiet before. "I had made myself a promise, long ago, that I would never create more of my kind. I feared she had not thought through the cost of it. That she didn't understand she was giving up every sunrise, every taste of food untainted by blood. That she would have to watch her family and loved ones grow old and die while she stayed the same. But she… She thought…" His words die off, and I can see him struggling for words. Shame creeps into his normally unreadable expression, and I realize what he's finding it difficult to voice.

"She thought you said no because you only wanted her blood," I say.

"So she left," he says. "She went to other vampires, seeking someone who would grant the request I denied. But it is… a difficult process, and it is not so simple to find someone willing to turn a mortal, particularly one who is new to them. I tried to reach out to her, to make amends, but she avoided me. And as she grew more desperate for what she sought, she turned to more dangerous avenues." He goes quiet, and I hold my breath, half afraid to hear what comes next. "When I heard from her again, years later, she asked to come see me. Of course I agreed. And when she arrived, I soon realized that she was very unwell. She was addicted to vampire blood, and it was killing her."

My stomach lurches. "Alexander," I whisper.

Sebastian nods, agony in his eyes. "Etta knew that she did not have much time, and she was afraid. She asked me again to turn her, and this time I said yes."

The quiet stretches out. I think of that gravestone, the sadness in his voice when he speaks of her, and already know how this ends. The process of turning a vampire is shrouded in secrecy, a mystery held tightly by the vampire courts, but there are many rumors about the difficulty and potential dangers of the process. I know that not even a strong, youthful candidate will always survive the transformation, let alone a woman who was already dying. Still, I wait for Sebastian to finish telling his tragic tale.

"Of course she did not survive it," he says. "It was foolish of me to try. Even if I had succeeded, I had not asked for proper permission from my court, and it would have been a legal nightmare. But as it was…" He shakes his head. "She didn't have a chance. I buried her on the grounds and swore that I would never let myself feel such a thing again. Both for her memory and for my sake."

I shut my eyes, processing that. The truth hurts, as I expected it to, as something finally slots into place for me. The puzzle piece I've been missing that gives the reason for Sebastian's volatile behavior. I am here because I remind him of *her*. My blood is enough to conjure the ghost of his love for this long-dead valentine, and *that* must be the reason for these moments of physical affection, where it almost seems like he sees me as more than a blood donor. And that, too, must be the reason he always flees shortly afterward—when he comes back down to earth and realizes that I am not her, and never will be.

I am just a replacement for his former love. Once, I would've accepted that. But now… now I think I deserve better. Leaving him after all that we've been through will break my heart, but sometimes it's necessary to break something before it can be rebuilt.

I force a smile that I'm sure comes across as small and sad, and reach over to squeeze his arm. I want him to know that it's alright, that I understand, and I don't hold it against him. As much as it hurts, I'm glad that he is being honest with me, and I'm sure it wasn't easy to share. I don't think Sebastian is a bad person, or that he meant to use me. We have an agreement, after all; I am the one who started to think we could have something more than our contracted relationship. "Thank you for telling me that," I say. "And for saving me from Alexander, and for being so kind."

Sebastian searches my face, a small furrow in his brow.

"Of course," he says. "And I…" His throat bobs. "I understand this is strange timing," he says. "But… in my initial plan for this night… I had also planned on asking you for a dance."

The request is so unexpected, especially in the context of everything that's happened tonight, it stops me for a moment. *A dance.* "You hate dancing," I say.

"I do." I would think the request was a joke if I didn't know him better, but of course he is all solemnity. "But I have never tried it with you."

It almost feels like he's trying to woo me with that line. My heart is a tangled mess of emotions.

But if this is our last night together, I won't refuse him. Perhaps it will grant closure to both of us. So I take his hand and let him pull me toward the party. I pause only to take his coat off my shoulders and offer it to him, to cover his torn and bloodstained shirt.

Then his cold, slender fingers twine with mine, and he leads me indoors and to the dance floor.

As if on cue, the formerly lively music takes a turn for the slow and almost sorrowful. Sebastian gently pulls me close and places a hand on my hip, ever the gentleman. His other hand still grips mine, holding it aloft as he pulls me into the steps. I drop my eyes to his shoes, worried about stepping on them.

A waltz. It's been a while, but my body still remembers the steps that Benjamin taught me during our training long ago. It is easier than ever with Sebastian leading me; he is stiff but perfect in form, and my body is all too eager to follow his. I know every move he is going to make just before he makes it.

In this, at least, we are suited to one another. The realization hurts, but I push it deep down, take a deep breath, and look up at his face. His eyes are already on mine; he has been studying me since the beginning, I realize, and there is a look in his dark eyes I've never seen before.

"I wasn't sure if you'd be here tonight," I say.

"Nor I you."

I swallow. I wish I could focus on the dance to distract myself from the surge of unwanted feelings, but the steps come as easily as breathing when I'm with him. "Why are you?" I ask. If he intended for this night to be a way to say goodbye, he could have done it elsewhere.

His brow furrows. "Why do you think?"

I bite the inside of my lip as frustration wells up in me. I wanted this last conversation to leave on a good note, a kind note, but *God*, this man knows how to drive me crazy sometimes. "I don't know, Sebastian," I say. "I never have any idea what you're thinking or feeling, particularly—" My voice thickens, but I blink away the threat of tears. "Particularly when it comes to me."

His feet slow to a stop, and mine follow seemingly of their own accord. We are left standing still in the middle of the dance floor, the eye of a storm of twirling partners. Glances are drifting toward us, but Sebastian does not seem to care. He stares at me, eyes narrowed in disbelief, before he grabs my arm and pulls me from the dance floor.

I'm surprised at how well he seems to know the layout of this place, since he seems to avoid parties as much as possible, but then he turns on a light and I realize where we are: the library. Of course. It's not as impressive as his own or that of the Celeste mansion we visited, but it stands to reason that this is a room he would be able to locate.

But we're not the only ones seeking solace here. There's a clatter of noise from behind one of the shelves, and Sebastian goes instantly still, his fangs sliding out. "Get *out*," he snaps at the darkness.

For a moment, there's nothing. Then Viktoria de Camelia strides out of the shadows, her lipstick smeared and one strap of her dress falling down her slim shoulder, yet looking entirely unselfconscious about the state she's in. One hand tugs her valentine Jonah along while he struggles half-heartedly to hold together the torn buttons of his shirt.

Viktoria eyes us. Sebastian lets out one of those low, dangerous hisses, but she only smiles in response. "Have fun," she purrs, and leaves, tugging her valentine along with her. He casts one last look back at us before they both disappear.

Sebastian slams the door shut behind them and then stands with one hand pressed to his temple, struggling to get his expression under control. He doesn't speak until his fangs have retracted and he looks a little less like he wants to tear someone's throat out.

"Amelia," he says. He runs his fingers through his hair. "It feels as though I've mis-stepped again. I have been trying to tell you—"

"Wait," I say. "I want to say something first." Before I end this once and for all. I fold my arms over my chest, hugging myself. "I'm sorry about the blog. It was wrong of me to post private things about you. It was meant to be a way for me to vent. I never thought it would blow up like that or get back to you. But I did scrub the identifying details from it before posting it, just so you know. You don't have to worry about blowback."

Sebastian's expression tightens. He looks down at his shoes. "When your sister mentioned it, I assumed the worst," he says. I wait, giving him time to speak; I've already said my piece. "I had always wondered why… someone like you would be attracted to someone like me." I open my mouth, but he hurries on before I can interrupt. "I assumed life at my estate would bore you, that my efforts to bring you out into society were too little, too late. So when I heard that you had been posting online, I thought my worst fears had come true. That you were only in this for a story to tell, and that you were divulging everything for money or fame."

"That was never…" I say, not even sure how to refute the ridiculous things he's saying, but he holds up a palm to halt me and I bite my tongue.

"Then I read the blog," he continues. "And I saw the truth. At first, I was embarrassed that any of that was available to public eyes. But when I started reading… I was so much more ashamed to see who I was from your perspective." He raises his gaze to mine. "It made me realize how terrible I had been to you."

My lower lip wobbles. I bite down on it, trying to wrestle my emotions under control. God, how very *stupid* both of us have been. We understand each other so little. I thought that hashing out our issues would make me feel better, but it only makes me more aware of this enormous gap between us. I was fully ready to own up to my mistake in the blog, but I know, deep down, that was far from the worst of our issues. And I'm struck with a sudden despair that we are just too different for this to ever work. We can barely even talk to each other honestly.

"Every time I get close, you push me away," I say. "I know you like my blood, and that I remind you of Etta, but I…" I have to pause as my voice trembles. It's humiliating, but this might be my last chance to let him know how he made me feel, so I have to press onward. "I need more than that, Sebastian. I need more than being used and thrown away again and again. And you deserve more than clinging to some shred of resemblance to your past love. This relationship hasn't been healthy for either of us."

For a moment, he only stares at me. Then he lowers his head, staring at the floor.

"It's past midnight," I whisper. "Our contract is done. If you have something to say to me, you're running out of time."

He raises his head to look at me. "I have behaved boorishly."

I huff out a small laugh. "That was *almost* an apology."

"I am sorry, Amelia." He meets my eyes, and I try not to look as surprised as I feel—and try even harder not to soften so easily. "I am sorry for everything that I have done, and everything I have not done. I am sorry, too, that I do not always know the right thing to say. You have been… an unexpected change in my life, and I have not handled it as well as I should have. I have been unreasonable and selfish."

"And cold," I say. "And volatile. And fickle."

"I will accept all of those charges but *fickle*. My feelings for you have not wavered since the moment I laid eyes upon you. If it ever seemed so, it was only that I struggled with how to handle those feelings. They frightened me. *You* frightened me."

My heart stutters, but I viciously shove the feeling away. "Because I remind you of Etta."

To my surprise, he laughs. "*No*," he says. "You are *nothing* like Etta. She was…" He pauses. "Etta was fair-haired and soft-spoken and gentle. She was everything I wanted at that point in my life, when I was still healing from the war. But you…" He looks at me. "You are bold and funny and charming, and everything I need right now. I would not change you for the world."

My poor battered heart is beating double-time in my chest. "Because of my blood," I say, the words almost a question.

"It is not just your blood that I want, Amelia," he says slowly, as if shocked that he has to explain it. "Is it not clear that I adore you?"

Chapter Thirty-Four

My mouth drops open. For a moment I can only stare, and then, sputtering, I ask, "In what way was that ever supposed to be *clear*?"

Sebastian opens his mouth, hesitates, shuts it again. Consternation clouds his normally stony features. "You mean you truly didn't know?"

My heart—my stupid, stupid heart—is still thumping. Part of me is desperate to walk away while I still have the willpower, but a fragile hope keeps me in place. "Know what, Sebastian?" I ask, my voice barely more than a whisper.

My own trepidation is reflected in his expression. He draws back a step, as if he means to flee. But then his expression sets and he steps forward, reaching for my hand. I let him take it.

"Amelia Burton," he says, his tone formal and fierce all at once. "As I said, words often fail me, but that does not mean my emotions are not true. It feels as though you have awoken me from a long, long slumber, and made me see the light in the world once again. But... I am a coward, it seems. It has been so long since I cared for someone that it made me terrified of you. Because you are *blinding* after spending so long in the dark." He brings my hand to his chest, pressing my palm against his sternum while his eyes search mine. "After all these years, I thought I had forgotten what sunlight felt like, but then I met you. And step by step, you have led me out of the darkness."

I swallow hard. I can do nothing but stare at him.

"If I had lost you tonight..." His voice trails off as an expression I've never seen before breaks through, an open vulnerability as he reaches to cup my face. "I am so glad you wore silver."

Finally, the realization hits me. "The silver you sent me," I whisper. It was never Alexander. It was Sebastian looking after me, right after the incident where he nearly lost control.

His expression darkens as his thoughts follow the same path. "I never wanted you to feel unsafe again."

"And you sent me the notebooks when I mentioned to Ellen that I was writing," I say, beginning to understand. "New pillows when I said I couldn't sleep. Soup when I claimed I was sick..."

I look back over our six months together with my newfound understanding of Sebastian. He's been paying attention to me from afar all of this time. Sending me affection in the only way he could manage, even when he was too afraid to be physically near me.

That book of poetry—that's *right*. He read one of them aloud to me in Latin, that night at the Celeste ball.

I stare at him, trying to wrap my head around everything.

"I wanted to give you space after what happened," he says, searching my expression. "But I was constantly asking the staff about you, trying to find ways to make you comfortable and happy. Yet I... I am beginning to understand that I have treated you even more poorly than I comprehended, to make you doubt me so." He stops, shakes his head. "That is no one's fault but my own. If you choose to walk away from me, I will not hold it against you. But before that happens… I want you to know that I love you. Not because of your blood, nor because you have the *tiniest* bits in common with my past valentine, but because of who you are. Because you are smart and compassionate and stubborn enough to have wormed your way into my long-sleeping heart. Because you embrace your feelings in a way I have always wished I could. Because you make me want to be a better man to prove myself worthy of you. Because, Amelia, you are truly and wholly like none other I have encountered in over two centuries on this earth."

When he finally stops, it's as if the world is holding its breath.

Part of me wants to kiss him. Part of me wants to grab him by the collar and shake him. How could he be this goddamn obtuse, and why would he wait until now to tell me how he feels? Now, after six months of living in some kind of agonized limbo, not understanding why he was so hot and cold, forced to come up with my own outlandish reasoning for his behavior just to cope with it. Now, when I finally decided I could let him go, he decides it's time to be honest?

What if I accept him at his word, just to travel back to his estate and be trapped there in seclusion for another year? I don't think I can take it. I am scared, so scared, that I am just being manipulated again.

And yet… and yet, when I look into his eyes, I recognize the same hopeful agony that I have been experiencing. Far too often his emotions have seemed completely closed off to me, but now he wears them openly.

My heart tells me that this is true. It wants me to choose him. Can I trust it this time? Because this is not about trusting him; it is about whether or not I trust myself, and my feelings. Whether I can put aside the hurt of Declan pushing me aside, and Alexander's deceit, and all of my insecurities, and let myself be vulnerable once more.

I hesitate, and Sebastian's face falls. He lets my fingers slip from his cold grip. "I am too late," he says. "I see. I have been a fool, and for that I will never forgive myself, so it is not fair of me to ask you to forgive me either. I will respect your decision, as I said before. I... You must have come here to find a new patron, and I've been..."

I step forward, lifting my hand to touch his face. "Sebastian," I say. It hurts to listen to his stream of consciousness like that, especially once I realize how much it sounds like my own inner dialogue. Both of us have fallen victim to our insecurities and fears. I look him in the eyes, making sure he's listening to me, and tap my finger against the black heart pinned to my chest. "I came here for you."

Uncertainly flickers across his expression. "How did you know I would be here?"

"I didn't. But I realized it didn't matter."

He tilts his head, waiting for an explanation.

"I remembered... the last time we attended a ball, you said you did it for me. Because that's what you thought I wanted. So I knew if you wanted to talk to me, you would be here." I search his face. He's still hard to read, but I know now to look for the slightest softening of his eyes, the faintest twitch of his lips. I see his emotions now. I see him. "And you did, didn't you? You came because you thought this was where I'd be."

"Yes," he says.

I smile, though there's a tinge of sadness. "I almost missed it, you know. I had to rush here. Because I was at the estate, where I thought *you* would be."

He blinks. "Oh. That… would have been unfortunate."

"Yes." I sigh. "This would've been easier if you had a phone, you know. Or…" I bite the inside of my cheek. "Or if either of us were better at communicating."

"I am aware that is not my strong suit," he admits. "I… didn't realize how badly it affected you until I read your blog." His eyes shift downward, and shame floods his expression. "I know an apology won't fix this, but again: I am so sorry."

"And I'm sorry, again, for putting that online without your permission," I say. "We've both made mistakes, I think. And plenty of assumptions, too." Again, I'm struck by what fools we have been. And yet… despite it all… we are both here, out of a desire to make this work. I know it won't be easy, but the worthwhile things in life never are.

I run my thumb over his cheekbone, and he leans into my touch, his expression soft and vulnerable as he looks down at me. "But I'm beginning to realize we may be more alike than we think. And maybe that's been part of the problem all along. And also part of why…" I smile, drawing closer to him and pressing myself against his chest. His arm slides around me. "I've fallen in love with you, Sebastian de Celeste."

His eyes widen. "You have?" He sounds almost disbelieving. Amazed. It makes warmth unfurl in my chest.

"Yes." I stand on my tiptoes and press my lips to his, in a kiss as brief and gentle as a flutter of butterfly wings. He kisses me back, slow and tender. I pull back enough to whisper, "I love you, Sebastian." And then I kiss him again, and again, and again, until I am sure he believes it.

Chapter Thirty-Five

When we arrive at the estate, the house is silent.

"I gave the staff the weekend off," Sebastian says as he shuts the door behind us. "It's just us until tomorrow."

I smile, turning to face him. "I know." I kick my sneakers off, and then reach under my dress and pull off my panties, tossing them aside as well.

As Sebastian stares at me, his eyes turn black. His fangs slide out behind his lips. He watches as I discard my dress in a similar fashion and stand naked before him. He approaches me, his hands reaching out to settle on my hips like I'm some delicate thing. I tilt my head back as he kisses my neck, his lips feather-soft, right at the spot where my pulse beats the strongest.

We kiss pressed against the wall in the front parlor, and then on the stairs. He spreads my thighs and dives between them right on the staircase. His tongue is slow and thorough and relentless as his hands hold me wide open for him, his cold mouth bringing me swiftly to a climax I don't bother to keep quiet. Then he scoops me up in his arms and carries me to his bedroom.

I've wondered for so long what was behind this locked door. Now that I see it, I find that I'm hardly surprised. The room has minimalist furniture, a nightstand heaped with old books in various languages. It's subdued and elegant. Very Sebastian.

He sets me on the edge of the big canopy bed and unbuttons his shirt. When he shrugs it off, my eyes catch on the bite marks on his shoulder.

"I forgot you were hurt," I say, brow furrowing in concern.

"It's fine," he says. "It will heal."

I bite my lip, watching him undo his belt. "…It'll be faster if you drink from me."

His hands pause in their work before resuming again. "It's really nothing. Hardly a wound."

"Sebastian." I wait for him to look up at me and then lie back on the bed, fully naked, and brush my hair behind my shoulders. "I want you to drink from me."

He sheds the last of his clothes and climbs onto the bed, his weight settling on top of me. His eyes are black with desire, but there's indecision as his gaze flicks from my neck to my face. "I am not sure if I can control myself."

"You will," I say, without an ounce of doubt. "I trust you." I reach up to grasp the back of his neck and lead his face down to the curve of my neck. A moment's hesitation, and he sinks his teeth into me. I gasp, my back arching, as he drinks.

I expected a bite to the neck to feel different, and it does. This is… transcendent. The sensation of being held, cherished, *possessed* floods through my veins. My entire body is achingly sensitive and tingling with pleasure. I'm aware of every inch of skin that touches Sebastian, and especially aware of the throbbing ache between my thighs. I grab his hand and bring it there, showing him how wet and ready I am for him. He groans against my neck and guides that perfect cock to my entrance.

When he pushes into me, inch by slow inch, I cry out with pleasure. His teeth in my neck, his thick length inside of me—I feel full, whole, in a way I never have before. Like he was made for me, and I for him.

He fucks me slowly as he sips from my neck, savoring both my taste and my body as I gasp and whimper and beg for more. Soon, I am incoherent with pleasure. His pace quickens, his hips snapping against mine. I rake my nails down his back. When he breaks away from my neck to kiss me, his tongue cold and tasting faintly of copper as it slides against mine, I come apart. My toes curl, my entire body trembling with the intensity of it. He follows me over the edge with a gasp of my name.

* * *

When I wake, it takes me a few moments to remember anything. I rub a hand across my eyes and blink up at the unfamiliar ceiling, wondering if it's really possible for everything to have changed. Then I shift onto my side and look over at Sebastian sitting beside me with a book open on his lap.

He shuts it, sets it aside, and smiles. "Good morning, my love," he says, leaning over to press his lips to mine.

I stare up at him. "Good morning, Sebastian." I bite my lip. "You stayed."

"So did you," he says.

We study each other. I'm vividly aware that this is the first time he's witnessed my bedhead, my morning—evening?—breath. The version of me before I put on all of the makeup and dresses that have become my shield.

And it is the first time I have seen him in the morning, wearing only loose trousers with his pale, muscular chest exposed. His hair is somehow still perfect. He is strikingly beautiful, and I would be self-conscious if not for the naked adoration in the way he's looking at me right now.

"If every morning will be like this, I'll stay as long as you want," I say.

"Hm. That was going to be my line." He reaches over to push my hair out of my face, his long fingers winding through my curls. "I know this isn't the most romantic pillow talk, but I have a renewed contract for you to sign."

"You prepared it last night?" I ask, surprised at how quickly he worked.

"Oh, long before then, Amelia."

I smile up at him. After a moment, he smiles back, almost shyly, and God, he is so blindingly beautiful.

"I'll sign it after my coffee," I say. "But first..."

I grab him by the back of the neck and pull him under the covers with me.

Epilogue

Six months later

I stand at the top of the staircase, looking down and listening to the conversation drifting out from the dining room just down the hall. My heart is beating so hard, I can hear it in my ears.

A cold hand gently grips my shoulder, and I turn to see Sebastian, dressed in a three-piece suit.

"You look stunning, my love," he says, drinking in the sight of me in my new yellow dress. I smile, doing a little twirl to show off the long skirts. He lets his eyes linger on me for a long moment before shifting to meet my gaze. "Are you nervous?"

I bite my lip. "A little. But mostly excited."

"As am I."

Despite the anxious fluttering of my heart, another broad smile unfolds on my face. "Our first dinner party at the estate."

"The first dinner party *ever* held under my ownership," he adds, and gallantly offers me an arm. I take it and squeeze him reassuringly as we walk down the stairs to join everyone.

"It's going to be spectacular," I whisper to him, knowing he's as nervous as I am, though he'd rather not admit it.

It's much easier to walk into a room and face a crowd when it's full of familiar faces. Our guest list is far from what one would see at a grand ball held by one of the courts—especially because the vast majority of attendees are human.

The entire estate staff is here, of course: Ellen, our dependable groundskeepers Trent and Tobias, polite driver Vincent, and Bridget from the kitchens. The latter is rather nervous about what the food is going to be like because she's so used to cooking herself. But tonight they're the guests rather than staff, all dressed in their Sunday best, because Sebastian and I want to spoil them.

My sister Maisy is also here; she's seated next to Trent, and he keeps stealing sideways glances at her and blushing, which is adorable. There are only two vampires in attendance. The first is Benjamin. The last time I saw him, when Sebastian and I renewed our contract, was awkward. He apologized for lying to me about Alexander's offer of patronage to protect me, and I've forgiven him, since I believe his intent was good. I'm glad to have him here tonight, with a sultry Lissa at his side.

The second vampire is Georgiana de Celeste, the only person from his court Sebastian wanted to invite when I asked him—and I was pleased to find out that she's the patron of Farah, the museum-curating valentine who was so welcoming to me at the Celeste gala.

A dozen people in all, including me and Sebastian. Plus one very dapper dalmatian, wearing a collar with a bowtie on it.

It's a good, manageable crowd for our first event, I think. I'm excited to have a chance to speak with each of them. And I can feel Sebastian relax at my side as he sees them all, like he was bracing himself for something terrible but has finally realized it might not be so bad.

We went all out tonight, hiring the human bartender and vampire pastry chef that work all of the big court events. I couldn't help but notice that there was some glaring and muttering between the two when they arrived—I thought they were used to working together, but I guess I was wrong, because there's clearly some resentment there. Despite that, the food and drinks both prove to be perfect as dinner goes on.

Everything goes fabulously.

It's such a pleasure to see the staff enjoy themselves, and to talk to Maisy, and to have an opportunity to get to know Farah and her patron better. Barnabas spends dinner under the table, his tail thumping against Sebastian's chair whenever someone sneaks him scraps of food.

We couldn't have picked a better bunch of people. But nothing warms my heart as much as hearing Sebastian's laugh ring out not once but *twice* from the other end of the table during dinner. The second time, I look over and grin at him, and he catches my eye and lifts his blood-infused wine in a silent toast; a moment of connection despite the table and the guests between us.

As midnight comes and goes and the early hours of the morning approach, we bid our guests goodbye. Everyone thanks us for a lovely night; Ellen even sheds a couple tears as she squeezes my hand and tells me what a pleasure it was.

The estate is very quiet once they're gone, but it's a comfortable quiet. A quiet I've grown accustomed to. Sebastian and I let the silence linger as we make our way to our bedroom. I take a warm bath while Sebastian spends time in the library to decompress. Then we slip into bed, and he reads a book beside me while I type on my blog.

I rarely write about my own experiences anymore, and when I do, it's always with Sebastian's approval. Mostly, these days, I prefer to use my platform to share other peoples' stories and give them advice about their own situations. The outpouring of attention from being a viral sensation faded away when people realized I was never going to reveal my identity or share any juicy gossip. But readership is still steady, and plenty of people take the opportunity to write in anonymously.

There are so many valentines out there who think they're alone in their experiences. It brings me joy to offer even the briefest moment of connection online. I want the community to know that my hand is always extended to offer a lift up if they need it.

The confessions in my inbox range from devastatingly sad to so raunchy, they make me blush even when I'm reading them alone. But a message I receive tonight *really* makes me do a double take.

"Oh my God, Sebastian, listen to this," I say. "Dear Anonymous Valentine," I begin. "I have a confession to make. My patron is an artist who views me as his new muse, but I want to be seen as more..."

Acknowledgments

I would like to thank:

My developmental editor Sarah Chorn and copy editor Claudette Cruz ("The Editing Sweetheart"). Both are, as ever, brilliant and delightful to work with.

My very talented cover designer, Mayhem Cover Creations.

My beta readers: Remarkable-Thanks480, Aggressive_feature94, skipthroughmordor, princesslemontree, jazz-music-starts (who told me about poem 5 by Catullus), Baine Fox, rusig, and pbny. Each and every one of you made suggestions that strengthened the story, and cheered me on when I needed it.

The Romance Author's Writing Group Discord, and all of the friends I have made there, who help me feel less alone on this self-publishing journey. <3

The Indie Authors Ascending Discord, an endless fount of knowledge.

My family, my partner, and my friends, for their support over my many years of writing.

And lastly: thank you, my reader, for making all of this worthwhile. I hope you enjoyed my story.

About the Author

Skyla Gray is a romance author fond of all things scary and steamy. When not writing, she can usually be found gaming, cooking, or binge-watching horror movies. She lives in Arizona with her partner and an absolute rascal of a dog.

Sign up for my newsletter for monthly updates and free bonuses, including a spicy deleted scene of Sebastian and Amelia!

You can connect with me on:
🌐 http://skyla-gray.com

Subscribe to my newsletter:
✉ https://skyla-gray.ck.page/e838b44108

Also by Skyla Gray

The Nightmare's Kiss
How can a living nightmare bring such sweet dreams?

Mara Vance never thought her "useless" psychology degree would lead to studying an actual monster. Subject X-13, aka "The Nightmare," is armed with sharp teeth, claws, and a constantly shifting form… yet Mara finds the huge shadow creature as intriguing as he is terrifying.

But as Mara studies him, she soon realizes that the Nightmare is far more intelligent than her shady superiors say he is. And every night, she indulges in twisted fantasies about the same monster. What happens in her dreams stays in her dreams – right?

Everyone says he's nothing more than a monster. But when dream and reality collide, Mara must decide how much she's willing to trust him – and herself. Will she risk setting him free, or will she lose him forever?